STEFI HART

Copyright © 2025 by Stefi Hart

All rights reserved.

No part of this book may be reproduced in any form or by any electronic or mechanical means, including information storage and retrieval systems, without written permission from the author, except for the use of brief quotations in a book review.

❦ Created with Vellum

ALSO BY STEFI HART

**Bennett Springs Series**

Country Charm

**Ravens Ridge Series**

Hidden in His Eyes

**Angel Cove Series**

Second Chance Love

**Single Titles**

Dating Game

*For Mr T*

# CHAPTER 1

*<I'm sorry that mitigating factors prevented me from indulging in such an attractive and tempting invitation as spending the night with you, Molly.*

*Allow me to explain over coffee? >*

Molly sighed as the screen of her cell phone darkened and then went black.

*Mitigating factors,* what the hell was that meant to mean.

"Mitigating factors." Aloud, the word combination sounded even more threatening than when it appeared in text. She flipped open the mirror on the back of her sun visor and applied lip-gloss to her already glossy lips. "Perhaps I don't want you to explain your *mitigating factors*, Mr. Jones."

Molly pressed her thumb to the screen of her cell phone. The message reappeared until she tapped on the photo identification. Carl Jones smiled back at her. "And, for the hundredth time—I. Don't. Drink. Coffee." As much as the brew was like poison to her lips, even a pot of strong black coffee sounded sweeter than what she feared he'd reveal, should she take him up on his coffee invitation.

She glanced up at the mirror again, checked that her hair and make-up was as it should be, and flipped the mirror shut.

There was no point avoiding a response, when Carl set his sight on something he was the most persistent person she knew.

*<I could lie and say I look forward to seeing you, but instinct tells me to run and hide... >*

Molly read over her message to check for error, then pressed send before she chickened out and hit delete.

Already fashionably late, Molly snatched her handbag from the passenger seat, dropped her cell phone and keys inside and pushed open the car door.

Six-inch heels weren't ideal attire when braving the loose stones of Shelley's driveway. Not unlike walking upon thousands of marbles, it wouldn't be the first time Molly rolled her ankle or had her feet slip out from beneath her. Today, she hoped for neither, but given her luck over the weekend, it'd be like the cherry atop a sundae if she landed on her butt.

The afternoon sun had a bite to it, even though summer was just beginning. The sudden warmth that replaced the icy chill wasn't something she intended to complain about.

Once on the path, Molly was able to lift her gaze from the ground and admire Shelley's garden that was blooming shades of purple, pink, and berry red. Bees hummed as they busied themselves amongst fragrant buds. How Shelley found time to maintain such an Eden was beyond her, especially when Molly struggled to keep her bowl of succulents alive.

Reaching the front door, having survived the walk, she rang the bell and waited. Molly was glad

Candice had beaten her there. Having stayed out the night before, she wanted the interview over with so she could go home and relax for a few hours before writing the article to make the press for Tuesday morning.

In a swirl of color, in fitting with her garden, Shelley appeared from around the corner. "Hello beautiful, we're sitting in the courtyard, I hope that's okay for you?"

"Of course." Molly wrapped her arms around Shelley in a tight hug. "How was your date last night?"

"Huh." Shelley snorted and pulled back from the embrace. "About as vibrant as the dead fish in his profile photos."

Molly couldn't help but laugh as she wrinkled her nose in disgust and shook her head.

"Honestly, there are so many men who could use a high voltage dose from a defibrillator. Even then I doubt it'd be enough to kick start a steady rhythm."

"That good, huh?" She didn't envy Shelley and the pool of singles. Even though her relationship with Carl hadn't gone beyond a lingering kiss on the lips, it was in the developing stages. Despite not being able to join her at the hotel, he teased her with sexy messages, and even went so far as sending selfies that weren't appropriate for public display.

"You have no idea." She shook her head as she led the way around to where Candice was waiting for them. "How are things with Mr. Jones?" She glanced over her shoulder and eyed Molly briefly.

"Not sure." She shrugged. "He should've finished his screenplay, so time will tell, I guess." As much as she tried not to get excited that he would now be free to spend time with her, she couldn't help but get her hopes up.

"About time." Shelley didn't bother to hide her disapproval. Three months from when they first met, a novel sized message each night, some rather suggestive photographs, and a few meet ups here and there, was enough to validate her impatience.

"No arguments from me." Her relationship, if she could call it that, wasn't up for discussion, especially not in the presence of Candice. The film industry was too small for her not to make the connection.

"Hi, Molly." Candice waved as they approached. "Thanks for doing this, I really appreciate it."

Molly smiled and settled in the chair opposite Candice. "You're the one doing me a favor. You're hot news, babe. Do you know what this will do for my ratings?" She winked across at her before reaching into her bag for her voice recorder.

"The magazine will have to double your wage if your ratings get any higher." Candice was a little gushy, but in an industry where so many were fake, she was one of the good ones.

"Huh, wouldn't that be nice?" Molly set the device on the table and glanced up at Candice. "You don't mind, do you? Saves me handwriting."

"Not at all—you do whatever you need to do."

Since her stage performance as *Nancy* in Charles Dickens classic, *Oliver Twist*, Candice had been in demand. Teamed with Shelley's designs, and new venture into recycled material costuming, the two were a force to be reckoned with.

As much as she should've been excited about the interview, and the two-page spread the magazine was running in the next addition, Molly struggled for enthusiasm. The idea of a career change had been haunting her for some time. Although, details weren't something that had moved beyond a faded sketch awaiting form and color. The change was inevitable. It was just a matter of time before she took the plunge.

Broadcast appealed, but also meant more study, and she didn't want to do that. Carl had suggested she write a novel. The idea wasn't too awful, but she had no idea on how to execute such a steep task. A journalist, even with the creative freedom to explore fashion and the arts, didn't equip her with the knowhow to become a novelist—at least not one that'd make a decent living off the royalties.

"Before you get started, can I get you a cup of tea and cake?"

Having skipped breakfast at the hotel, for not wanting to dine alone, Molly's stomach grumbled as if a warning that calorie counting was overrated.

"That'd be great, thanks." The cream and strawberry filled sponge was her favorite and Shelley knew she wouldn't be able to resist. With a bit of luck, the interview wouldn't take long, and they could push work aside for a while.

"So, Candice, tell us about the project you're working on at the moment."

Candice grinned, the spotlight was on and she loved nothing more than to be in it. At the rate she spoke and the enthusiasm in which she gushed, Molly was relieved she thought to bring the recording device. Hand-written notes left too much room for misinterpretation, and her reputation as a journalist who reported the inside truth gave reason for her popularity and ensured job security in a sketchy industry.

There was a time when the acting industry intrigued Molly enough to attend an audition for a short film. It was short-lived. The moment the director requested she act as though she was licking ice-cream from a cone, center stage, and in front of more than a hundred other candidates, she made a beeline for the exit and never went back. Too many eyes focused on her, too much attention all at once, did little to entice her creative side to shine.

Behind the words she could hide, and from that point she could improvise and create something for her readers to enjoy, but still it was lacking the spunk she believed possible if she were connecting with her readers in a way that inspired or excited them.

"Any new projects on the horizon?" Molly was prying for information juicy enough to inspire a lead for her next story, and Candice was the best person to provide what she was looking for. Her ability to keep a secret seemed to be non-existent.

The sound of bells indicated a message had come through on her phone. Out of habit, and eager to read Carl's response, Molly reached into her bag and pulled her phone from where she'd dropped it. "Sorry, could be work." The excuse rolled off her tongue without much thought to what day it was. A quick glance at Shelley told her she wasn't buying the excuse for a moment, but she ignored her and turned her focus to the words displayed on the screen of her phone. *Journalists still worked on Sundays.*

*<Well you should deny that particular instinct...Besides, I was always pretty adept at Hide and Seek, so I'd find you in no time at all. >*

There was no denying Carl had a way with words that made every nerve ending in her body stand to attention.

Molly knew Shelley was reading her like an open book, but she didn't care. So what if the man made her happy. He was charming, well respected in the artsy world, and, despite him being so far from her usual type, his attention was flattering, to say the least.

Candice didn't seem to notice that Molly's attention shifted elsewhere. She continued with enthusiasm about the growing film industry in Western Australia.

"Now, he's someone you should be interviewing." Candice claimed her attention. "He's hot news."

Molly frowned and looked over at her recording device to ensure it was still rolling. A blossoming romance was enough to cause a flutter to pulse through her from a simple text message, but it wouldn't pay the bills at the end of the month.

"Molly already knows Mr. Jones *very* well." Shelley supplied the information with a little too much emphasis on Molly's familiarity with Carl.

"Oh, really?" Candice arched one eyebrow and grinned. "Then you would know his girlfriend, Sally, she's another interesting character for you to do a story on. Such a mixed bag of talent—" At that point, Molly zoned out. Mitigating factors suddenly made sense, and like her initial reaction to the words, dread replaced the flutter in the pit of her stomach. The jam and cream sponge threatened to make a reappearance. She swallowed, picked up her cup of tea and took a sip.

The frown on Shelley's face showed that she was as confused by the news Candice had delivered as Molly.

"Candice, why don't you tell Molly about the

production you've written and will perform, and how the recycled costumes fit in."

Now wasn't the time, but Molly would have to remember to thank Shelley for saving the interview, and diverting the conversation away from Carl's *little miss perfect*. Jealousy wasn't something she'd ever suffered before, and Molly wasn't convinced it was what she was feeling at that moment. Whatever emotion it was, she never wanted to experience it again.

# CHAPTER 2

"Oh, beautiful, I'm so sorry."

Puffy eyed from crying, Molly answered the door despite knowing she looked a wreck. Shelley had been phoning and leaving messages on her answering machine and inundating her with text messages, so she had no doubt that she'd followed through with her threat to bring over her answer to every situation—Chinese takeaway, chocolate, and wine.

The combination usually appealed to Molly, but not so much when she felt as lousy as she did at that moment.

She'd narrowed down the mix of emotions to the one flashing neon in her mind—*humiliation*. What a fool she'd been to believe someone so successful and admired in the creative circle would be interested in pursuing a relationship with her.

In so many ways, everything added up. His *sneaking away from the desk* to meet her for coffee wasn't a cute, nerdy way of him being spontaneous. He was actually sneaking away. The late night text messages and photographs made her cringe the most. Where was *Little Miss Perfect* whilst he was making suggestive passes at her? Probably in his bed, waiting for him to put into action the words of desire he'd been declaring to Molly.

The whole situation grew from something sweet and innocent to a sinister act of regret. He'd played her all the way. The worse part, had he taken her up on the invitation to join her at the hotel, she could've added home wrecking whore to her list of not so proud moments.

Shelley didn't wait to be invited in, instead she stepped around Molly and headed for the lounge room. As if on autopilot, Molly closed the door and followed. Numbness blanketed her, and, for the first time, she wished Shelley hadn't come.

In the hours she'd spent wallowing in self-pity since she left Shelley and Candice to go over costume details she didn't need to be a part of, Molly had come to the conclusion that the relationship she and Carl had been developing was simply a figment of her imagination. A pretty story created by her, which had resulted in a one-sided love affair. Humiliation stung, and Shelley's presence was like salt in the wound, rubbed in deeper with every sympathetic look she threw her way.

"You know—" Shelley paused as if searching for the right words, or else a delicate way to deliver them. She placed the box of food on the coffee table she'd slid close to the couch so they could reach without having to get up. "I'll get us some plates and cutlery, you can grab the glasses." The no nonsense tone and dishing out orders was Shelley's way of showing that she cared. Lingering on the verge of depression wasn't an option around her, which was why Molly had been hesitant to answer her calls and open the door in the first place. For one night, at least, she wanted to wallow in self-pity. To watch unrealistic romance movies and go through a box of tissues feeling sorry for herself whilst hating on the world of men.

It seemed they were in for a long night. Shelley's distracted manner was a sure sign she had a lot to say, and once she got started exhaustion or severe drunkenness was the only hope for the conversation to come to an end.

Molly took her time retrieving glasses and a bottle of sparkling water from the fridge. The worse part about the whole situation with Carl was that she always had her doubts about him, doubts she'd shared with Shelley on more than one occasion. Doubts she'd talked herself out of having despite the constant nag that all was not so rosy as it appeared. Titled Bachelor of the Year, it seemed she wasn't the only one confused about his relationship status, but sadly the only one stupid enough to be misguided by the media without question.

More unsettling than a lecture, or an attempt to cheer her up was Shelley's silence, but as excruciating as it was Molly did nothing to fill the void. Shock still lingered, as did an element of doubt. Carl didn't seem the cheating type—and technically he wasn't, but his lack of action wasn't without intent.

"So, have you finished your write up on Candice?" Small talk rarely clouded their communication, but Molly was grateful for the distraction—silence when overanalyzed seemed louder than sideshow alley.

"Almost." Truth was she hadn't started, but, with the risk of the lecture she'd been waiting for, a white lie was ample to cover the state she hoped would remain a secret.

Shelley speared a piece of chicken with her chopstick, lifting the capture to her mouth she took a bite and chewed. The frown creasing her brow indicated an idea was brewing, or else a thought was being edited and refined internally before spilling from her mouth, at risk of being taken the wrong way.

She swallowed. "I think you need to get out more. Have fun. Sign up for *Craze*." She shrugged as if nothing about what she just said stooped to a whole new level of *not her thing*. Online dating didn't interest Molly in the slightest.

"Terrible idea. You know how I feel about online dating. It's for desperadoes who don't have a life—or a personality—or the ability to meet someone the old-fashioned way."

"So, I'm a *desperado* now, am I?" A grin teased the corners of Shelley's lips, indicating the insult hadn't been taken further than an opportunity to tease Molly for her negative attitude. "You'll see that it's a respectable way of perusing the opposite sex without the risk of making a move on a married man, or having someone you're not interested in making a move on you and embarrassing himself."

"With the apps we have access to these days, how can we even be sure the photo looks like the real thing?"

Shelley tipped her head back and laughed. "You may have been playing the innocent card in that hand, but be careful how you dish out the comments." Shelley winked, and for the first time that night, Molly managed an unforced smile. "Careful what you wish for. After a day on *Craze*, there will be nothing left to the imagination." Shelley let out a hoot of laughter as Molly screwed up her nose and shook her head.

"Stop with the details if you really want me to sign up." Molly leaned forward in her seat to load her plate with fried rice, topping it with satay chicken and stir-fried greens. Shelley knew how to cheer her up, Asian cuisine, wine, and conversation that pulled her from a place of self-pity to one where the heavy in her life seemed to detach and float away.

"If dating sites are so worthy of your time as you say they are, why is it you're here with me and not out on some hot date this evening."

Shelley picked a prawn off her plate with her

fingers, popped it in her mouth and took her time chewing as if contemplating a justifiable answer. She swallowed and then grinned. "I need a time out—I need sleep." She groaned as she tucked her feet underneath her. "Going out every night until after midnight gets to be too much. A few nights off will be as refreshing as a holiday."

"Why date if it's a chore?" Given Shelley's busy schedule, Molly could see how the late nights would become taxing, but it wasn't as though dating was compulsory. Shelley was the most independent person she knew. A man in her life, one on a permanent basis, would cramp her style.

"I've got seven years on you. I need to start thinking about children whilst my maternal clock is still ticking." She shoveled a large scoop of rice and chicken into her mouth and shrugged.

"Thirty-six isn't too old to have a baby." Molly hadn't even considered the family side of a relationship. Finding a suitable guy to date was difficult enough without the thought of a baby looming in the background.

"Maybe not. But, by the time we get to know each other and settle down a bit, a few years will pass by, and I'll be forty before my legs even hit the stirrups." From frown to grin in a moment, Shelley was trying to make light of a situation that Molly knew must be bothering her more than she wanted to let on. Shelley hadn't always been the maternal type, something Molly hoped she didn't regret if the opportunity for children passed her by.

"Any possibilities?" Leading Shelley down the path to talk about her love life, or lack of, wasn't her intention, but diverting the attention away from hers was a bonus. Molly tucked her legs up on the couch when Shelley rolled her eyes, knowing she was in for a long story. Or, given the number of dates she'd been on lately, a *string* of long stories.

"The pool is full, and I'm sure you won't have any problems finding someone decent." There was no doubt she was trying to soften Molly up enough to join the craze. "But, by the time you get to my age, most of the guys have baggage or they're so set in their ways I don't think they really want a woman around at all. At least not for anything more than a romp between the sheets." Shelley sighed, and for the first time in her quest for a match, Molly recognized a sadness she'd failed to see before. Whether it was always there, and she had been too caught up in her own failed attempts to notice, or if it was the strain of constantly fighting the negative that never seemed to progress enough to meet her usual outlook on life.

"That bad, huh?" Stuck for a comment, Molly encouraged her to elaborate.

She shook her head and sighed again before taking another mouthful of rice, using the time it took to chew to decide the direction of their conversation. They'd known each other too long, been through too much heartache, pain, and even good times not to recognize the meaning of the silences between them.

"Sometimes I think I'd be in a better place if I learned to love my own company and turn my back on the dating game once and for all—perhaps I could seek a donor and settle on having a baby—someone to divert my love to. Someone I could spoil and not be disappointed in return."

Molly knew disappointment all too well, having invested too much time and emotion in those not meant for her.

"All I'm trying to say is don't wait until you're too old. Take a risk, even if it means getting hurt a few times. Finding that special someone to share the rest of your life with will be worth every second of hurt. Take it from me. I put career and everything else before love, and look where that got me—don't make the mistakes I've made."

Shelley wasn't the sort to deliver a sermon, to harp on a belief, if it wasn't coming from a place for the better good. She'd been a mother figure, a big sister, a confidant—her best friend—for more years than Molly could remember. A message was not something for Molly to ignore, but a lesson learned through her longtime best friend's suffering.

## CHAPTER 3

Like an alarm, a consistent tone from her cell phone penetrated her dream state and pulled Molly back to reality. Darkness, so thick and black, only the red numbers glowing on the face of her alarm clock were visible.

Five thirty-three.

Molly reached out and picked up her cell phone up off her bedside table. *Let the Craze begin…* repeatedly appeared on the screen. Scrolling down confirmed she'd not set her alarm for some ungodly hour, an interview she knew hadn't been planned, but the alert had come from beside her.

"*Craze* alright—or maybe crazy would be a more fitting name." Molly pulled the unoccupied pillow from beside her and, sitting forward, tucked it on top of her own and slid herself up to a sitting position. Curiosity overruled the need for sleep despite having turned in after midnight.

Molly swiped the screens of her cell to where the last app she downloaded occupied a page of its own. The blue square with an arrow pierced heart now had a red circle with numbers, ninety-nine and a plus sign, showing the number of matches, or messages, she didn't know.

*"Let the Craze begin..."* She muttered the words of the alert as she clicked open the app. As if loading, a red circle appeared against a white background. The circle changed into a blinking heart, red on white. Molly watched and waited. She liked to think *patiently*, however, the patient part was debatable—a trait she hadn't been blessed with, but fought to acquire on a daily basis.

Across the top of the screen, and down the side, images of the men she'd swiped right to the night before had appeared, some with messages alongside and others not. Overwhelmed by the amount of matches she'd received, Molly scrolled through the faces, squinting to see the small images. Some she recognized straight away, especially those few she thought to be particularly gorgeous, and silently hoped would swipe her back.

It seemed there was an easy way to make her feel seventeen again. All it took was a little app called *Craze*, and to be inundated with attention from the opposite sex.

Too intrigued to sleep, she padded barefoot to the kitchen and flipped the switch off the kettle. Nursing a delicate head after too much wine and not nearly enough sleep, a cup of tea was a must.

Having left her cell phone on her bedside table was a good thing. The temptation to sift through her messages would've been too much to resist whilst she waited. Instead, she wandered through the house to the lounge room, where Shelley had fallen asleep and insisted she was comfortable when Molly suggested she take the spare room instead of the couch.

It wasn't often they drank so much that either couldn't drive home, but it seemed they were both as unlucky in love as the other. Shelley just wasn't so willing to offer the information so freely as Molly did, kept the cork in the bottle, wax sealed, until the pressure got too much, and months of misery was revealed in less than an evening.

Covered with the blanket Molly had draped over the back of the couch, Shelley was breathing heavy enough to hear, but not so heavy to be classed as a snore. Molly left the room and entered the kitchen as the kettle came to the boil.

From where she stood, preparing a strong blend, Molly could hear the notification on her phone going off again.

"Early risers," she muttered. "Already a negative in their favor." Pressing the tea bag against the side of her mug before discarding it in the sink. "You can stay there until an hour more appropriate for cleaning." Talking to herself may have been considered a sign of madness for which she was willing to claim, too often, not having anyone else to talk to.

Such thoughts highlighted the loneliness she too often felt these days. Was it desperate to want to be with someone, to share an evening, a weekend, a life with that special someone who made you smile even when they weren't around—the mere thought of him and you're beaming like a lighthouse guiding a ship home.

Molly sighed. Perhaps it was time to trade her rose-colored glasses for a reality check. Stooping so low as to hope to find her happily ever after from a stack of selfies didn't sit so well as she hoped it would, no matter the flood of attention she'd received.

With both hands hugging the mug, Molly took a

sip of tea and closed her eyes. The pull to sleep was almost too great to resist, but she knew that if she went back to bed before drinking her tea she would wake to feeling even more lousy than giving in to her early morning wake up call.

Already the day was shaping up to be warmer than she cared for, and the sun hadn't even come up. She was convinced that summer was the most complained about season until the gloom of winter set in and she made enough noise for everyone. Balmy nights that saw it light until after nine in the evening gave more reason to stay out and socialize, although, the sheer lack of a man in her life saw her spending too many of those possibilities at home, curled up with a good book or watching romantic comedies on television, wishing her own life was so exciting as the heroine. All it managed to achieve was to enhance the fact that her life couldn't have been further from the leading lady if she tried.

Maybe *Craze* was the answer to her lonely spell after all. She'd never live it down if her happily ever after was discovered online. Shelley would remind her daily to thank her.

Molly rolled her eyes and shook her head. Shelley would never change, larger than life, too good, and not nearly appreciated enough by those who breezed in and out of her life. Finding a partner for Shelley would be as satisfying, if not more so, than finding one herself. She was so good, thoughtful of others, Molly just wanted her to be happy.

The screen of her cell was lit up as she walked into the dark room and flicked the light on—more messages or matches, she assumed.

She took a sip of tea and placed the mug on her bedside table before climbing into bed. There was no point being uncomfortable whilst she sifted through the possibilities.

A twinge of what she assumed to be guilt, for her shallow attitude toward the guys who'd taken time to message or swipe her, was quickly consumed with nervous excitement.

Scrolling through, she didn't know where to begin. Too many to choose from. It was overwhelming. So, she decided to start at the bottom, the first message she would've received had she been awake.

*Doug*, not what she imagined the man of her dreams to be called, but when he looked like that, there were some things Molly was willing to make allowances for. Sandy blonde hair, too long to be taken seriously but not so long that she'd deny the urge to run her fingers through it, should she succumb to kissing him on the first date.

"Bloody hell," she muttered. It seemed a pile of matches was all she needed to picture herself locking lips with the first guy who bothered to send her a message. There were names for girls like her. *Desperate* was the first one that sprung to mind.

Before opening his message, Molly browsed through Doug's photos. There was no denying he was gorgeous looking, but there was sadness in his eyes that made her hesitate. A man with hang-ups wasn't high on her list of priorities to tackle at this point in her life. Carefree and relaxed appealed.

His profile was vague. *Pubs over clubs...barbecue with friends' beats them both. Family comes first. Smokers swipe left.*

Didn't give away much, yet his fifteen words spoke volumes.

Molly paused before she opened his message. What was the protocol, or general consensus, of polite *Craze* etiquette? If the first guy appealed and she struck up a conversation with him, was it wrong to chat to another at the same time? In a bar she'd get a name for herself, but in the privacy of her own room it seemed that she was free to chat with as many as she could handle at once.

The sinking feeling in her gut indicated that she wasn't comfortable stringing more than one guy along at a time, but perhaps that was because she was new at this game. She paused. Thinking of the dating scene as a game felt wrong as well. Having been hurt over again, mind games in the emotion department weren't much fun and not what she signed up for.

Over thinking wouldn't help her through the growing list of messages.

"Let's see what you have to say for yourself, Doug," she muttered and pressed her thumb to open his message.

A brown bear sitting in long grass waved at her. Beneath the image were two words,

*<Hello Molly. >*

She smiled. The simplicity of his message sure beat the corny pick up lines Shelley often shared from her own account.

As if he was standing before her and delivering his greeting in person, a flutter of nerves made her hesitate. Keeping it casual, and as simple as his message, wasn't so easy if she wanted the conversation to move past a polite hello.

<Hi Doug, how are you?>

She frowned at her screen—boring, but polite and open for him to advance the conversation if he was interested. It wasn't like she didn't have a list as long as her arm to choose from if vivacity was what he was chasing.

His response, just as boring when he pinged backed immediately.

<Great! How are you?>

Pleasantries were a given, but she couldn't help but wish there was an easy way to meet singles. Or, else, a way too fast forward the small talk and skip to having fun and being comfortable with someone. Even the flirt, the anticipation of whether a second date would happen, wasn't an appealing thought. Awkwardness had a way of slipping in and sucking the thrill out of the moment.

Being a klutz as she was, she feared what was bound to happen when she was consumed with nerves or flustered from saying the wrong thing.

Not knowing sense of humor or the quirks of a random stranger, especially after only having exchanged a few messages, misinterpretation was practically a given. Even more so in a text message than when meeting face to face.

*<Nothing to complain about at my end. >*

She responded so as not to leave Doug hanging in hope of moving past formalities.

*<So, tell me, what do you do when you're not perusing Craze? >*

Anything was better than enduring the weather conversation, so she got in quick in order to avoid the subject altogether.

. . .

*<Argh, that sounds terrible. I'm rarely on this app. >*

Far out. Molly shook her head. She had a defensive one on her hands. After pushing the temptation to ignore him and push him to the side, she wrote and deleted her response a few times before pressing send.

*<No judgment—after all, I'm the one at the other end of your conversation. Just interested in knowing more about you. >*

For her, there was nothing natural about getting to know someone via text. Certainly not so easy as when you meet someone in a bar, offer up an exchange, and within a few moments you're able to make an assumption whether you're keen to go out on a date, even if only based on something so shallow as instant attract.

Whilst she awaited his response, Molly tapped the heart icon in the corner of the screen to take her back to the profiles she'd not yet viewed—photographs of guys with dead fish bigger than a small child, or puckered up for soggy doggy kisses, or else risking their lives whilst participating in extreme sports. Few weren't so flashy or trying to be adorable, offering a selfie or two accompanied by photos they'd cropped friends or ex girlfriends out of.

Those with only one photo didn't stand a chance with her, especially if they'd failed to offer a short write up about themselves, as suggested. Stock photos were too easy to come across these days, and she wasn't taking any additional risks.

The ping of Doug's response caught her off guard, and she jumped. Eager to know what he wrote, she touched the message icon on the opposite side of the screen as the heart. Even if she pounced on the message straight away, it didn't mean she needed to respond immediately. Gone were the days she'd give a man the upper hand and be at his beck and call. If she'd learned anything from her encounter with Carl, it was to make them work for her attention.

*<I have my own business, so work keeps me busy. >*

. . .

That was it.

From the three photographs Doug had posted, Molly was keen to meet him, but if conversation was as miserable as his messages then she'd be in for a one hit wonder. Shelley had prepared her, as most of her dates never flowed over to a second date or another romp between the sheets.

*<Messaging isn't really my thing. Would you like to go out for dinner tonight? >*

His second message took her off guard, although she wasn't disappointed. She could think of worse things to do on an evening that she'd otherwise be sitting at home, alone.

*<Sounds good to me. >*

. . .

Momentarily forgetting her vow not to respond too quickly, she cursed herself as soon as she pressed send.

"Bloody hell," she muttered, then followed up with *where and when?*

Discarding her phone on her bedside table as soon as their date was set, Molly wandered out to the kitchen for another cup of tea. Still feeling a little precious, she popped two pieces of raisin toast in the toaster whilst waiting for the kettle to boil.

Glad to have an excuse at the end of the day to abandon the story she still had to write about Candice, inspired her to get an early start in hope to get it out of the way before lunchtime. Not including the few *coffee* dates she had with Carl, she couldn't remember the last first date she'd been on.

# CHAPTER 4

Molly stared back at herself in the mirror, it'd been sometime since she got dressed up for a dinner date with a man. Carl had always been a daytime meet up, in addition to his lack of height, heels and fancy dresses hadn't been the attire she opted for. A pamper day was exactly what she needed in order to prepare, and for the first time in a long while, she felt feminine—almost sexy.

With hair scooped up, exposing her neck and the drop earrings that hung from her lobes, Molly turned her head, first right and then left, altered the angle and repeated the process a number of times before she was happy that all was as it should be.

Nerves were beginning to kick in and she was

glad she didn't have long to wait before the taxi arrived. Not that she intended to drink, but a few quiet ones to help her relax wouldn't do her any harm. Besides, parking wasn't always so easy to find close to the restaurant, at least not in Fremantle, even on a weeknight, and she had no intention of walking the back alleys alone.

Shelley suggested she ask Doug to walk her back to her car after the date was over, but having watched too many crime television series, she didn't trust that a strange man in a deserted car park was much safer than facing a stranger in a dark alley. Who knew what he was capable of. At an influential age during the time that the *Claremont Serial Killer* was on the loose, Molly trusted no one whilst out and about at nighttime, despite the crime rate for local murder being nowhere near the statistics of other states in the country. It was far from the top of capital cities under the radar of high risk.

Still, the idea of going out with a complete stranger she met online left her on edge. Who was to say that the profile and photographs he was hiding behind were legitimately him? She could be meeting anyone, capable of anything, at the other end.

The doorbell interrupted her thoughts, making her jump. No doubt her cab had arrived, and in the nick of time—any later and she probably would have talked herself out of the date on account of it being unsafe. It wouldn't take much to back her argument, although nothing would've been so drastic to convince Shelley she had made the right decision.

It was too warm out to bother with a jacket, so Molly left it on her bed and snatched her clutch from the dresser and left without a backward glance. Anything to stall her would also see to her making an excuse not to open the door before the taxi driver declared her not home and left for his next waiting passenger. No doubt he had a long list in need of his services.

Molly released a breath as she opened the door and attempted a smile. Not that she had to impress the taxi driver as she would if she'd allowed her date to pick her up as he first suggested—which she found a little creepy. What sort of idiot did he think she was, expecting she would allow him to come to her home on the first date they ever went on? Recipe for disaster would be the headlines reporting the discovery of her body in the entry of her own home. She shook her head. No one could ever accuse her of having a boring imagination. The thought alone was enough to have her in need of sleeping pills to get to sleep for the next six weeks, at least.

Fear of the unknown had always filled her with dread. Never the dark, but what could be in it. Even in relationships, it was the unknown that always drove her to near insanity. Mixed messages and mind games were the bane of her existence, and all too often grown men loved to behave like adolescence and use such tactics in adult relationships. There was nothing more confusing, nothing more annoying, and the easiest trait to dislike, backing her decision to move on to a more palatable candidate.

Molly slid into the backseat and smoothed her dress, not wanting to look like she had dragged herself off the laundry floor only moments before their scheduled meeting time.

He'd seemed so nervous, Doug, the adorable blondie with hair too long and dimples deep enough to pull you in and claim your heart with the flash of one grin. From the moment she saw his photograph, Molly had felt seventeen again. A sucker for the surfy type she imagined they wouldn't have anything in common, but even if he didn't stimulate her on all levels, she was content to compensate with sex appeal.

A whirl of information was floating around in her head, proving it was difficult to keep up with what guy belonged to what information. Snippets of conversations with more than twenty different men made online dating so much more difficult than she anticipated. Molly flipped open her clutch and rummaged around in search of her phone. The easiest way to remember details that belonged with Doug was to read over the messages they had exchanged. The beauty and the downfall of meeting someone online was that you always had a record of information exchanged—useful, but potentially dangerous at the same time.

Molly frowned, then peered into the small space, willing a hidden compartment to miraculously appear and reveal the cell she knew was on her bed, no doubt concealed by the jacket she was originally convinced she'd need but thought better of taking.

No idea of the time, her only source of time-keeping on her bed at home, Molly guessed she wouldn't have time to turn around to retrieve her lifeline. Too worried about walking to the car and encountering an unfortunate incident at the hands of her date, and she leaves her phone on her bed. The night hadn't even begun, and already she was regretting her decision to meet up with this strange man that was too cute to just leave on the shelf.

Too bad if he was caught up and tried to contact her, she would be sitting like a loner and everyone else would be as aware as her he was a no show. A stand up that would crush her confidence not nearly so much as Carl had, but up there all the same.

The thought of Carl and what he'd done still made her wince. She liked to think he was everything she wanted in a man, but she knew he was quite the opposite. Too short, too nerdy, too caught up in his work for any sort of real fun. Molly was well aware that the boredom would probably get to her long before their relationship diminished, not that she had admitted so much to anyone, not even herself, before that moment. It was funny how such intellect, such creative genius, could scatter her thoughts and entice her to believe there was more to her feelings than admiration for brilliance in an artist's craft.

Her train of thought unnerved her. How she hadn't seen this sooner, she didn't know. Not that she had spent months, weeks, days even, pining for him, but three months dangled on a string was long enough to be declared a waste of time.

Molly held her breath when the restaurant came into view. Bold cherry red letters against the white background wasn't easy to miss—although the cab driver seemed to manage it and sailed straight past.

She cleared her throat, mouth dry from not

speaking and stressing the entire distance they had driven.

"Um. Excuse me. The restaurant is just back there on your left." Obviously, he too had been in a world of his own. It was a good thing she was familiar with the place they were going or else she would've ended up in Rockingham before either of them registered they had gone too far. She scowled as she realized that would've been the perfect excuse for not turning up, no matter how unbelievable it may have sounded that she had not only got lost, but left her phone at home and couldn't message him to let him know.

A pang of guilt surged to the pit of her gut. Poor unsuspecting guy had no idea she was such a novice dater, although, truth be told, he was sitting in the restaurant, or in whatever means of transport he had opted for that evening, and was as much a wreck as she was. A comforting thought, even if it was nowhere near the truth of the situation, and one she intended to go with, at least until she got out of the taxi and inside the door of the restaurant.

Still ahead of time, Molly paid the fare and hesitated a moment before opening the door. Not having her phone with her, she wondered if she should ask the driver to wait in case her date didn't show.

He glanced up, peering back at her in the rear vision mirror. "Is everything okay?"

Molly sucked in a breath, nodded, and exhaled slowly. It'd be easy enough to arrange another taxi. She was being overcautious, which wasn't a bad thing, but when paranoia took over all else, it wasn't ideal.

"Thanks for the lift." Opening the door, she slid from the backseat and closed the door before she could change her mind. Moments after taking a step back from the car, he pulled away. No doubt eager for his next fare.

Molly turned to face the restaurant. From the outside it appeared not so intimidating as she guessed the man who awaited her company inside.

"Be brave, for Christ sake," she cursed, frustration masked anxiety.

She shivered, despite the night being balmy, then rubbed her hands up and down her arms for warmth.

A mix of spices she couldn't determine teased her senses and her stomach ached from hunger. Eating had been furthest from her mind all day, and if for nothing else, the food would be worth the effort she'd made to get ready.

As she entered, Molly glanced around to see if anyone stood out as familiar.

"Looking for someone?" A voice more husky than she imagined caught her off guard as he approached from behind. Her instant reaction was to say no, but she thought better of it and turned to face the direction in which it'd come. Molly couldn't help but smile. Leaning against the wall, *Surfer Boy* looked every bit as appealing in the flesh as he did in his profile. Perhaps the effort would be rewarded with more than just good food.

"It seems I've found him. Nice to meet you, Doug." Molly stepped toward him and offered her hand to shake. Doug slipped his into hers, gave a gentle squeeze as he leaned forward and pecked her on the cheek.

"Pleasure is all mine."

*His voice.* Goosebumps pricked her skin, and she fought against shivering for a second time.

"Shall we?" He gestured for her to take the lead into the main restaurant where he spoke to the waitress about a booth for two. She nodded.

Having got what he wanted, he turned to Molly and smiled. *There it was.* That smile. As effective as it threatened in a photograph.

*Why the hell was this guy single?* Instantly charmed,

he intrigued her, as would a crime committed in the opening scene of a movie. She needed more to work him out and wasn't going to stop until she had all the answers.

Doug stood until Molly was seated before he slid in alongside her. *Old school gentleman.* She'd not picked it, but his manner added to his charm.

Instead of being nervous as she had been when she left home, Molly found herself relaxing and laughing along with Doug's attempts at humor, most of which were more ridiculous than funny.

"So, tell me, why *Craze?*" Doug held his hands up and impersonated quotations as he said the name of the app that had bought them together.

Molly laughed and shook her head. "Not a lot to tell. A friend convinced me it was a good idea, and after a few wines over Chinese takeout and a chick flick, I relented."

Doug raised his eyebrows and grinned. Dimples exposed, which charmed her more every time they made an appearance. "Moment of truth." Doug paused for effect, struggling to keep a serious face. "It's not the first time I've heard that excuse."

"So, tell me, how long have you been on *Craze?*" She mimicked his quotation gesture and smiled, knowing too well that hers didn't come with the added advantage of dimples.

"A few months." He shrugged, looking uncomfortable for the first time since they met.

All Molly managed was to nod. Too many questions rushed through her mind at once, none of which were appropriate to say out aloud. Of course, she'd heard talk about online dating sites being the place to fill your bed with a variety, but that wasn't what she was looking for. Perhaps it wasn't a bad idea to add the intention to her profile. She'd noticed many guys made it clear if a one nightstand or friends with benefits was their desire. Just as, if a relationship was what they were looking for, they mentioned it in their profile.

"I haven't been on many dates, if that's what you're thinking," Doug added after the silence between them lingered longer than comfortable.

Relieved the waitress chose that moment to interrupt, Molly picked up the menu she had neglected from the moment she sat down.

"Beer for me. Molly?"

"Sauvignon Blanc, please."

"Would you like to order meals, or do you need a few moments?" Young and sweet, the waitress directed her question at Molly.

"Extra time would be great, thanks."

Tapas were something they needed to discuss. Not so easy as ordering a separate meal on a first date, they were heading for sharing territory straight up and they had no clue as to what the other liked to eat.

"Have you eaten here before?" At least if Doug had a sense of what he liked on the menu, then they were in for less of a challenge.

"Um, yeah." He fidgeted in his seat and searched the room, as if willing for another interruption. "I used to come here with my wife."

Molly raised her eyebrows. She hadn't seen that one coming. Home wrecker wasn't a title she ever wanted to be given, however, it seemed to have attached itself to her back and didn't want to shift no matter how hard she tried to resist.

"Your wife. No ex in there, or perhaps estranged?" Remaining calm, voice kept low, was not so easy when Molly wanted to scream like a lunatic. It wasn't any wonder he'd been on the dating site for so long.

"No. Deceased."

Words were her life, and yet the right ones escaped her. Molly sat forward in her chair, elbows on the table; she cupped her hands over her mouth and looked into his eyes. The laughter and dimpled grin had hidden the sadness, but for the first time she recognized heartbreak—a man who lost his love and was still feeling her absence.

"I'm sorry." What else could she say? The beautiful stranger she so superficially picked from the pack was as available as Carl turned out to be. Obviously, not of the cheating type, but still he was as spoken for as he would've been if his wife was sitting at home waiting for him.

He shook his head, fighting the tears that threatened to spill. "She's been gone for two years. Cancer." Minimal, but enough detail to hit home that this guy needed a friend, a shoulder to cry on, not a replacement wife.

The waitress approached, but with a shake of her head, she deviated toward another table.

"Such a rotten disease. I'm sorry she had to go through that—for both of you." Not wanting to appear heartless, Molly toyed with the corner of her menu, but didn't open it.

"Thanks. It was a horrible period in my life, that's for sure."

Although she knew the wife conversation wasn't over, she was relieved when Doug suggested they place their order. After a quick discussion, they opted for the bread platter and assorted dipping sauces, mixed greens, pork belly bites, and chicken breast fillets with pomegranate sauce.

"So, what sort of business do you run?" She figured work to be a safe topic and steered the conversation away from the ghost that seemed to have taken up residence in the center of the table. The thought of dating someone else's husband, deceased or living, left an uneasy feeling over her. She couldn't begin to imagine how Doug was feeling.

Once the meal was served, he dished up his emotions on a silver platter—tears and all. The man was a mess before he downed one beer.

Heavy and exhausted by the time the waitress offered them the dessert menu, Molly opted out of her favorite course despite sticky date pudding served with vanilla bean ice-cream being on the menu. Doug ordered a black coffee with an extra shot. No doubt he'd be heading home for another night of watching the recording of his wedding day, alone.

## CHAPTER 5

Disappointment about summed it up for her. So sweet, yet so damaged. There was no competing with a ghost who died perfect, in his eyes. Two years later and it was as though she'd been gone a few days.

Molly ran a brush through her hair and applied a smear of pale pink gloss to her lips. *Two dates in two days. She had to be mad.* Although Doug fit the mold of her type, the hauntings of his past would be prominent in her future, and she wasn't keen to come second to a memory.

She'd made no promises, and despite having no intention to see him again, guilt gripped and momentarily consumed her. Perhaps dismissing one and moving on to a second so soon after they met wasn't the best way to handle the dating scene. It'd been so long since she went out for the evening, having hung around waiting and hoping for Carl to be available. Time wasted frustrated her, and Carl was nothing more than a waste of her time.

There was no point adding Doug, who'd never be more to her than one date, to the list of time wasters. Moving on and not dwelling was a much better use of her time.

Molly left her bathroom in chaos. Discarded outfits draped over the edge of the bath, and makeup littered the usually cleared bench top. As always, she was pushing it to be on time.

With her cell in hand, so as not to forget it again, Molly decided it'd be best to take her car. *The Grosvenor Hotel* was one of her favorite places to go for a quiet drink and a light meal. Set on the beach and less than fifteen minutes' drive, it was the closest thing to a local she had.

Molly slid into the driver's seat as her cell phone began to ring. Shelley's name displayed across the screen. After a moment's hesitation, she swiped to answer the call.

"Hey gorgeous." Bright and bubbly, as always. "You keen for takeout and a movie at yours tonight?"

Shelley always invited herself over, insisting that Molly's house was more fun to be at.

"Sorry, lovely, I'm on my way out—I have a date."

The shrill echoed down the line. Molly jerked the phone away from her ear and cringed. The last thing she needed was a burst eardrum before her date with Simon. Deliciously cute, this guy looked too good to be true. So much so that Molly hesitated to swipe right, convinced his account was a scam.

Doug was everything she thought her type to be, and Simon was his complete opposite. Taller and bigger built, the manual labor of his work obviously kept him in tone, as his photos indicated.

"A second date with the surfer boy, or a newbie." The giggle that followed was proof enough that Shelley was getting more out of Molly dating than she was.

"Nah, pity about him, he was cute." She paused a moment, not wanting to get into details about the previous evening whilst she was driving to meet someone else. "I'll tell you all about him when we catch up next. If this guy turns out to be a dud, then I'll call you and we can have a late-night movie minus the meal, if you want?"

"Sure, sounds good—I want every detail as if you're writing me a report. No censoring, my date card has reached expiry. I think we need a girls' day out—an adult toy shop is at the top of the list of places to visit."

Molly tipped her head back and laughed. "If that turns you on, sure." Shelley was as flamboyant in nature as she was in her clothing designs, and reason the tabloids never tired of her creations. Difficult to pick what she'd bring to the table next. Kind-hearted and loyal to a tee, Molly wished she'd find the sort of man she was looking for. Although, something told her that even Shelley wasn't sure what she was looking for.

"I'm running late. I'll call you later if it's not too late, or else tomorrow."

"Fine, Miss popular, whenever you've got a free moment."

Molly tossed her phone onto the passenger seat before backing out of the driveway. At the rate she was going, he'd think she was a no show, especially if parking was anything like she imagined it would be so early in the evening. The popular after work hang out, so close to the city, would be packed to the brim, but the atmosphere never disappointed no matter what day or time she visited.

The car park was empty. The establishment more deserted than she'd seen it before, which wasn't altogether a bad thing. There was nothing worse than having to shout through a first date, and a pub wasn't the most intimate of places.

Not sure where to wait, Molly found a seat out of the direct sunlight, but close to the front entry. She assumed he'd wait outside. Perhaps he was even tardier than she, which she'd much prefer than being stood up.

Ten minutes waiting seemed like an hour; especially when she checked her phone for the time every minute or two. She didn't fancy wandering around the premises on the scout for a man she had never seen before. Photos had a way of concealing true identity. The embarrassment of mistaking Simon for another guy would almost be comparable to being stood up.

Fifteen minutes late wasn't outrageous, but enough time passed to send a polite *where the fuck are you* text...not so crassly put, but hopefully he'd get the general gist.

*<Hi Simon, not sure where you wanted to meet so I'm sitting out front in the shade. I'm the loner in white... >*

. . .

Subtlety was never her strong point, but given that Simon only knew her from a few texts, perhaps he'd miss the point that waiting around for a man was no longer her thing. For too long she'd jumped through hurdles, danced to the tune of another—those days were gone. Online dating had Molly writing her own rules, and Simon had assisted her to set the first one.

Rule Number One; more than half an hour late without a text or call and the date is over before it even begins.

Molly watched as couples walked past, hand in hand, laughing or talking—prams seemingly the accessory of the season. The fact that she was sitting alone, out the front of a bar, enhanced the rejection building in the pit of her gut.

Half an hour passed and after sending a brief text to tell Simon she was leaving, she awaited his response. It didn't come.

Breaking the first rule she set, an hour late and she'd had enough. Dating a guy hung up on a ghost wouldn't be so bad as one who presented as one, but neither was a contender for a second date.

The blow to her ego kept coming at a rate she hoped would slow down. The temptation to hang up her dating shoes before she managed to wear them beyond blister-givers, had increased over the past few days, even more in the last hour than since she first downloaded the app. A mistake she knew she'd regret and did.

Surely the brief flirtation they'd exchanged via text wasn't enough to put him off. She'd kept her correspondence light and fun. He'd sent her emojis blowing kisses and laughing faces after most comments.

Humiliation was beginning to kick in, and the time to leave had long past. She was better than the loser she felt. Not that she had any control over him not turning up, even so, it wasn't her finest moment. Almost as bad as the swift kick she suffered when she found out the reason Carl avoided contact with her was because physical attention was being provided by another source.

Not wanting to go home to spend another evening texting random men, she headed for Shelley's instead of inviting her over to hers. Dinner and a movie with her bestie beat the delectable Simon any day.

Chinese takeout twice in one week was a little too much, so Molly opted for another favorite and stopped at the Thai restaurant two streets away from Shelley's house. At least the green curry would add some spice to her life. She certainly wasn't getting it from any other source but her palette.

Quick to deliver her order, Molly was back in her car and pulling into Shelley's driveway in a matter of minutes. It seemed so long ago that she was here, interviewing Candice, and stumbling over information she didn't want to discover, when only a few weeks had passed.

Knowing that no one else would be visiting so late, she parked up close to the step, so she didn't have to fight for balance as she walked across the stones with their dinner in hand.

She'd not thought to make the detour to buy a bottle of wine. With the mood she was in, a bottle of gin wouldn't have been enough to numb the humiliation cursing through her veins.

Nothing about being stood up was good for boosting esteem, and Molly was beginning to feel the effects of being a dud in love. She just hoped that not all men would see her as such.

Shelley took her time to answer the door. No doubt peering out the window first to see who was intruding on her space. She wasn't much for having people over, despite having hosted some of the most memorable events Molly could remember.

"I know you said you'd come to mine, but I was

in my car already, so I thought I'd bring us dinner—" She paused and held up the bag of food. "I forgot to get wine, but I can go out now if you want me to." She lowered the bag and shrugged her shoulders. "I hope you don't mind me dropping in on you without prior warning." Tears pooled in her eyes, and she blinked rapidly in hope they'd go away before they spilled down her cheeks.

"Of course I don't mind. Come in." Shelley took a step back and opened the door wide enough for Molly to slip past her and inside. Candles lit up the entryway, and the rest of the house she noticed as she walked through to the kitchen and placed the food on the granite bench.

"I didn't interrupt a hot date night, did I?"

"Nah. I thought it'd be nice to do this for me. I was just about to open a bottle of wine, set me out some cheese and crackers, and have a romantic evening for one. But, even better, we have Thai food, and mood setting candles for two." She smiled as she picked up the bottle of red she'd set on the bench before opening the door.

"You okay with red to go with curry? I'm not really in the mood for white."

"I'm up for either. So long as it doesn't dry up

and evaporate before I lift the glass to my lips, I'm happy."

"What's that all about?" Shelley retrieved a second glass from the cupboard and poured them each a glass.

"Well, given my track record over the past few days, anything is possible." She sighed and took the offered glass and took a sip, then reached into the bag for their food, passed one box to Shelley before taking cutlery out from the drawer.

"Simon, that bad you did a runner?" She jutted out her bottom lip and tipped her head sideways in sympathy.

"Huh. Who knows? He didn't bother to show." She passed over the cutlery and they each carried their food and drink to the couch in the next room. *More candles.* "He didn't even bother to message me either."

"What a prick." She dropped down onto the sofa, careful not to spill a drop. "Sadly, the site is full of them."

"And joining the *Craze* was such a good idea *because?*" She raised her eyebrows and awaited Shelley's response.

"It'd be a suitable topic to write about." She flashed a smile, then shoved a large fork full of noodles in her mouth so she didn't have to speak any time soon.

"Oh yeah. I'm going to start a blog to warn the innocent singles of the nightmares they're wasting hours conversing with. I mean, why do these guys even sign up to these sites if they have no interest in being decent enough to show up."

Shelley chewed as she mulled over Molly's words, swallowed, and then took a large gulp of wine before she answered. "You don't have to convince me. I don't understand it either." Another mouthful of wine. "But, I like the idea of the blog—you wanted a career change. I think you've just discovered a way to become a celebrity blogger instead of writing about fashion and entertainment for *The Times*."

"I've got as much chance of becoming a celebrity blogger as I have of scoring a decent date that leads to a second, and eventually a sexual encounter."

"If anyone has enough luck to find a keeper, it'll be you. Give the blog some thought, it could be fun."

"Oh yeah? And what would I report on, my disastrous love life.

"Well, there would be a market for it. You're not the only one with a sucky love life."

"Problem is, you have to have a date turn up to

claim you have a love life in the first place—" She raised her eyebrows and took a huge bite of noodles and chewed.

"Um, honey, if you do go on a date, don't eat like that or he won't come back for a second."

"What's wrong with how I eat?" Mouth still full, chewing action exaggerated.

Shelley groaned. "My point exactly." She held her hand up and gestured toward Molly as if showcasing her mouth. "I present to you exhibit A."

# CHAPTER 6

Molly decided to put *Craze* on hold for a few days, exhausted from too many late nights answering the ridiculous amount of messages she'd received. How she'd swiped right for so many men, she didn't know. Some were an accident, and, although she felt bad, she unmatched with them if it was an instant match. Others she had second thoughts about, so they were weeded out as well.

The entire process made her wince. Like livestock at a market, she was picking and choosing guys based on a few photos and, if she was lucky, a few sentences about their likes and dislikes. *Craze* about summed it up, she'd doubted her sanity since the app became a part of her daily ritual.

Ensuring her cell was on silent, Molly tucked it in the back pocket of her purse, and zipped the compartment shut. A few hours out with her besties was exactly what she needed to distract her from the miserable dating game that was messing with her head. There was no doubt she would never get used to this way of finding a date, and the appeal of a single life was growing on her. Not that she would admit that in front of Shelley, who'd drag her out on double dates for the rest of her life if she didn't at least try to find an eligible suitor.

Molly groaned, even tucked away and zipped tight, that bloody app still haunted her thoughts. It was a good thing work was quiet or else shades of craze would no doubt shadow her articles. Although, any excuse to spice up the tedious task she endured in order to pay the rent and put food on her table was a good one. Goodness knows, it'd add a little color to an already colorful industry.

In her experience, with said screenwriter, the industry already had plenty of spice to contend with. Spice she could do without being a part of.

It's amazing how quickly a negative experience in an industry she once respected could tarnish her entire outlook. Maybe it was petty, to want a change of scene just because of a man, if she dare grant him such a title, and his ill-intent, to draw her into a word of deceit. A home wrecker, had Candice's revelation not set her free of the title before their relationship ventured further than a lingering kiss.

Still, she liked to think Carl would've told her about the woman sleeping in his bed whilst he busied himself sending selfies and monologues via messenger each night. Restoring faith in the industry she once admired wouldn't be so hard if that were the case, but deep in her gut she didn't believe it to be true.

For too long she'd been cooped up indoors, her thoughts stuck in a loop on replay, she couldn't wait to get out. Walking was the best way to clear her head, so despite the restaurant they were going to being a good half-hour walk, Molly opted to for clarity.

There was an element of comfort about her shoes, lightweight, wedged heel, made for an easy walk. It was the six inches added to her height that encouraged her to take a cab home. Especially with a few wines in her, there'd be no other way she'd make it back to her apartment intact.

Dating game on or not, a cast and crutches wouldn't do much to enhance sex appeal, and given the luck she had in finding love, she didn't need anything else to work against her.

Mind working overtime, a common occurrence of late, Molly ran her morning over as if on reenactment. Not that a lot happened, it was rather uneventful, in fact. But her thoughts were becoming destructive. *When did negativity become such a huge part of her routine? Was there a moment that wasn't devoted to feeling sorry for herself or hating on the world of men?* Better to realize it now than to end up a bitter old lady even cats couldn't tolerate.

She had to get off the dating train, no matter how much Shelley pushed her to lower the boom gates. She just wasn't ready to put herself out there—to trust someone again so soon.

Molly was a wreck by the time she arrived at the restaurant. Hair windblown, mind a muddle, and blisters threatening. Her desire for a glass or two of wine had increased to bottles.

"Look at you, all ruffled and sexy in your get up." Shelley stood and offered a hug as Molly approached the table. Karina, renowned for being late, was yet to arrive.

"I needed the exercise, so I walked." She shrugged, not bothering to elaborate that *Craze* was pushing her over the edge, the fact that she'd walked kilometers in heels was all the supporting evidence required.

"Pftt. That's what *Craze* is for." Head tipped back, she laughed, deep and from the gut causing other diners to turn in their direction.

"I have enough trouble getting them to turn up, I'm certainly not going to rely on the app as an exercise regimen." Molly sat in one of the two seats that were vacant and waited for Shelley to do the same.

"Karina's running late. Surprise, surprise." The *tut* in her tone was in good nature. Karina's tardiness had rubbed off from her mother back in the days of high school when she'd rarely arrived before the siren sounded. Often having to manage the tedious task of getting teachers to sign her late form.

"There's comfort in predictability—you know what I'm like, creature of habit and all."

"Yeah, well, it's about time you step out of your comfort zone and break those habits." Shelley tilted her head to one side and stared at her a moment. "So, when's your next date?"

Molly shrugged, not wanting to get into the conversation with her, but knowing she'd have little choice. "When's yours?"

"No, no, no. We're not talking about me—I hope

you didn't delete that app." The frown on her face was just the beginning of the disapproval to come.

"Settle down, *craze-y* lady. I didn't delete anything."

The lines smoothed from her forehead, and a smile touched the corners of her mouth. "Don't hold back any new suitors worth pursuing?"

Molly toyed with the lie that threatened to roll out of her mouth.

"I'm waiting." She thrummed her fingertips on the tabletop, indicating her impatience.

"Sorry I'm late." Out of breath and obviously rushing, Karina announced her arrival when she was more than a meter from their table.

Molly released a sigh. "Not at all, perfect timing." *In more ways than one.*

"Oh yes," Shelley gushed. "Perfect timing to hear all about Molly's new men." Heads pivoted in their direction again, only this time Molly wished the ground would swallow her whole so as not to suffer the humiliation of being titled the restaurant's biggest floozie.

"She means lack of. Now that we're up to speed on me, sit your skinny butt down so we can get this party started." The exchange of kisses didn't take long. Nothing ever did when Karina was involved.

Fast-paced and never tired, she reminded Molly of the *Eveready Battery* ad on television when she was a child. *The bunny that never ran out of steam.*

Three kids underfoot, she made juggling motherhood with her own online business look like a walk in the park. Despite being late to every event she'd ever attended in life.

"Come off it. I've been married for-*ever*, and the most exciting thing in my life is when Oscar doesn't miss the potty." She rolled her eyes, more dramatic than Shelley, but not so loud.

"How's he going with the toilet training?" Babies weren't her forte, nor were the mechanics of the training process, but anything to distract Shelley from *Craze* was a perfect conversation to elaborate on.

"Oh, you know—" Karina paused mid shrug and turned her gaze to Shelley. "I get it—avoiding the *man.*" Lifting her hand to shoulder height, she signaled inverted commas around the word before continuing. "Confessions. I do hope they're sinful enough to be worth the suspense." The wicked glint in her eye proved that she was eager to hear about something more exciting than the toilet training she was dealing with.

Molly arched one eyebrow and looked pointedly

at Shelley. "Nothing sinful on my behalf—but being stood up isn't the most pleasant date I've ever experienced."

"I don't know, in my experience I'd bet it was a blessing," Shelley scoffed. "Did simple-Simon bother to offer an apology or make an attempt to come up with a viable excuse?"

"What do you think? A man capable of pulling off such a dick move doesn't have an apology in his narcissistic mind." Molly released a deep breath, an attempt to cool her heated mood. Sometimes she wished Shelley would back off with her prodding and allow her to share private moments when she was ready to share them. "I need wine."

It seemed that exchange of glances was going to be a thing between Shelley and Karina today. Tiptoeing around the *crazy* member of the party, who couldn't even manage to get a simple first date right. Pity was plastered all over Karina's expression when her eyes met Molly's again.

"I don't need a man in my life to make me happy, so there's no need to feel sorry for me." Molly signaled a waitress as she headed back toward the bar.

"That makes one of us. Seems a man is my only missing ingredient to make a baby." Shelley's laughter was cut short whilst the waitress took their order.

"There are other options, you know." Karina's focus honed in on the baby comment and, for the moment, Molly was safe to simmer her thoughts on the online dating situation.

"I've actually been looking into them," Shelley admitted, tone a little more hushed than usual. "My biggest fear is what to tell the kid as it grows up about who the father was."

"That's an easy one." Karina flipped a hand in Shelley's direction, as the waitress returned with the bottle they'd ordered and began pouring them each a glass.

Shelley was the first to pick up her glass and offer up a toast. "To the three crazies." Clinking glasses as they laughed.

"So." Shelley set her glass back on the table. "Tell me this easy solution."

"Tell it the truth."

"That's it?"

"Yeah. Honesty is the best policy." Karina took another sip before setting her glass down too. "There is nothing wrong with a woman grasping hold of what she wants in life, even if it defies nature. I mean, you wouldn't hesitate a nip and a tuck if it was offered to you later in life, would you?"

"Well, no, but—"

"But what? It's no different. Defying nature in that department is exactly the same as wanting a baby and making it happen no matter what."

"True." Molly piped up. "And it's not like you'd love it less. Who cares how it came about so long as you give it the best life you can."

"To be honest, I think it'd show the child exactly how devoted you are to having one when you had to go to such measures to become pregnant in the first place."

"Ha. That makes my speech an easy one then, doesn't it? *Desperate Mommy went to desperate measures to have you, no man required.*"

We may have been laughing, but the glassing over with tears in Shelley's eyes indicated she'd prefer conventional methods as a way to start a family.

"So, are you serious about having a baby?" Karina picked up the lunch menu and perused the options on offer.

She was the heart of our little threesome. Always knowing how to open up the conversation so we wore our heart on a chain around our necks whenever she was around.

Karina placed the menu on the table and turned her attention back to Shelley.

"I have an appointment at the clinic next week." Exposed and vulnerable pushed Shelley way beyond her comfort zone. The tear she swiped from her cheek was the first of many to follow.

Karina was usually the one in need of tissues whenever they caught up, emotional from too little sleep. She was always equipped with a supply, so she pulled one from her purse and passed it to Shelley. "Need a support crew?" She glanced at Molly to confirm she wasn't out of line with her offer.

Shelley smiled through her tears. "I'd really like that," she admitted.

"Good. Now that we have you all sorted, Molly, tell us about your love life."

*So much for avoiding the limelight.* "Nothing to tell. It's as happening as ever—not." Avoiding eye contact, it was her turn to grab for the menu and act as if she were focused on what she intended to order.

There was no doubt in her mind that Shelley had been keeping Karina updated with date reports, or that they were exchanging glances whilst she concentrated on what she wanted for lunch.

"Well." She began slowly. "There's this guy, Zakary, who works with Matty. I think you'd like him," Karina suggested. "Not that I've met him, yet, but no doubt he'll be at the next business dinner we have to go to."

"No set ups. You know how I feel about dating friends of friends. It just wouldn't work for me."

"He's not really a friend, just a colleague Matty sometimes grabs a beer with after work."

"Oh, I assume you're saying that the minor technicalities of their relationship makes all the difference?"

"Something like that." She looked doubtful, but Molly had to score her high for being persistent. She was always trying to set her up with these really *great* guys, but there was no way she'd agree.

"Thanks for thinking of me, but no thanks. Fix him up with Shelley."

Karina glanced over at Shelley and winced. "I would, but he's into blondes and won't date women older than him."

"He sounds like a nice guy—*deep*. Wouldn't you agree?" Molly arched one eyebrow, a smile teasing the corners of her lips as she tried to remain serious.

## CHAPTER 7

There was nothing about being set up with a friend's friend that appealed to her. Molly's less than positive attitude toward the whole dating scene saw the rest of the conversation focused on Karina and her *Mary Poppins* life, or gossip about one thing or another.

After too many wines and a cab drive home, Molly decided to check the action on *Craze*—for something to do in her otherwise less than exciting life.

*Okay, boys, who's looking for a dull lady to share your extreme sporting, fish gutting, dog kissing life.* Surely there was a manual or a blog out there telling these dateless individuals how to complete their profile to set them apart from the next. Because, *they all listened, and, honestly, it ain't working for no one.*

The wine didn't help her cynical side, it enhanced it, although it also enticed her to agree to going on another date. *Third time lucky.* This would be the decider date. If all went well then she'd continue her hunt for Mr. Right. But, if it turned out to be as much a disaster as the other two, then she was throwing in the towel and calling it quits on *Craze*.

As she put the bottle of wine back in the fridge, she spotted an unopened brie and a bunch of grapes that'd make the perfect light meal after a big lunch. Crackers and a few almonds from the cupboard finished her platter off perfectly. She admired her creation as she carried it and her glass to the couch where the *Craze* awaited her return.


The date preparation process had lost its appeal for Molly. Going to too much effort seemed a waste if the guy was a no show, or such a dud that the temptation to run and hide in the ladies' restrooms would win out.

Deep in the pit of her gut, she still hoped to meet a keeper. Someone she'd be content to share her life with. Someone who made her happy. Someone who made her like herself more because of who *she was* when she was with them. Someone to prove to herself that *happily ever after* wasn't reserved for fairytales.

It was the possibility of meeting a keeper that drove her to put effort into getting ready that night. To pick the black dress over the white to make her feel better about the *fat-day* she was having, and to disguise any bloating she may suffer from too much wine the day before.

Prepped, polished, and as bright as she could manage whilst suffering a hangover, she snatched her purse from the kitchen bench at the sound of the cab driver blasting the horn out front of her apartment.

There was no point taking a jacket. The evenings could still be chilly, but she opted to suffer from the car to the front door, because once inside the restaurant she'd be fine. The best part about meeting her date at an arranged location was that there'd be no lingering moments when he dropped her off, walked her to the front door in hope to score a kiss or an invitation inside her apartment.

Keith wasn't her usual type in looks or personality, from what she could tell via text, but, determined to take two steps out of her comfort zone she overlooked a few minor details and went for the guy she thought was self assured enough to, at least, make an appearance.

Since before he stood her up, she hadn't heard a peep from Simon. Super keen met with such disappointment made a lasting impression on her, that was for sure. The saddest part about their almost encounter was that she allowed his actions and lack of character to reduce her to feel as if she was the one that wasn't enough, which was all kinds of messed up. Truth was, a guy like him wasn't worthy of her time, and any dud would run rings around him anyway—even if, from his photographs, he appeared to be beautiful looking and had a body resembling that of the Greek God Poseidon.

Letting things go was something she needed to work on. Being stood up was currently at the top of the list of situations she needed to let go of. For the moment, at least, she needed to push all thoughts of Simon to one side or else there'd be a strong chance she'd reveal her thoughts were elsewhere when she greeted Keith.

*Keith. Keith. Keith.* She chanted his name over in her head in hope it'd stick, and she wouldn't slip up and call him the name of one of her other suitors.

It wasn't until the cab driver pulled the car to the

verge and she reached into her purse for her credit card that she realized she'd done it again and left her cell with her jacket, carefully laid out on her bed.

"Shit," she muttered, loud enough for the driver to glance back at her in the rearview mirror.

"Is everything okay, Madame."

She was positive he would've locked the doors of the cab, certain she didn't have money to pay for her fair, if he could.

"Oh, sorry, I forgot my cell phone, is all." She tried to sound casual, but inside her stomach felt to be twisting in knots. Of all dates, this was the last one she wanted to attend without the option to abort if things went downhill.

Handing over her credit card, Molly paid the driver and then climbed out from the back seat and into the brisk night air. She wrapped her arms around herself in a tight hug and hurried to the front door where an elderly gentleman, wearing a suit with tails, a top hat, and holding a cane in one hand, pulled open the door with the other.

"Good evening." He dipped his head and greeted her the moment she stepped upon the velvety red carpet that led the way from the sidewalk.

"Good evening." She mimicked his move, dipping

her head, and walked through to the open bar area where Keith indicated he'd be waiting.

She spotted him from across the room. As per his photographs, Keith did nothing much for her from a physical perspective. Not entirely a brilliant start, but showing up was a tick on the side of positive, so she decided not to keep him waiting any longer.

Crossing the room, she took him in. There was no doubt he was good-looking, with dark hair and olive complexion, despite her usually leaning toward fair looks. Even though he was sitting down, she could tell that he was tall and lean, more athletic than bulky and big. And he was nicely dressed. Formal, more than the casual attire she was used to a partner wearing through choice rather than what was expected according to dress code.

So far, there was little she could pick as a negative in his favor. She exhaled as she approached, hoping to calm the pounding in her chest—not a reaction as to who was waiting, but first dates made her nervous.

"Keith?" She was cautious in case today, of all days, his doppelganger was in the house and caught them both by surprise.

"Molly." He grinned as he stood, placed a hand on

her shoulder and leaned over to kiss her on the cheek.

A polite notion he executed with ease, as if he were a seasoned first dater. He was on *Craze*, after all, so perhaps this was his hobby. Her cynical side was clawing its way to the surface as if taunting her to find fault in this poor unsuspecting guy.

He moved around her and pulled a chair out from under the table and waited for her to sit.

"I'm glad you showed up, I've been stood up a few times, so this makes for a pleasant change."

Molly sat and was relieved to learn so soon into the date that she wasn't the only one who'd endured the *loser tune* of a no-show. And, as negative as the topic was, at least they had something in common.

"You too, huh?"

"Oh no, don't tell me?" he raised his eyebrows and tipped his head slightly to show his disbelief that he wasn't alone in the experience.

Molly nodded, but didn't offer an explanation. She didn't feel comfortable elaborating on past date experiences, even the dates that didn't eventuate. However, this didn't stop Keith from expressing his disapproval.

On and on he harped, only stopping briefly to speak to the waitress, order two espresso martinis before waving her off so he could continue the one-sided conversation he was having *at her* rather than *with her.*

The exchange between Keith and the waitress happened too quickly for her to argue the order he placed for them both. Molly sat in disbelief as he continued to talk so fast she couldn't find a break in his sentence long enough to offer a comment.

The arrival of their drinks didn't slow him, as he reached up and took both drinks from the tray and flicked his head as if dismissing her services.

Molly was certain her mouth was agape, but shell-shocked by his rudeness and the rate at which his conversation was being flung her way, rendered her speechless.

Instead of passing over one of the martinis, Keith placed two fingers on the base of the glass and slid it across the shiny surface of the table. Obviously, a practiced party trick because he didn't spill a drop of its contents.

"Thanks." Molly muttered, but he didn't acknowledge that she'd spoken. His stories continued, from one subject to another, to another.

As soon as he paused to take a sip of his drink, Molly jumped in with a comment, which was met with a *hmm, as I was saying.*

Like a slap in the face, nothing could have come as more of a shock. After her initial irritation, she made a game out of the exchange, jumping in and offering comments here and there, most of which were met with the same response. Raised eyebrows, or a *hmm*, or *as I was saying*, and on occasions he combined all three.

His stories were boring, mostly about people she didn't know, his work colleagues or friends of friends. Negativity seemed the common connection between the stories, and his sense of humor spiked at the expense of others.

Even his good looks irritated her as he twisted his face into odd expressions to accommodate the impersonations and voice changes he made whilst imitating another.

Delete was the only reaction from a first date with him stimulated, and Molly couldn't wait for it to be over. She was grateful they'd opted for drinks rather than dinner—the expected time they spent together not so long.

He'd avoided the usual, getting to know each other topics she expected to exchange until he broached the *Craze* subject. "So, you've been stood up too?"

Before she had time to open her mouth, he

launched into a tale of his own. *Honestly, why did he bother to ask a question in the first place?*

"I don't know about you, but head shots alone, with no full-length photo sparks a few questions in my head—mostly, *how fat are you exactly?*"

Molly didn't bother to hide her irritation. The frown clouding her expression would've been enough to warn a normal, socially appropriate individual that her patience was growing thin. The fact that Keith was inept for society enhanced her motivation to bring the date to an abrupt end. Fed up listening to his shitty stories, she devised a plan to aid her escape—*if only she had her cell phone*. It'd make the process a whole lot easier.

From across the room, he caught the waitress's eye, pointed to their empty glasses and held up two fingers to indicate replenishments for them both.

Despite espresso martinis being one of her favorite cocktails, it wasn't enough to soften the blow any more than if he ordered her liquid nitrogen to drink. Online dating, or any dating for that matter, may not come with a do's and don'ts manual, but it wasn't cool to take such control on the first date, or any date with her. She had a voice, and if he didn't want to hear it, then perhaps he should stick with the *online* part of dating, and skip out on real life.

A few minutes later, after he dished out countless insults about the women who uploaded photos that weren't recent on their *Craze* profile page, the waitress appeared with the replacement drinks.

Again, Keith lifted the two glasses from the tray and waited as the waitress cleared the two empty ones and disappeared.

He was predictable, too caught up in himself to register that she knew what was coming next. What she imagined he thought to be a suave maneuver, Keith push the glass at the base and let it slide across the table to her.

Molly reached out, finger in the path of the glass. It collided, tipped and spilled all over her. It was the only thing she could think to do having left her cell phone at home.

Glass shattered as soon as the brim came into contact with the tabletop. A large shard flicked off to the side and nicked her arm, deep red against the cream of her skin, which added to the drama of the situation. It looked worse than it was, but it was another thing she could play up if necessary.

Liquid momentarily pooled in her lap before seeping through the thin fabric, saturating her from front to back. Fluid dripped from the table and fell to meet the two coffee beans resting like a set of balls in her lap. She tried not to smile. There was no denying she'd taken the situation by the balls and nailed the perfect escape plan.

# CHAPTER 8

Building a site for her blog didn't take long, but, with her stomach threatening to eat itself, she wandered to the kitchen to make grilled cheese on toast and a cup of tea—her own version of a nightcap.

Keith was the deciding factor to inspire her to take what was initially intended as a joke to actually building a blog. Online dating didn't have to be such a solitary ride, or an experience that stripped one of their confidence, or faith in the opposite sex, to the point where they began to feel like they're the dud and not the person sitting across the table.

Molly couldn't deny she'd toyed with the idea of writing a blog in the past, but never had she imagined it'd be based on such a personal aspect of her life as dating. The thought of others being in the same position as she was in feeling lousy as though she was a dating dud, inspired her to spread the word that they weren't alone. Not to mention that those who inflict such trauma upon others may stumble upon the site and take a hint that their behavior is inexcusable.

Keith was the turning point for her. Full of his own importance, and too ignorant to realize that he was the one with not much worth listening to. Too many women would've gone home from a date with the likes of him feeling worthless, despite not getting a word in during the entire date.

With plate and mug in hand, she ventured back to her computer, eager to write her first blog.

After a brief introduction to what *Join The Craze* was about, Molly set to work outlining the content of what she was offering beyond her welcome.

*Tips, bits, and real-life stories...*

*Life is often broken up into categories, and, in my opinion, online dating shouldn't be an exception, so I propose a way to make sifting through your matches an easier way to manage the masses.*

*If I were serious about this as a means of testing the*

*waters of all eligible fish in the search for my Poseidon, then I would draft a spreadsheet and split my options into three categories.*

*Number One; Dud... it'll take a special person to embrace the attributes of such a being...stands you up, makes unreasonable demands, displays aggressive or sexually explicit behavior...someone you believe is best avoided at all costs.*

*Number Two; Stud... gorgeous, and he or she knows it...nice to look at, but, if a relationship develops, you'll spend half your life fighting for mirror time.*

*Number Three; Keeper... the happily ever after kind, either for yourself or a special someone you'd love to introduce to your best friend.*

*I guess there are times when one category may encroach upon another, or perhaps be in disguise. Time and trusting your gut turn the key to reveal truth. Sometimes there is no quick way to discover hidden secrets, and you won't know unless you put yourself out there and give it a shot.*

*Feel free to share your experiences in the comments below, or head over to my contact page, send me your story to feature as a special guest on my blog. Share with us your experience...dud? stud? or keeper? And, remember, discretion is imperative for your story to be heard and not hidden. We all have feelings, even if those you've encountered resemble the spawn of Satin...*

*BIGGEST TIP EVER—ignore advice offered in 101 Tips to Online Dating via blog, book, or well-versed friend—no matter how late you're going to be, turn around, go home, and get your cell phone. Never go into a date unprepared for escape. Take it from someone who knows dating disasters better than anyone.*

Molly pushed her chair back from her desk and turned to face the window. Opening the floodgates seemed a good opportunity to draw readers to her blog. More readers meant more money pouring into her bank account. A career change, an out she had been searching for, yet hadn't thought to explore. For the first time since she could remember, Molly was excited about the path she was on. Now all she needed was to line up enough dates to keep the wheels turning, which shouldn't be too difficult, at least, not the arrangement part. Men seemed to flock to her like seagulls to a chip. Setting dates up would be a breeze, it was the tornado in waiting that wasn't so easy to manage.

The idea for readers to contribute their own experiences came to her whilst she was writing. At least if she sourced some of the content from others, she'd cover herself for dry spells. Goodness knows she couldn't keep reporting on no-shows or else desperate and dateless would make for a more accurate spreadsheet than the categories she pitched to her readers. Doom dating wasn't something she wanted to promote either. Fun, flirty stories to inspire singles to explore the possibility of online dating, or to provide a good laugh, was her aim. She'd already established, lining up the dates wasn't posing to be a problem, it was actually experiencing a date that seemed her downfall.

How many others out there were experiencing the same difficulties as she was? The disappointment and hurt from such rejection was almost enough to have her throwing in the hope of ever finding a decent guy to spend time with. Had she not been hounded by Shelley, and now inspired by her blog, Molly would have ditched the dating scene days after she joined the *Craze*.

With the blog up and running, Molly was more committed than ever to explore the world of singles. If she could adopt Shelley's earlier method, and schedule back-to-back dates, then she may have a shot at some readable content. No longer just abut finding herself a partner, someone to keep her warm at night and to share a laugh with until the end of their time. She was a blogger now, and a blogger needed something to blog about.

It wouldn't take her long to decide if she was on to something that others were keen to read or participate in. This was the beauty of managing your own at the likes of *Wordpress*, which was her preferred provider.

For now, with the help of Shelley, the experience would be entirely personal, but she hoped others would join her own minor element of *craze*. If desperation set in, she would head out into the streets and ask the public for their opinion on the world of online dating, if they have firsthand experience with the process, and any survival tips they have to offer.

As much as Molly liked the idea of meeting by chance, falling in love the old-fashioned way, it didn't seem the done thing any more. The more out in the open the subject became, the more it'd be accepted as the norm.

The more she thought about the process, and the more involved she became, she wondered if it was really such a bad way of putting herself out there as she initially thought. Letting other singles know she was keen and available certainly beat the risk of hitting on some other woman's man because he looked appealing and wasn't wearing his relationship status in neon across his forehead.

The grounds of approach, when left up to the traditional methods of finding a date, came with as many, if not more, pitfalls than the way of modern. Either way, the duds would be out there, as would those undesirables she hoped not to encounter. Although, she couldn't deny that a few disaster stories would make for interesting reading. With her blog now taking priority, in an attempt to host a hit and not have to continue working as a journalist, not all would be lost if she happened to stumble upon a dud or two.

Molly picked up her cell and the dishes from beside her computer, and carried them to the kitchen where she flicked the switch for the kettle to make another cup of tea before heading to the sofa for some serious date scheduling.

A hard copy plan was her first step. She worked best on paper, where she could see all of her workings in front of her before adding the details to her cell so she could refer back, especially if she was out and about. For her blog was to be successful, loaded with content, back-to-back dates would be necessary for a while.

Grabbing a packet of chocolate biscuits from the pantry on her way to the lounge room, Molly settled in and got comfortable for the night. Feet tucked underneath her, she leaned forward and gripped the large sketchpad she slid under the sofa the week before when she'd been working on the write up on Candice. Too caught up in her newfound interest in *Craze*, she hadn't even thought to pull up her article and check out the end result. Even Shelley hadn't mentioned the piece over lunch, but baby brain seemed to be affecting her even though she wasn't yet pregnant.

Molly sat back and set to work. She doubted the online dating world wasn't one that many would classify as work, and as much as she thought she'd feel guilty for what she was doing, it hadn't set in as yet. There was an element of truth in her search for love. She was just making the most of the leftover bits along the way—one could call it recycling, but that'd make her appear heartless. Although, at times, she felt broken, heartless she wasn't.

The offer to add extra options to her *Craze* account didn't appeal. A locked in contract for six months almost screamed she was wasting her time looking because it wasn't bound to happen anytime soon. She could understand how the packages might appeal, unlimited swipes, unlimited matches, and the opportunity to see who was keen before they hit the stack of possibilities being offered to the public. A subscription just wasn't for her, not that there was anything wrong with it, but it felt a little desperate when she was being bombarded with more than she could keep up with, anyway.

Molly drew a makeshift calendar, allocating three time slots of brunch, half nine to midday, lunch from one, and after six for dinner. Brunch with a random seemed unlikely, and lacked appeal, but it'd be another variation to write. Especially if she was the one titled dud, at least that's how she felt when early morning encounters were inflicted upon her.

"Where to start," she muttered. Living alone for so long, it wasn't unusual for her to speak to herself. "The first sign you're crazy, apparently. The second is joining the *Craze*." She shook her head and smiled at the pathetic joke she found incredibly amusing and couldn't work out why.

She opted to start at the top. The last message she received was from a guy called Tim. He too went against the grain of men she'd usually find appealing, but his message was nice. He looked clean, and he pulled off olive skin, dark hair, and blue eyes with ease.

He pounced on her message as soon as it went through and responded in less than a minute. There was no accusing him of being slack or unresponsive. Obviously he wasn't out on a date, or else it wasn't going very well and he was being rude.

Having an app downloaded to your phone, with access to it at the click of a button was a recipe for addiction. Like reading a book, just one more page before closing it for the night saw her with a reading hangover on many occasions, just as *Craze* was beginning to do to her too. How many users became addicted? Ruining relationships because they couldn't break the habit of swiping the stack of new offers every day.

She'd been accused of over thinking in the past, and this had cause for paranoia written all over it. She shook her head as she tried for a light response to his flirt. It was all well and good going out on a first date with these guys, but could she really continue a relationship knowing her knight in shining armor was just an app away from replacing her.

# CHAPTER 9

*Mommy's Boy*

*On time and as good-looking as his photos promised, Tim was waiting on the steps inside and to the right of the cinema complex as we'd planned.*

*When he suggested a romantic comedy as a good way to end a busy week, I jumped at the chance. Rom-coms are my movie genre of choice, and the week had indeed been busy, 'Craze' wholly and solely responsible for my lack of sleep. Besides, a movie first date had me betting that not much could go wrong, and if personality matched his online persona, there may be a second date in me despite my insecurities of being replaced by the next one on his list of matches.*

*As much as I hate to admit, it was as much an addiction as I expected it to be—swiping late into the night and chatting to random strangers, mostly about the weather, or how busy our lives are. Scheduling dates with some, whilst others seemed keen to linger in the chat room. Most of my matches appeared too good to be true and more adventurous and exciting than a superhero.*

*The thing that I can't really understand, about the contenders on the site, is that they all seem to live complete lives, not really in need for more. How they intend to fit a significant other into their full and exciting life seemed a challenge that didn't add up to possible in the measly twenty-four hours granted each day.*

*A cold Friday night saw to the cinemas being a popular choice of entertainment, so how close people were standing, jam-packed and waiting in lines to enter theaters, or to purchase tickets or food at the candy bar, didn't strike me as strange. That was until I approached and saw that the older woman smooched up against Tim wasn't only standing close, but her arm was linked with his.*

*I know I wore a frown as I approached. But unless he failed to disclose that he was a Siamese twin with a much older female, then he had some explaining to do.*

*"Molly." He greeted me as if an old friend, smile wide and endearing, and held his free hand out for me to grasp, which, as if on autopilot, I did.*

*His grip was tight as he leaned in and kissed me on the*

*cheek. The attachment to his arm leaned also, enabling him to close the distance.* "This is my mom, Sian. When I told her about you, she was so excited that she insisted on meeting you, so here she is."

*I smiled to be polite, but seriously, was this guy for real?*

*Sian certainly didn't look excited to see me. Her face was as sour as if she sucked an unripe plum.*

"Nice to meet you both." *There was no point hiding the obvious. A first date was hardly the time to venture so far as meeting the parents. Instantly, sex on a first date didn't seem such an outrageous option in comparison. It wasn't any wonder this guy was still on the shelf if his handbag insisted on attending all outings. And, if that were the case, he could very well be the only thirty-year-old guy with a gunning chance of being a virgin. Not that a lack of experience appeals to me, merely an observation.*

*Tim glanced at his mother when she failed to respond and gave her a little nudge which initiated a forced smile and,* "likewise."

*I wanted to turn and run, but I didn't have the guts with the likes of Sian on my tail. Her piercing eyes were enough to freeze my soul in a heartbeat.*

"Shall we?" *Tim ferried us through the crowds, arm still linked with mommy, and the other he pressed to the small of my back as a guide. "I already bought tickets, would you like anything from the candy bar?"*

*He was polite, and seemingly sweet. On first impressions of Tim I would probably have been keen for a second date, but the puppet at his side convinced me otherwise. At this rate, he was lucky to be getting a first date.*

*Mommy sat on one side of Tim, and I on the other, nearest the aisle. The pull to leave increased as she dominated the conversation in a tone audible enough for Tim's ears only. When the lights went dim, I did just that. Too far from the exit to escape before the screen lit up the theater, I leaned in close enough to Tim's ear and whispered that I was ducking out to the bathroom. He patted me on the knee, told me to hurry because the movie was starting, and then I escaped.*

*Not going to lie, I still feel a little guilty, but there was no way I was going to endure coffee and small talk after the movie if Mommy planned to stay. And, with the hold she had on Tim's arm, he was going to need a pot of butter to loosen her grip and pry himself free. Before deleting him from my list of matches, I sent him a quick note to apologize and suggested he purchase a man bag instead of his current fashion statement that wasn't working for him.*

. . .

*Take-home lesson...leave your mom, dad, or anyone else for that matter, at home if you're wanting to make a 'positive' lasting impression.*

*Although he wasn't a dud as such, his choice to bring a plus one dragged him in that direction. Tim, I wish you good luck...and even more luck to whoever you find brave enough to take on Sian.*

Molly sat back in her chair and read over the blog post. Although she'd offered most details of their exchanged, she held back on some of their conversation. Despite keeping their encounter as close to the truth as possible, she wanted to keep some of the special moments for herself.

It was a pity about Tim. Sweet and good-looking, and not to mention that he turned up, were traits she was looking for in a partner. Most times, an overbearing mother-in-law would be enough to create grief for the rest of their time together, especially if she didn't understand boundaries associated with unwritten first date protocol.

Before she pressed publish, Molly wandered into the kitchen and made herself a cup of tea. A half hour break prior to a last read through had always served her well to eliminate her work of error, and to fine-tune her words to their best possible combination.

With her next few days already schedule for back-to-back dates, Molly left her cell on charge beside her bed and tuned out the regular ping that accompanied an incoming message, a new match, or *I'm crazy for you,* notification. Why anyone would be so eager to indicate their obsession with a complete stranger by clicking that particular button based on a maximum of six photos and a few line introduction, was beyond her understanding. She avoided those who expressed such enthusiasm for fear a stalker may reside at the other end.

A craving for vegetables topped with natural yogurt and pan-fried chicken, Molly pulled open the fridge to see what she had that could be classified as edible. Too focused on her newfound passion for dating, even the disasters that came with it, food shopping was the furthest thing from her mind.

Scraps more than fresh options would have to do. A carrot, a potato, and a small piece each of pumpkin, cauliflower, and broccoli made the meal preparation seem worthwhile. Living alone, it was too convenient to opt for pre-prepared or takeout food rather than taking the time to fire up the stove. Not that she didn't like to cook, quite the opposite, but there wasn't much satisfaction in cooking up a feast for one. Sharing the experience was much more fun, and in many ways, she couldn't wait for that to be the norm in her life. Until then, she had *Craze*, her blog, and the dregs from the bottom of the veggie draw.

Dinner sorted, and steaming on her plate, Molly wandered into the lounge room to enjoy her meal in comfort. The television was her company for the evening. Nice and quiet, as she intended, had she remained at the cinemas with Tim. Switching to Netflix, she opted for the latest release romantic comedy and settled back to relax.

Who would've thought dating could turn your life upside down and inside out in such a short space of time? Usually she'd be pursuing social sites and events to claim the first interview with up-and-coming fashion talent, or showcasing a household name after the release of a new collection. Unlike the chase for dates, she hadn't bothered to follow up a single lead since Candice.

She'd had a few emails, requests from the head of editing, but a quick response stating she was on vacation saw the threat of an avalanche in her inbox stabilizing.

To make a career from blogging wasn't an easy

feat, but one she wanted to tackle all the same. Writing was her passion, it was the world of journalism that stifled her creativity, making the process into a chore.

Dregs or fresh from the market, she enjoyed her dinner all the same. Once finished, she set her plate down on the coffee table and tucked her feet up on the sofa and settled back to watch the rest of her movie. The latest blog post could wait to be published until after the happy couple on the screen declared their undivided love for each other and preceded to live happily ever after.

## CHAPTER 10

*He's a Keeper!*

*Have you ever met the man who ticks all the boxes except the one that determines the difference between friend and love interest? Well, tonight was my turn to discover a keeper. Toby restored my faith in online dating as a possibility to meet my happily ever after—a man worth settling down with.*

*If I weren't so stubborn and curious, then he would've been the perfect candidate in my best friends search for love. He was exactly her type, and I spent most of the evening wondering why he wasn't mine.*

*On time and smelling like heaven, he greeted me out the front of a quaint little inn that had been his choice. I liked the fact that he didn't play the usual 'but, where would you like to go' game that so many of the indecisive men of today seemed to play. He took control, named the time and place, minus the arrogance in which the tone my words may portray, and the date was planned. Easy as that.*

*Guiding me inside and over to the bar, we made our drink selection and then carried the poured glasses to a quiet corner at the back of the room. Usually I'm not the submissive type, but being in the company of a stranger who didn't mind making the decisions, yet consulting me before they were set into action, was more appealing than I expected. I had a voice, yet I could relax and go with the flow.*

*Toby was an old school gentleman. He held my chair as I sat and invited me to speak first if we both started to speak at the same time. His tone was soft, and yet there was a determination about his nature. He was an impressive date, to say the least.*

*Simple seemed his way, a share platter ordered for starters with the option for more if we so desired, which was a good thing because the platter was equipped to serve four.*

*More wine and ongoing conversation and laughs saw the minutes slip into hours before we decided dessert was a must, as was a hot chocolate. His taste reflected mine, so we ended up ordering the same. Time spent with Toby was not only enjoyable, but it was easy, as if we were a well-oiled machine that had shared company for a long time.*

*Moments after our dessert was served, the large party beside us got up to leave. The grandmother of the group somehow managed to catch the heel of her shoe in the strap of her bag, and she hit the floor with a thud. Without a second thought, Toby was out of his chair and ready to assist whilst the rest of her family looked on as if in shock and uncertain what to do to help.*

*Shaken up and more than a little embarrassed, the elderly lady was so appreciative of her savior, and even went so far as giving him a hug, whilst sons and grandsons clapped him on the back and offered their thanks.*

*Once they left the restaurant area, Toby took his seat opposite me and picked up the conversation from where we'd left off. Given the commotion, and all that happened, I'd completely forgotten that we were discussing the intricate details of rock climbing, a passion of his I was fascinated by.*

*Dessert finished and a mug of hot chocolate drained, we were the last to leave the restaurant, although the bar area was still crowded.*

*Toby was everything a girl could ask for, and yet there was a best friend's brother feel to our interaction so far. But it wasn't enough that I didn't experience that longing for his touch, the desire to reach out, push his hair from his face and to kiss him long and slow. I did it anyway. I kissed him on the first date because I needed to know why I wasn't feeling it. The man was gorgeous, intelligent, and he made me laugh.*

*He seemed as surprised by my forward approach as I was by my lack of response to the contact. Now, don't get me wrong, the man was a great kisser. Soft lips and a confidence in the way he handled a woman I hadn't seen coming, but that was where it ended.*

*Curiosity satisfied, I broke the kiss off short. He was too sweet, too wonderful to be used as exhibit A. My lack of full body response to one of the most genuinely nice guys I'd met since signing up to 'Craze', perhaps in my whole dating life.*

*Innovative and driven, I have no doubt he's going places. Pity I just didn't feel 'that' way for him. He is going to be a mighty fine catch for the right girl. I just hope, being such a nice guy, that he doesn't get chewed up and spat out on his way to finding his happily ever after.*

*So, to all you Craze—y ladies out there, if you come across the beautiful Toby, be sure to swipe right, he could be the man you've been searching for, and you may be the lucky girl for him.*

*And, remember, men are just as vulnerable on this journey to find love—so, ladies...be kind.*

. . .

Molly closed the screen of her laptop and pushed away from her desk. Toby was everything she was looking for in a guy, perhaps it was her and not him that fell short of the passion straw.

She hadn't entertained that thought before, that maybe she was categorized as a dud in his book and not the keeper she pinned him to be.

For too long she had settled in relationships that didn't tick all the boxes, and the results had been brief and disastrous. After the experience with Carl, there was no way she was settling for less than she deserved, and there was no way she would set someone so deserving as Toby up for disappointment. Even though it was just one kiss, her body's response was no more than if she'd puckered up and made contact with her own arm—not even the slightest spark with the potential to be ignited.

Disappointed he wasn't the one, but not so much so she let her confidence slip, Molly wandered to her bedroom to sift through her wardrobe to find the perfect outfit for her date the following night. Who knew how long she would be caught up at the fertility clinic with Shelley and Karina in the morning, and for lunch after. Molly just hoped she managed to keep her glass on the side of full to avoid top ups that'd see her staggering, instead of walking, to meet her date.

What did it matter if she wore the same outfit over and over again, so far, not one of her dates had advanced to a second meeting? If she were smart, she'd divide her wardrobe into dresses based on the number of dates the guy had advanced to. Only problem she'd face would be that the first date batch would be tattered before the month was over.

Molly sighed as she pulled out a seemingly conservative dress. Figure hugging to below the knee, and with a modest neckline, the dress appeared simple, but it was the showstopper back line that made it her favorite. Scooped low, to the base of her back, simplicity went out the window and sexy stepped in. There was no doubt this was a one-year anniversary number, so she returned the dress to her closet. Tags on and never worn, she wondered if it ever would be.

Carl had promised her a red carpet event, the dress intended for the event, nothing too showy, but costly all the same. She didn't even want to think about how much the promised evening set her back. The shoes remained in their box, and the dress reminded her that not everyone stood by their word, and yet the world still spun. The sun still came up in the morning, and there was breath in her lungs. What Carl did to her said more about his lack of character than hers. Candice did her a favor with her big reveal, even if it hurt at the time. Better after a few months skirting around the possibility than years down the track when real feelings came into play.

As quickly as he came into her life, he disappeared. The late night, novel length, messages stopped, as did the inappropriate selfies he'd been sending. Why, when they'd not been requested, he sent those Molly would never know. The last photo type she'd want from any man was a nude from the chin down. At least if he was going to press send, have the guts to make eye contact and own the image, or else keep your pants on.

Toby was at the opposite end of the spectrum, charming, sweet, and physically attractive. The perfect man to remind her she deserved more than just settling with someone less than perfect for her. Carl never appealed on a physical level, and yet, she was willing to take the short fall because he was—what—*famous*?

Too much of her life was consumed by online dating, something she never predicted to part of it in the first place. Now, her entire life seemed to revolve around it—starting a blog, *what was she thinking*. Surely one day someone would come along and sweep her off her feet. What would she do for income once dates ran out and her blog dried up?

## CHAPTER 11

*L*ike a hospital, the fertility clinic smelled sterile, stark white walls against pale gray linoleum floors, the waiting room choked with patients and partners. The reception staff seemed gentler, more compassionate—more human than the ones who mostly failed to grunt an audible *hello* at the practice Molly attended.

They were the only group of three, and Molly couldn't help but wonder what the other patients were thinking when the lady behind the desk asked which of them was there to see the doctor, and Shelley responded that they all were.

Molly grinned when she was handed a file to fill out as a new patient. "Shelley is here to see the doctor, we," she pointed from herself to Karina. "We're the support crew."

The receptionist smiled as she withdrew the clipboard and set it on the desk beside her. "You're all welcome, the more the merrier." She smiled and handed Shelley a pen. "If you could fill out the first two pages with as much detail about yourself, Dad, if you know his details, and your family history. Dr. Stu is running on time today, and will see you in fifteen minutes."

"Thank you." The color faded from Shelley's face and Molly was almost certain she was going to faint, so she linked her arm through hers and, with Karina on the other side, guided her to where there were two seats together and another one opposite.

Molly sat facing them and watched as Shelley's hand moved across the page in swift, confident strokes. That is, until she reached page two. "What the hell am I supposed to write in the *Dad* section?" She whispered loud enough for half the waiting room to hear. A trace of a smile touched the lips of a few neighboring patients. The man seated beside her frowned as he glanced over his shoulder at Shelley.

"Tall, dark, and handsome." Molly offered. "Oh, and preferably intelligent." She was trying hard not to laugh, despite the situation being serious and not a laughing matter.

Shelley shrugged. "Sounds good to me. Washboard abs would work."

"Hell, whilst you're at it, you should request a good sense of humor. That one's a deal breaker," Karina added.

"Really? That's all you've got to add?" Molly scoffed.

"What? Laughter is key to a long and happy relationship. Trust me, I've been with Matty forever, and if it wasn't for his sense of humor, I'm sure we would've been in divorce courts numerous times by now."

"So you reckon without his sense of humor you'd be doomed?"

"His. Mine. How can you stay angry at someone who makes you laugh so damn much?"

"Wow. Well, that's where I'm going wrong. Perhaps put a request in for a sense of humor for me too." Molly checked her cell for time, then tapped the screen. "Hurry along, Dr. Stu won't have much of a sense of humor if you make him late, and neither will the rest of the mob." She glanced around the waiting room at the amount of patients awaiting treatment. How sad that so many struggled to fall pregnant without assistance, and usually those who'd make some of the best parents.

Shelley filled out what questions she could before returning the clipboard and pen to the receptionist and then sat quietly next to Karina until she was called. All three of them stood and, arms linked, they followed the nurse down the corridor to Dr. Stu's office.

His office was large and spacious, which was a good thing considering there were three of them. Dr. Stu stood as soon as they entered the room, walked around his desk and held out his hand in their general direction, not knowing who's to shake first.

Shelley stepped forward and took his hand and introduced herself. "These are my best friends, Molly and Karina." He smiled and shook their hands.

"Find a seat, ladies, and we'll get down to business." Despite looking too old to practice, he was spritely and had a warmth about him that could settle even the most nervous patient. He slid into his seat and turned his attention over to them. "Tell me a story. What brings you here today?"

Shelley didn't holdback, poured her heart out onto his desk and spilled over to the floor, the hallway, probably all the way back to reception. Tears, laughter and so much hope interjected into a story worth hearing.

There was so much she'd not shared with Molly in the past, but her story only enhanced her reason for not wanting to linger if she felt her maternal clock was ticking.

Dr. Stu was as compassionate as he was matter of fact. "Without the support of tests, I'm speaking off the record." He paused and waited for his words to sink in. After Shelley nodded, he continued. "I believe you still have time, but I also think you've given this a lot of thought and you're not taking this light heartedly."

Shelley nodded her head again, but didn't interrupt.

"I'd be happy to assist you, to make your dream of being a mom come true."

Tears streamed down Shelley's cheeks, but she was laughing through them, no doubt pleased with his acknowledgement of her wishes.

"There will he hurdles, small ones, along the way, but with the support of me and your friends I think we will have a smooth run to making this happen for you." He grinned, like a proud grandfather to be.

"I don't know what to say—thank you so much." Shelley sniffed, taking the tissue Karina pulled from a small packet from within her handbag. There was no denying she was the mother of the group, Molly still wearing trainer wheels and struggling to get past self absorption. Selflessness was a necessary practice she needed to learn.

Dr. Stu didn't rush them, but they were back at reception in record time, especially considering the amount of information they'd covered in their first meeting.

Tear-streaked cheeks and eyes bloodshot from crying, Shelley slowed to a stop when the guy at the reception desk turned and looked at her. First Molly and then Karina collided with the one in front like dominos set in a line. Not that Molly could blame her. Despite fashioning the complete opposite of what appealed to her in a man, he was a creature worth appreciation.

Spectacular looking with a smile to dazzle, Prince Charming acknowledged their presence. "Ladies." He nodded, flashing another winning smile he then turned his attention back to the lady behind the desk.

. . .

"Oh. My. God. He was so gorgeous. I totally want to have his baby," Shelley gushed as soon as they left the building.

"Then why didn't you put in a request?"

"That, Karina, would be a demand, not a request. Forget the profile book, I pick him."

"Well, his swimmers, at least." Molly piped in. There was no denying the guy was hot, and completely Shelley's taste. With the glances they shared, it was a pity they didn't exchange numbers and baby make the conventional way.

"When you put it that way it makes an awkward situation a whole lot more awkward." Shelley screwed up her nose and glanced across the road at the busy cafe on the corner. "Know of a quieter place to eat than there?"

Molly shook her head and looked to Karina. "I'm not familiar with much around here."

"Nope, me neither," Karina admitted as they approached the corner and turned in the opposite direction to the cafe.

"How about Italian?" Molly spied a sign less than fifty meters up the street.

"Perfect." Karina and Shelley chorused and then laughed. For so long the three of them had been the best of friends, similar in so many ways, yet different. In a crisis they were there for each other, as they shared their most special moments too.

The Italian restaurant was dimly lit, a more intimate atmosphere than the crammed cafe down the street.

"I have a feeling we're going to spend a lot of time here over the next few months." With one quick swoop, Shelley took in her surrounds and gave the nod of approval. "It'll be the only intimate and romantic part of my baby making process." She burst out laughing, as did the others, just as a waitress appeared to take them to their seat.

"So, do I dare ask how the dating game is going?" Karina picked up her napkin and waved it like a flag above her head.

"Ha. Ha. Very funny." Molly picked up her own, wadded it into a ball and threw it in her direction.

"Honestly, you two, I can't take you anywhere. Behave, why don't you." Shelley plucked the napkin from the middle of the table and threw it back at Molly.

"Yes, Mommy."

"Your punishment is to spill the beans on all the dates you've been on since we caught up last week."

"You should consult my blog if you're so interested in the facts. I can't remember them all. Do you know how exhausting it is to be a full-time dater and blogger of the shit I have to put up with?"

"You started the blog? Oh my god. I seriously didn't think you would have it in you." Shelley shook her head, a grin spread across her face. Molly couldn't tell if she was impressed, shocked, or a little bit of both.

"I felt I owed it to all the other desperate and dateless out there. I was so sick of feeling like I had leprosy, or some other fatal disorder that was hindering me from a normal or enjoyable dating experience. Do you know how brutal this online dating system is—someone need be held accountable, or else we all need to stick together. Out the duds, laugh about the studs, and hold out hope to find ourselves a keeper."

Karina sat in silence, exchanged a glance with Shelley, who wiped a tear that escaped and slid down her cheek before she managed to get to it.

"Oh, trust me, I know exactly where you're coming from and I couldn't agree more. It really is a brutal world to be a part of."

Molly reached across the table and gripped her hand. "You're not in this alone." She was trying for comforting, but that just seemed to make Shelley cry harder. "I'm sorry. I didn't mean to make you cry."

"No. No. Not your fault. I'm just feeling super sensitive today."

"I bet you are. How about a drink?" Karina picked up the wine list, glanced at it briefly before handing it over to Shelley.

"I think I will stick with orange juice or something. I have a date tonight with a Chris Hemsworth look alike. I need to be on my best behavior."

"Oh, really." Shelley wiped her eyes with the back of her hand. "If that's the case, get her a bottle. She needs to lighten up, don't you think."

"That may take a little more than a bottle, but if we start now, she may stand a chance of hitting the level of slightly chilled."

"Remind me why it is that I call you two my friends." Molly scoffed, snatching the wine list from Shelley before she had a chance to even glance at it. "How are you going to commit to nine months without a drop of wine? Maybe you should start practicing."

"Ha. When a baby is the price I pay for nine months sober, commitment will become my middle name."

"So tell us more about this guy. Where are you going?" Karina leaned forward, elbows on the table as if moving in to hear a top secret.

Disappointed was all she'd be when she earned that Molly had so few details. He wasn't much of a texting type of guy. Took control, organized a date, and that was about all she could tell them.

"I don't have many details about him. He doesn't seem to be ruled by the online chat rooms, as so many of them seem to be. Never jumps on a message. He seems normal. Hot as. And, I hope I'm not disappointed as I have been with most of the other guys I've been out with."

Karina jut out her bottom lip, the corners of her mouth turned down in sympathy.

"You're lucky Matty was the one from the get go." Molly always thought it strange that the two of them had been together for so long without having been with anyone else, ever. But, since the online dating thing, she discovered there was a lot to be said for finding that special someone and being strong enough to stick by them. To love and trust them so openly as Karina and Matty had since they were kids.

"No argument from me." Karina held her hands up, sat back in her seat and let her hands drop to her lap. "He's a good guy, and I'm lucky."

The waitress appeared to take their drink order. A bottle of red seemed the obvious answer when a pasta dish of sorts was almost a given. The smell of Napolitano sauce wafted through to the restaurant, and Molly had to hold back a moan of sheer delight just from the fragrance. It'd been a long time since she'd eaten such a carb heavy meal in the middle of the day, and she planned to enjoy every mouthful.

"So, how about sharing this hottie with us? Really not fair to keep us hanging."

"Hmm. I don't know. I'm not much into sharing, you should know that."

"That's not what the rest of the world would be thinking. From what I have heard, you give all the gory details on that blog of yours."

"Oh, trust me baby, if there were gory details, the last place they would end up is on my blog. That's a place for others to feel they aren't alone in this dating game. Not a play site for those not getting enough action on their own."

"Ha. Maybe I need to be reading it. What did you say the blog was called?"

"Join the Craze."

"Of course it is." Karina attempted serious, but the smile tainted her tone and laughter gave her away. "Oh, I have to have a look at this." From her bag she pulled her cell phone, typed in the web address and waited it for it to load.

Molly glanced in the same direction as Karina did, both seeing him at the same time.

"Oh dear. It looks as if the Italian stallion from the clinic needs a little romance in his life after filling his quota in a jar, too."

"What?" Shelley craned her neck to follow the gaze to see what had pulled their attention from the website in question. "Hmm. Yes, I will have a baby with you anytime. You don't even have to open your mouth. I like you exactly as you are." She sighed, and Molly and Karina giggled. Her support crew to the end, they too approved of her choice in quality daddy material.

"Ask him out," Karina hissed.

"Get out of it. He came here to eat pasta, not to be hit on by a desperate looking for a donor to fertilize her eggs due to the human kind of exchange not being an option. Imagine how desperate he would have me pegged as. He'd be too scared to go out with me for fear I might prick holes in his condom as I slip it on."

"Eww." Molly shuddered, the image too much for her to handle in such intimate surrounds. As much as she loved her, Shelley never failed to leave out the details that made her cringe and wish she could rewind time enough to cover her ears and blur the words before they escaped her lips.

"How would he know that you were there to proposition microscopic swimmers?"

"Well, he wouldn't, but as soon as I proposition him, he will have me categorized as either desperate or unfaithful. As sad as this is to admit, I would take desperate over the later any day."

'I'll drink to that." Molly reached for her glass as soon as the waitress filled it with the red of their choosing.

In turn, the others raised their glasses. "Here's to being desperate over being unfaithful." They clinked glasses, then took a swig.

Molly glanced over to see the hottie heading through the door of the kitchen. "I think he works here." She glanced at the waitress, who followed her gaze.

"Nick? He owns the place." A frown crossed her expression momentarily before she took their order.

They were all waiting for the waitress to leave and started talking as soon as she left the table.

"Oh yes, this is definitely our new go to restaurant. Have I ever told you how much I love carbs and miss having them in my diet?"

Shelley laughed. "Oh my god. I'm going to be the size of a barn by the time I work up the courage to ask him out. Why did you girls suggest we come here? What if all I get is the fine delicacies that come from his kitchen and never experience more than that?"

Well, you'll have twenty or more kilos to thank him for. You'll have your baby as you planned before you set your sights on him, and you'll live happily ever after without the man you never knew, but could cook like an Italian food God."

"Honestly, the guy is probably a wanker, anyway." Molly near spat the wine she sipped when she realized how accurate her comment was.

"You're terrible." Shelley shook her head, sipped her wine and sat back, seemingly more relaxed than she'd been all day.

## CHAPTER 12

*Oh. My. God!*

*What can I say—the world of online dating has more than one keeper in the pool of possible happily ever after's. All you need to do is reach deep, because they are out there searching for you.*

*When you discover one so fabulous as I did tonight, you may feel a little bit giddy, like the cork of a champagne bottle bursting free after being wrapped and caged, keeping the bubbles trapped inside. A sense of freedom to be yourself, and a longing to learn more about the person sitting opposite. There's no need to share a kiss for the body to react because the desire to lean over and touch your lips to his will be almost impossible to resist.*

*If this happens to you, be warned, you're probably not*

*drunk...you're at the beginning of something wonderful... that is, if the feelings are mutual.*

Molly hit the button to publish her post, shut down her laptop, and wandered over to her bed. Sprawled out, she gazed up at the ceiling, a smile played at her lips as if she were a love-struck teen, but she didn't care. She was too caught up in the thrill of meeting someone wonderful to even string enough coherent sentences together to share her joy with her readers.

It was one thing to share the duds and studs with the readers of her blog, even the keepers she'd happily hand over to another, but to exploit such raw feelings, ones she had no desire to share with anyone, was a new experience for her. It'd been a few hours since he kissed her goodbye and they parted ways and, yet, she was no cleared than she'd been when the haze, cloaking her rational mind, accompanied his kiss.

There was no denying that Zak was the *oh my god* guy she doubted she'd ever stumble over, especially whilst relying on a dating app. Too good to be true, she wasn't getting her hopes up. There had to be a good reason as to why he was single and relying on an app to find a date. Why he was on the market was a mystery, one she didn't bother to ask on the first date, because no matter how she delivered the question it would sound corny, like she was desperate to boost him high upon a pedestal. She'd learned from past mistakes that once up there she may struggle to get him off should he not be all she thought he was after their first encounter.

Molly rolled onto her stomach, stretched out to grab her cell phone from where she'd left it on her bedside table, and pressed her thumb down on the button to access apps. Legs swinging in a gentle rhythm behind her, she opened *Craze,* and, bypassing the stack of possibilities awaiting her attention, she clicked on existing matches to check that Zak hadn't raced home to give her the flick as she had done to the many guys who fell into her dud category.

She scrolled beyond all of her most recent messages and breathed a sigh of relief when his profile came into view. She touched his face, and his photograph filled the screen. Strikingly good-looking, yet the image didn't do him justice.

Like a lovesick puppy, she returned his smile. Even though it wasn't meant for her, a little burst, like bubbles popping, tickled inside her stomach. There was no denying this guy had awoken the sleeping siren and Molly was keen to unleash her inner goddess.

The shrill of the ringtone scared her, and she dropped her phone, faced down, light flashing like the paparazzi up close and in her personal space. Holding her breath, Molly reached for the phone and flipped it over in hope to see Zak's name on the screen. Instead, it was Shelley.

Tempted to ignore the call for not wanting to share her date with anyone else, but knowing she'd spent an emotionally taxing day taking in all that would happen if she decided to pursue her parenting adventure. Molly swiped to answer the call, a smile touched her lips as she made the connection to swiping for Zak the moment his picture flashed onto the screen.

"Hey lovely, what's up?" Molly rolled onto her back, with her knee bent up she rested her right ankle high on her left thigh.

"How was your date?"

She could've guessed it'd be Shelley's opening question, however, there was an offhanded note to her tone, which indicated there was more on her mind than discovering the nitty-gritty details.

"It was okay. How was your night?" Offhanded

was the best response, as was turning the direction of the conversation back on to Shelley.

She sighed loudly before she answered, and Molly wondered whether crying made up a large portion of her night. "Lonely." Her voice broke. *"What is wrong with me?"* she wailed. "Why can't I find a man and do the baby thing the traditional way?"

There wasn't room in her question for Molly to respond, and she knew that a response wasn't what she sought. It wasn't the first time she'd phoned late at night, after one wine too many, confessing how lonely she was.

Great personality with a wicked sense of humor, and gorgeous looking in an exotic eastern European way, Molly never could understand why men weren't flocking at her feet begging her to have their babies. Sure, she'd left her search for Mr. Right to a little later in life, but thirty-four was far from over the hill.

It broke her heart to witness her friend so sad. She wished more than anything there was something she could do to turn her luck around.

"Oh, Shel, you know it's not you, babe. I stand by what I've always said, you scare the shit out of men. They're too weak minded to see your intelligence and beauty, inside and out, as a positive rather than an intimidation."

"You only say that because you're my best friend. There really can't be that many weak men in the world." She sniffed. Nothing Molly said would comfort her tonight. A venting session rather than resolve.

"What about Mr. Italia? He was checking you out from the moment we approached the desk. Don't kick him off your radar just yet. He might be the reason we were at the clinic today, even more so than the need to pick up brochures. If you don't remember, let me refresh your memory—he was pretty bloody gorgeous."

Shelley giggled through her tears, a splutter more than the shrill of a schoolgirl, but a giggle all the same. "He was, wasn't he?"

"Yep, so I think a follow-up visit is necessary, just to make sure the gnocchi is as good as I remember it being."

Shelley's tone changed from desperate to hopeful. "Sounds good to me."

Molly hoped her suggestion didn't lead to further disappointment. But, like the feeling she got from the moment she laid eyes on Zak, she sensed Mr. Italia was smitten as soon as Shelley came into view.

"I'll tee it up with Karina for as soon as she can make it. Unless you're pressed for time on your latest collection."

"My latest collection is done and ready for the runway, so all I really have is time—it's my patience that's wearing thin."

"Huh—you're not alone there. It'd come in handy sometimes, but I wasn't blessed with patience either." Molly laughed as she pulled the phone away from her ear so she could put Shelley on speaker, then flipped to her messages. Multitasking whilst on the phone had become a habit, but all the talk of patience had her willing Zak to contact her, even though she'd not long left him at the restaurant he'd chosen for their first meeting.

Not too flashy seemed to be Zak's way, which appealed to her so much more than if he'd tried to impress her with falsities. Besides, there was no way up if he started at the top of places to go. Something else she could relate to. There were occasions when nothing but the best was appreciated, but, in her opinion, a first date wasn't the time.

*Zanders* was set on the upper deck of the *Zander Bar*. The view of the sunset over the ocean was spectacular. The tropical atmosphere set off the illusion of being somewhere exotic, relaxing, far from the hustle and bustle of her everyday existence. Cocktails to compliment every dish, mostly seafood, were suggested on the menu, and Molly didn't hesitate to slip in to the mood, as did Zak.

The meals were substantial, as were the bowls they were served to drink from. She was glad she'd opted for a cab or else she would've been in a bind. The Caribbean blue liquid was too good to waste. Not a drop escaped her lips and was delicious enough to entice her to have another.

"Are you still there?" Shelley's voice broke through her thoughts.

"Sorry, what did you say?" A pang of guilt surged through her as Molly aborted the speaker option to better tune in to the conversation she was supposed to be having and not the memories she was keen to relive—over and over again.

## CHAPTER 13

*Second Date Material*

*And so we have ourselves a keeper...I'm not sure if he's quite my type, or if he's meant for someone else, but he's definitely worth a second date.*

*Gorgeous looking. Good sense of humor. Good job. Good kisser. He ticks all the right boxes, yet I wonder if good indicates I am settling for second best.*

*Sure, I could live with good, it certainly beats mediocre, but it's not quite great, and it's far from...Oh. My. God.*

*Still, there is something about him that caught my attention, made me stop and think, 'hey, this guy has potential'. Is it so bad that I am tempted to encourage my best friend to accidentally on purpose bump into us on our next date in hope the two of them hit it off?*

*Charming from the get go, Michael stood when I approached the table, stepped out from in front of his chair to greet me with a polite kiss on the cheek, hand on the shoulder. He moved to pull the chair out for me and stood, supporting my chair until I was seated.*

*"Thanks for agreeing to meet with me." He returned to the other side of the table and sat. "I've not been on a first date in many years, so forgive me whilst I fumble my way through this one." When he laughed, his eyes danced through mixed emotions, having a snowball effect and enticing a wide grin from me.*

*Chitchat went uninterrupted, except when he ordered us a drink, and suggested we get something to eat, and the waiter returned with our order. He asked a lot of questions. Not so many that I felt like he was interrogating me, but enough to know he was keen to get to know me.*

*He was nervous. I could sense it a mile away, and he didn't try to hide how he was feeling, which made him even more appealing. There was something about a man putting himself out there and allowing himself to be vulnerable that really appealed to me. It was as though he was opening a door and allowing me in to see what was really going on beyond an otherwise confident exterior.*

*Before moving on with my post, I just want to reinforce that there is absolutely nothing wrong with admitting you are less than comfortable in the dating realm. It's actually a refreshing change to connect with people willing to show their true self, so don't hide who you are.*

*Michael was a delight to spend time with. Passionate about his work, he openly spoke about research he was conducting as part of a team working to cure epilepsy, and about life in general. Although that little bit of spark between us was missing, he is someone I would like to get to know. I'm curious to see if nerves got in the way of chemistry, or if every guy beyond Mr. Oh. My. God., is going to pale in comparison. Michael was lovely, but Mr. OMG was WOW!*

Dating had taken over her life. Shelley steered a wider birth than usual, perhaps because the baby venture had stolen her focus and she no longer cared to have a man in her life to share the experience with or not. Still, it was odd not to speak with her, exchange a mass of text messages, or see her at least once a day.

That was the relationship she shared with Karina. Once a week, sometimes stretched out to once a fortnight even, they'd pick up the phone to call each other, but not Shelley. It wasn't that she liked one better than the other, but it had always been like that with them.

Now, when she wasn't racing off to another date, Molly spent more and more time alone, closed off from the world outside of *Craze* and her blog. Even her editor hadn't been in touch, at least not since Molly ignored a week of emails and the odd call here and there.

Fashion reporting was a thing of the past. Not a job she regretted, but one she did out of habit. Blogging wasn't a whole lot different, nor did it pay so well as what she'd earned in the past, but it was still early stages. The biggest difference for her was that an editor no longer dictated what she could and couldn't write, nor did they have the final say over how an article was executed. Freedom, at long last, to write what she wanted to write, made all the difference. It was no longer a chore to settle in front of her computer and churn out a couple of hundred words before she drifted off to sleep. Working around her lifestyle was the only way she intended to do it from that point on.

Where she'd once been scared of having to date for a lifetime if she wanted to continue to feed her readers, she didn't have to worry. Stories from all over the world were being sent her way, and guest posting was going to make up half of the content, so long as the readers kept coming. And, she had no doubt they would because compared to many she'd received, her experiences walked on the side of boring. Some of the encounters she read were worse than her imagination was capable of stretching and kept her entertained for hours each night as she read them before bed.

Too late to phone Shelley, or to settle in front of a movie, Molly opted for a hot soak in the tub to try to settle her mind. More restless than usual, she added a scoop of Epsom Salts and a few drops of lavender oil to the water in hope to find calm before she attempted sleep.

The date with Michael was nice, however it was Zak who'd made the lasting impression. Chris Hemsworth look alike, he was not only big and beautiful to look at, she clicked with him in a way she'd not experienced with a man before. Admitting it, even to herself, made her feel even more pathetic than she did over fantasizing that he may have felt the same way about her and might step outside the awkward zone to instigate a second encounter.

Without knowing much about him, she caught glimpses of a future. But a one-sided affair wasn't one she was interested in experiencing again, as she had with Carl, hence the reason she had no intention to make the first move. Besides, it was a sure sign he was keen if the invitation came from him, and she wanted to be certain he was seeing her again because he wanted to and not out of obligation. Not that one date granted her grounds to be owed a damn thing.

Despite not being in a relationship, Molly had been out of the dating scene for a while, but she never remembered the traditional way of meeting someone to be so frustrating and confusing as what the online version managed to inflict. Meeting a guy in a bar, the flirt was on, numbers exchanged, and a first date arranged—if he called. With the process came less doubt. The likelihood of him going home to arrange a date with the next on his list wasn't a thought that had ever run through her head. Now, a simple thought was completing a marathon, circling round and round until a headache threatened, and then took hold.

Self-confidence wasn't something she suffered so much in the pass as she did now, and, yet, until Zak, she had treated her online experience as a career change with the possibility of meeting someone nice enough to go out with for a second time. She, of all people, would be a hypocrite if she point the finger at anyone else for browsing the app until late after returning from a date that hadn't gone to plan. Which was every one of them besides the night out with Zak, she was yet to share with any one. There was something about him she still wanted to keep to herself—the only aspect of exclusivity she was within her right to claim.

Still, Zak aside, Michael was the only date she could imagine spending another evening with by choice. There was a quiet charm about him that appealed, and Molly guessed that, in time, he would slip into the *Oh. My. God.* Category if she gave him a chance.

Unlike many, she wasn't so naïve to recognize there was more than one way in to the minority, especially when he was within a stretching distance of her measure.

Exhausted, and head still pounding, Molly collapsed into bed, her cell phone still in the purse she'd taken out on her date with Michael. *Craze* was the last thing she wanted to deal with when her mind was already overflowing with doubt and uncertainty as to what her next move should be. Besides, Ainsley was on the agenda for the following evening, and unless she was willing to stand him up, which she wasn't, then she had her blog content for yet another day.

Was it bad to hope a dud was on the cards, too many keepers meant decisions had to be made if they thought she was a bit of all right too. So far, she hadn't had to deal with choosing between two, with little background to base her decision on. But, without a doubt, she knew that if Zak appeared in the midst of the choosing pot, she wouldn't hesitate to take a chance on him. There was something that set him apart from all the rest, from the moment she set eyes on him—and it was more than just lust.

## CHAPTER 14

*Animal!*

*When a man speaks about the mother of his children with such disrespect as Ainsley, my defensive mechanism kicks in and boots all tolerance for him out of the room.*

*I mean, what was he thinking, sharing personal details about her lack of hygiene, and situations where her odor was almost unbearable. It was enough to make me gag on my salad, defusing my appetite in an instant.*

*Mocking her and demonstrating her eating habits seemed to be his party trick, buying a bag of crisps for the rendition, crunching noisily with mouth open, allowing for crumbs to litter the front of his black shirt. Not only did he manage to make a spectacle of himself, he boosted my opinion of him to a whole new level that gained momentum as the night dragged on.*

*Ridiculing his ex for gaining weight whilst pregnant with their second child tipped me over to feeling sorry for the poor woman—that was until he detonated the final explosion. Get this, he signed up for Craze whilst she was pregnant with his baby. His excuse—he had needs, and she became too fat and lazy to satisfy them.*

*That was the point I shifted from sympathy to relief that she'd kicked the bastard out.*

*How my wine glass remained intact from the pressure I applied as my grip tightened, rage pumping through me, was nothing short of a miracle. I guzzled what remained of my drink in hope it would wash the foul taste, and words I feared might spill out involuntarily, to the pit of my gut. Of all the dates I'd been on, no other spurred me on to leave so fast as this one. However, nothing repulsed me so much as when he leaned across the table to brush my cheek with the back of his knuckles, as if preparing to deliver a kiss.*

*The bathroom was my first thought, and the best excuse I could come up with to vacate quick.*

*He sat back in his chair, lifted his glass to his lips, and smiled. "Don't be long or I may have to come in after you."*

*Too disgusted to respond, I ignored his comment as if he'd not spoken and made my dash.*

&lt;Give me fifteen minutes, then abort mission&gt;

*In passing, Shelley suggested we make up a code to drag the other out of a lousy date, but we never got around to what the code could be. I went for dramatic in hope that she'd add creative flare and throw me a lifeline secure enough to save me from the slime awaiting my return.*

*From over his shoulder, I could see the familiar app filling the screen of his phone. "Checking the menu for tomorrow night?" I didn't care if I came across jealous, because the opinion of a douche like him meant absolutely nothing to me.*

*"It's addictive, don't you think?" He grinned, not at all embarrassed that I'd caught him out lining up dates whilst I was supposedly in the ladies' room.*

*"Perhaps if I had nothing better to do with my life." My inner ice queen was out, and nothing he had to say would warm me.*

*It took all my will not to thrum my fingertips on the tabletop as I awaited Shelley's call to bail me out of the disaster in which I'd landed.*

*Ainsley made small talk, and although he tried to act carefree, his eyes told another story. Ten points for trying, though. He left no room for awkward silences, and the subject matter switched from crass conversation about his ex to the cars he took pride in rebuilding.*

*I don't think I've ever been so grateful for Shelley's vivid imagination as I was at that moment—academy award candidate, for sure.*

*So frantic was her voice that even I was worried something terrible had happened.*

*"Slow down, Shelley, I can't understand a word you're saying."*

*"I've been arrested," she wailed. "Molly, I need you to come down here and bail me out." She was so convincing it made for an easy show on my behalf.*

*Reassuring her that I was on my way, I pulled my keys from my purse before I hung up the call.*

*Ainsley was on his feet, offering to drive me as I shook my head and apologized for the abrupt end to our date.*

*"I had a great time and hope to see you again." He smiled. Toned down, he almost appeared sweet.*

*In such a rush to leave, I ignored his comment, flipped him a wave and rushed out the door.*

*What a disaster that one turned out to be. Honestly though, did he really think his shitty revelations were going to win me over, or any woman for that matter? All I learned from him was that if I did pursue a relationship with him, upon breaking up, I would become the focal point for future first date material.*

*Not an ounce of remorse for cheating on his family, not a care for anyone other than himself and his needs, pushes him to the top of my list of duds I've encountered thus far.*


Molly read over her post, mostly to check for error, but contemplating whether she'd gone too far with this one. There was no room to sugarcoat his behavior and glorifying online dating for the sake of it wasn't the nature of her blog. She was dishing up real life. Putting it out there so that others caught up in such negative experiences didn't start to think their lack of luck finding a keeper was a reflection of their behaviour, but the shitty attitude of those whom they were encountering.

The *Craze* alert on her phone pinged and an explosion of fireworks filled the screen.

"Not another one," Molly moaned. It was taxing enough to keep up with two and yet her match list had grown to more than two hundred. Even doubling up on some days with back-to-back lunch and dinner dates, there still wouldn't be enough days left in the year to get through them all.

The only consolation being that it'd keep her blog in good supply, if she didn't burn herself out in the meantime. It's not like she could take stress leave if she needed a time out. Dating was an exhausting game, and it was the one area in her life that she had no interest in building stamina.

Molly allowed her mind to wander to Zak. The only keeper she'd met and wanted to do just that—keep him. At least for a few more dates to see if the *wow factor* wore off with time, or if it grew.

As if they shared a telepathic connection, her phone pinged with a message, and not one of the *Craze* kind. He was the only date who'd asked for her number, and he was the only one she would have given it to. Hope shifted to delighted that he didn't take too long to use it—fingers crossed he was as keen to see her again as she was.

The giddy feeling she experienced at the thought of him or moments of the date they shared were foreign to her. If she'd not become such a seasoned dater over the past few weeks, then she would have put the release of butterflies down to lack of experience, but this was entirely something different.

She stared at the screen a long time before daring

to open the message which would enable her to read it in its entirety and tried to guess what was beyond the politeness of his first line.

*<Thank you for a lovely evening, Molly, you certainly gave me...>*

Her mind raced as she toyed with the possibilities of what she'd *certainly* given him.

*<...much to contemplate, despite being sure I wanted to get to know you within the first hour of meeting you. Which leads me to hope that I made a positive enough impression for you to agree to another date...>*

Molly released the breath she held longer than necessary. It wasn't as if he would hear a rapid increase in pace, or a change in volume as she waited for his words to sink in. That was the one thing about communicating in such a way, there was little room for anything more than the words typed upon the screen to influence meaning. Helpful in some instances, not so much in others. But, for this message at least, there was nothing more than a yes or no answer required. Of course, she knew her response as soon as she realized the message was from him, in hope that he was keen to catch up again. And although she wasn't keen for mind games, she had no interest in him thinking she was a sure thing. Not until she was certain he was as wonderful as he appeared on first impressions. As negative as the thought was, and she didn't want to entertain more than necessary, not everyone showed their true colors as upfront as others. For the first few dates, Molly was proceeding with as much caution as she took for the first timers.

Time ticked away so slowly when she was watching the clock. So instead of prolonging the agony of holding out on him, she rolled off her bed and headed for the shower. There was nothing quite like hot water streaming over her, steaming up the room, to draw her away from reality and allow her to slip into her own imagination.

With so many dates scheduled for the near future, she wondered how she was to fit in a second date with Zak without pulling out of plans with someone else.

It was a good thing she was meticulous with

detail, and had a fool proof scheduling system, or else she'd be destined to mix up the men somewhere along the line. As it was, she struggled to remember specific details that fit with each date she had coming up, but reading over a quick brief before she left the house brought her up to speed in a flash.

Guilt plunged deep in her gut. Although it was good for her readers, treating men like cattle at the market wasn't something she was proud of. In too far to back out, she couldn't stop until regular posts were rolling in from the community she was building.

The moment posting didn't fall so heavily on her shoulders, she was willing to abandon *Craze* to get caught up in the whirlwind of love. Since meeting Zak, she believed there was hope for her becoming a positive example of what could come from the new age version of chance meetings.

Not able to wait any longer, Molly responded to Zak before turning in for the night.

*<Positive impression made...another date sounds good to me>*

## CHAPTER 15

*<Is 7:30am too early for a date?>*

Molly considered the message for a moment. Despite an early start being a torturous thought, she wanted to see Zak again and would've agreed to five in the morning if it meant seeing him sooner.

*<I'm intrigued...not too early at all...>*

She hit send and waited. Breakfast was an intimate meal to share—more so than the standard dinner date. At least she thought it would be, no one had ever asked her to breakfast before.

*<Are you free tomorrow morning?>*

He was a fast worker, she had to give him that. Rarely did she make an appointment for early morning Saturday, but she checked all the same.

Dates were building up. Her blog was a hit, yet all she wanted to do was spend time getting to know Zak and ignore the responsibility of being a serial dater and dishing up the dirt on the single scene.

*<It appears so. What did you have in mind?>*

She sucked in a breath, hit send, and waited.

*<It's a surprise>*

Text having no tone, Molly sat reading the message over and over, not sure if she was hoping for a clue to be hidden in those three simple words, yet knowing, no matter the tone of the text or how she read it, no clue was given.

Born curious, surprises had never been her thing. Even Christmas hadn't been safe. Late at night, once all presents were placed beneath the tree, Molly would sit peeling away sticky tape to sneak a peak at what was hidden behind foil wrapping. It never dawned on her mother that, by using foil instead of paper, she was providing perfect snooping grounds.

Three simple words to anyone else would have seemed harmless, but, to her, they were enough to ensure a frustrating day of creating possible scenarios and a sleepless night to follow.

*<Any clue as to what I should wear?>*

She didn't expect he'd give away much by revealing a dress code, but at least she could be dressed appropriately. Too much angst came with a surprise date, especially with one she hoped to impress as she did Zak. Tall and handsome loosely summed him up. Eyes she first thought to be hazel were a mesmerizing shade of green with blue highlights, and flecks of liquid amber. As if it wasn't enough that stunning eyes were her weakness, to add intrigue to the mix she was a goner upon first meeting.

*<Something comfortable, appropriate for the outdoors, and be prepared for lots of photographs>*

If there was one thing Molly disliked above all others, including surprises, it was having her photograph taken. As long as the lens was pointed in the opposite direction, then they would get along fine.

Dread began to creep in. Zak's date sounded more and more daunting with each message he sent. She had to admit, messages formed the majority of their communication, which wasn't so appealing as catching up for a drink or even a telephone conversation. It may have been the way of society, but there was something lacking in communication via text—something she didn't want to get used to.

The simplicity of an 'okay' was all she sent back for fear that elaborating on what she was really thinking may result in him taking cover, never to return.

These *Craze* boys weren't the sort she was used to, and she wondered if loneliness had anything to do with it, or if life had been overtaken by electrical devices. They all seemed too eager and jumped on messages as soon as she sent them their way. Not that she was much better, but hers had now become about work—being paid to write a blog was like a dream come true. For how long she could sustain something based around dating, when she hoped that Zak would result in her officially being off the market, she didn't know.

Second date in the planning and she was already bundling her heart up for the risk of being broken. He was like quicksand to her, and she sensed it from the moment he first smiled in her direction. His style she noticed from afar, but his eyes saw her spellbound and she couldn't wait for a second dose of the charm he cast her way.

~

*Big Daddy*

*Six foot two, my ass. What is it about online dating and the fascination with height? It seems to be the most asked questions so far, especially as I hadn't included specific details in my profile. I could understand if you're a guy and only five foot two, you might be looking for someone on the petite side of the masses. But surely being more than six foot puts you in the running to be taller than the majority of the female population.*

*The most bizarre thing about this instance was the big deal he made over his height, and the emphasis he placed on how my measure of five foot six was pint size in comparison. Small talk about height wasn't the most stimulating conversation in history, but not everyone was comfortable striking up a topic with a complete stranger, so I gave him the benefit of the doubt that an evening spent in his company couldn't be any worse than his messages.*

*Even from a distance, the first thing I noticed about Ryan was that his measuring stick had been tampered with. My observation was confirmed the closer I got to where he stood by the bar. Once by his side, despite wearing my shortest heels, I was just shy of matching his height.*

*Why exaggerate when you intend to meet a person? Adding six inches to your height and expecting no one to notice is bold and certainly takes you aback. The thing that got me the most was when he accused me of exagger-*

*ating my pint size and told me I was bigger than most girls he dated.*

*Well, buddy, there's the door, you know how to use it.*

*It wasn't the first time I'd been wrong about the date not being so bad as the text. Something I intended to be more mindful of in the future. Bore me on the screen and you will not pass go...nor will you collect two hundred dollars...consider yourself banished from my list of men in waiting.*

*If I'd known the height thing wasn't going to be the worst of the date, I would have turned and run before we secured a booth and took menus for dinner.*

*Conversation was stilted. Ryan seemed more interested in ogling young waitresses in short skirts than he was in carrying out anything with substance. Now, don't get me wrong, I can handle a glance here and there at a passing beauty, after all we were granted the gift of sight. Losing his train of thought, pausing mid sentence and inserting a 'damn' or 'come to daddy' comment, pushed the action of looking to blatant fantasizing. When they were barely of legal age, I instantly felt queasy about what type of guy was perched across the table from me—not one I wished to know anything more about.*

*I excused myself after I finished my drink, he wasn't one I was leaving my glass unattended around, and headed for the bathroom. Dinner was ordered and on its way, and I was hungry, so he had until my last mouthful before I was sliding from that booth and running for the exit. He wasn't even that good-looking, and the touch of youth wasn't on his side, despite him being a year younger than me.*

*He painted the clearest picture of any guy I'd been on a date with before, that his only intention was bedding as many women as possible, because he was too slimy for anything long term or with substance. Truth is, he made my skin crawl.*

*There was nothing self-conscious about Ryan. He was like the cock in the henhouse, flirting openly with the waitress who was delivering our food. This didn't irk me so much as his wandering eyes because I could rest assured my food was safe to eat.*

*Ryan pulled out his wallet, removed a business card, and the trail end of their conversation was all I caught—give me a call sometime.*

*Turn and leave was tempting, but so was the gnocchi steaming on the plate in the seat that had been mine. Surely I could endure his shitty company for half an hour more as I worked at devouring my meal, and his mouth was full enough to prevent further interaction.*

*"You know, you're much hotter than I first anticipated. Your ass all tight and inviting in those wet looking pants of yours. Why don't you come and sit on this side*

*and give Big Daddy some sugar? You're far more appetizing than this muck." He nodded his head, indicating he wasn't at all enthused by the meal before him.*

*Little did he know, I had no interest in sitting opposite him, let alone close. And, the only sugar he would be receiving, if I had anything to do with it, was his drink splashed in his face.*

*Instead of standing with my mouth agape, I slid into the booth where I'd been sitting before the bathroom stop and shoveled a mouthful of gnocchi in and began to chew. The flavors exploded in my mouth, but the saucy dish wasn't enough to moisten my mouth. I signaled to get the waitress's attention, ordering just water whilst Ryan added another bourbon and coke to the tab.*

*I don't think I've ever eaten a meal so fast. Ryan watched on with amusement evident in his expression. "Hungry?" He raised his eyebrows, but didn't allow me time to finish what was in my mouth in order for me to respond. "Or keen to drag Big Daddy out of here for dessert."*

*He was lucky the gnocchi didn't return to my plate. Only a few forkfuls left to go to waste, I picked up my purse and stood. Ryan scooted over, making room for me to sit next to him on his side of the booth.*

*The look on my face must have shown my confusion because Ryan seemed momentarily confused, and then he grinned. "Let me guess, you wanted to sit on Big Daddy's lap."*

*How do you tell someone that being in their company was the last place you wanted to be, let alone on their lap, without hurting their feelings?*

*I made a quick mental calculation of the rough cost of my meal, took the notes from my purse and placed them on the table. "I have to go."*

*I made my escape before he had time to register what I was doing. I had no interest in making a scene, nor did I want to verbalize what I really thought of the hours I'd never get back, if a confrontation was his style.*

*He didn't call out after me. He didn't follow, for which I was grateful. Never again would I have to endure the repulsion of his Big Daddy reference, which was a relief.*

## CHAPTER 16

The sun had been up longer than Molly, but there was nothing warming about it. Crisp breeze pricked at her skin, making her shiver, as she stepped out on the street in hope of hailing a cab so early.

Molly glanced up to make sure the weather looked as clear as the report indicated it'd be and was pleased to see it was. Not knowing where she was headed, her only hint being that it was outdoors, she turn back to her apartment, unlocked her door and ran inside for a jacket. There was nothing enjoyable about shivering through breakfast, especially if Zak didn't carry a jacket to offer in case of an emergency gentlemanly act.

There was no doubt she was more nervous about meeting him for a second time. He'd made an impression on her, there was no denying the draw she felt toward him from the moment she saw him, yet, still, she wasn't sure if she'd colored the moment to be more impressive and vibrant than it was, on account of dull dates prior.

Time would tell if he was worth the boost she gave him to the top of the pack, or if desperation was beginning to cloud her judgment. Besides, there was no rule to say that a second date must be followed by a third if he wasn't worthy of the pedestal she seated him upon. She just hoped that when she did see him, she'd get a hold on her nerves and not babble so much aloud as she was in her head. Mind racing too fast, she almost forgot what she'd come back inside for, but spotting the jacket on the hat stand provided a quick reminder.

Not wanting to be late, she grabbed the jacket and ventured back out to the street. There wasn't a lot of movement in her neighborhood so early on the weekends, but being so close to the city cabs frequently passed by. At least she wouldn't have to compete for a ride.

In less than two minutes she was heading toward the coffee shop where she agreed to meet Zak. Even though he didn't seem the type to stand her up, there was a slight nag in the pit of her gut that she might be met with a no show. Once was enough to instill the possibility, which was hardly fair considering he was early to meet her the first time they went out.

She spotted him the moment the cab driver turned onto the street, propped against a pole on the sidewalk, he looked every bit as good as she remembered—maybe even better. Olive colored chinos teamed with a fitted navy sweater, an advert for men's casual wear never looked so appealing.

The smile spread across his face as soon as she stepped out of the cab. *Yep, even better than she remembered. Chris Hemsworth fans eat your heart out.* A doppelgänger suited her better than the real deal, no flock of fans or pestering paparazzi to contend with.

His approach was as casual as his appearance. He leaned in for a peck on her cheek and then folded his arms around her, crushing her to his chest, and dropped another kiss on the top of her head. Warm and strong, she could've stood that way for a long time, her body and mind protesting as soon as he loosened his hold and took a step back. She smiled up at him, and he reached out, took her hand and led her away from the cafe strip.

"You look great." He openly appraised her from

face to foot. "Glad to see you're wearing shoes you can walk in. We have a bit of a trek ahead of us."

"Still no clues?" Looking up through her lashes, she tried for endearing in hope he'd cave and let her in on his secret.

"That is a clue. We're not going to one of the cafes along the strip."

"That's not a clue—not a good one, anyway." Head tipped back, she laughed. Even being in the area, she couldn't fathom where he could be taking her. Cafe strip aside, there was nothing prominent she could think would be open so early in the morning.

He wasn't wrong when he said they were in for a trek. Twenty minutes later they were still working. Sure, the pace was set at a stroll, but the distance she'd not been expecting. The warmth of the sun felt good on her shoulders and back, as did the breeze as it prickled her skin—cool in contrast.

Molly recognized the zoo, even from the side opposite the entrance.

"Do you like animals?" Zak drew her attention to the only attraction she associated with the area, but knew it would be closed for another few hours, at least.

"Love them—although, I don't have any because it'd be cruel not to give them the attention they deserve, and that takes time I don't have."

"Yeah, I'm the same. Although, I have thought about getting another dog. Mine died a few years ago—he was the best." The wistful expression on Zak's face was enough to indicate the loss he suffered. "It's saying goodbye that the hardest part."

Molly nodded, touched at the softer side of Zak that was coming through. "It is—" she paused, not wanting to come across as though she was disregarding his feelings. "But, the time shared is so wonderful—surely that's worth the heartbreak when it comes."

"Take the good with the bad, you reckon?" He sent a sideways glance her way.

"Something like that." She shrugged. "As with most good things in life, they're often tainted with a little bad, just depends on the way you look at it I guess." Deep and meaningful wasn't her intention, but given the subject matter was death of a much loved pet, light didn't cut it.

"I'd agree with that."

They wandered the next twenty, or so, meters in silence, each lost in their own thoughts.

"This is us." Zak gave her hand a little tug and veered toward a gate in the fence she would otherwise have missed.

"But, that's the zoo—it's closed until nine, isn't it?" There was no hiding the confusion in her tone. Unless he had contacts on the inside that could pull some strings, she'd never known the zoo to open early for VIP events.

"For the general public, yes." Still, he didn't offer her insight.

"Well, my shoes may be adequate for climbing fences, the dress may be a problem."

"The dress looks great, and, unless you're part monkey and climbing is your thing, I thought it best we enter the conventional way." He reached out, gripped the frame, and pulled the gate open. "After you, madame." He bowed his head and swished his hand as an indication for her to lead the way.

His lighthearted banter relaxed her. Zak was the right combination of serious and playful. Only time would tell if there were any boxes he didn't tick, but so far, on paper, he appeared too good to be true.

It seemed he was privy to the back entrance, even though anyone could waltz in, the grounds were deserted.

"Are we supposed to be in here?" Molly kept her voice low, barely above a whisper.

"Nah, I thought it'd be fun to do something illegal on our second date—I'm aiming for memorable." Zak attempted to keep a straight face, but the corners of his mouth gave him away.

"You already achieved that by dragging me out of bed before nine on a Saturday morning." She laughed, no longer worried that someone might hear them.

"Know the feeling. Early starts near kill me."

At least they were in agreement, there'd be nothing worse than dating someone opposite. Time spent together would be so much more restricted.

Zak seemed to know the way, and was clearly set on keeping the surprise of where they were headed for as long as he could, so Molly fell into stride with him, veering according to the slight tug at her hand.

Nestles in an alcove at the edge of thick rainforest stood a lady dressed in zoo keeper attire. Her warm smile indicated she'd been expecting them.

"Welcome to the Perth Zoo, I trust you found me without too much drama?" Her smile was as bright as the morning sun, and she genuinely looked pleased to see us. She was obviously of the *morning-person* species, or else put on a good show.

"No drama at all. Perfect instruction." Zak matched her perky mood with ease.

"Excellent. Thank you. My name is Kylie." She pointed to the name badge on the left side of her shirt. "And you are?" She glanced down at the list on the piece of paper she held.

"Zak and Molly."

Molly smiled when Kylie glanced up again.

"Well, it's nice to meet you both. If you follow me, I will take you through to your table."

"Thank you."

Molly remained silent, the smile still fixed to her face. Kylie radiated the sort of energy that you couldn't help but smile whilst in her presence.

Behind the thick of the forest entry, the tree-line met an open grassed area, the outer edge trimmed with tall trees, casting shadow over the space where round white tables were dressed as if in a fine restaurant.

"Wow, I didn't know you could dine at the zoo." There was no hiding the awe in her voice. To say she was impressed was an understatement. The sound of animals at close proximity, and not the annoying yapping type that reacted to every noise within a one-kilometre radius, added to the ambience of the early morning.

"Nor did I until I made it my mission to find something a bit different for today."

Kylie stopped at a table dappled with shade. "You're the first here, so would you prefer sun or shade?"

Zak glanced at Molly. "Up to you."

The breeze was still cool, and she couldn't imagine they'd be there long enough for the sun to develop the bite of the early afternoon. "Sun?" Put on the spot for a decision when she didn't know much about the man standing beside her was never a comfortable place to be.

"Good choice." His smile seemed genuine, confirming he too would've opted for the sunny position.

Kylie wandered over to a table more suitable, still dappled with shade, but not nearly so much as the previous one. "This will be in full sun in no time," she insisted.

"Lovely." Molly said, as she put her purse on the table next to the seat Zak pulled out for her. "Thank you."

"I hope you enjoy the show, and if there is anything I can get you don't hesitate to get my attention." Kylie didn't linger off to greet and seat more guests.

"Show?" Half knowing a clear answer wouldn't be given, she quizzed Zak in hope he'd drop his guard since she knew the destination.

"You'll see."

*Huh. Not a chance.*

"It's really beautiful here at this time of morning." She glanced around the clearing, then set her sight on a thick clump of bamboo swaying in the breeze. "This might sound strange, but it feels fresher than it does when it's crowded."

"Not strange at all. I agree." Zak relaxed back in his chair, hands clasped in his lap, he gazed at her as if she were the show he was supposed to be watching. "Have I told you how beautiful you look today?"

Molly felt her cheeks heat, the compliment unexpected and seemingly out of nowhere. She shook her head, not knowing what to say. *Why did she feel so shy around him?*

"Well, you do." He didn't bother to look away, staring at her as she struggled with the intensity of his focus.

"Thanks." Their eyes met, and the intensity of the moment increase. "You look pretty good yourself." She added. It was best she nip the shyness in the bud before it bloomed. Insecure was so far from who she was, she felt pathetic under the hold it seemed to be taking over her.

A satisfied smile broke across his face as he continued to stare. Eyes locked, as if looking beyond the surface for more.

Zak was the first to look away. The other tables were beginning to fill, and drinks were being served.

Molly gasped as an elephant, walking alongside a zookeeper, rounded the corner, followed by a calf clinging to its tail with its trunk. By the time they entered the clearing, she could see there was not one, but two babies in tow.

Kylie wandered from table to table, leaving a bucket of leafy green vegetables in front of each couple, two or three where there were groups of four or more.

"We get to feed them?" Molly gasped.

"Looks that way—a surprise to me too."

"But, you knew about the elephants?"

Zak nodded, the smile on his face widened.

"They're my favorite zoo animal, along with the giraffe." She was babbling, but excited didn't touch how she felt about the wow-factor date he'd organized.

*Not only sexy, he was thoughtful too.*

She'd been delighted by the prospect of a second date, but for him to go to such lengths to make it as unique and special as the experience they were sharing, she felt more special than she had to any man.

"I like giraffe's too, but the big cats are my favorite."

"They're pretty awesome—their size gets me. Especially when you see them all just sitting around, chilled and harmless looking." She shook her head and shuddered as she imagined the alternative to the behavior she witnessed.

"Yeah. Not sure I'd be so fond of them in the wild —the zoo suits me fine." He laughed at his admission. "Big coward over here."

Molly grinned. *Big softy is more like it.* But she kept that one to herself.

The buzz of excitement, as the elephants meandered amongst the tables seeking treats, was electric. Laughter and chatter didn't deter the animals from claiming their prize.

Molly giggled like a five-year-old as the trunk of one of the babies skimmed her hand as it wrapped tight around the leafy greens and drew them to its mouth.

With one hand draped around Molly's back, hand rested on her hip, Zak leaned forward and rubbed the calf between the eyes. "Its skin is as rough as it looks." He laughed as the calf nuzzled his chest, obviously searching for food.

The size of the elephants, infants at that, uncaged and up-close was breathtaking. Gentle giants that appeared to be having fun as they roamed the clearing for food and charmed the guests whilst doing so.

Art easels, with large canvases set upon them, were being set up in the middle of the clearing. The tables, spaced ten or so meters apart for privacy, formed a semicircle around the makeshift artists space.

Molly watched the staff as they worked, curious if artists would appear to sketch portraits for those interested in taking their turn to pose with the elephants. Instead, it was the large elephant that took her place at the easel. Trays of watery color were set on the grass beneath the canvas.

To the left, Kylie, with a microphone in hand, welcomed the crowd, then introduced the elephants by name. *Patricia, Ebby, and Charles.* Patricia, the largest of the elephants, swayed as the staff fussed around her. Ebby and Charles, having had their fix of treats, meandered over to stand one on either side.

Once the staff had finished what they were doing, they stood clear. Kylie gave her command and Patricia dipped her trunk, first in yellow, and then sucked. Head lifted, she sprayed the fluid over the canvas, Ebby and Charles spun circles beside her and raised their trunks as if excited. The guests laughed and clapped. Patricia dipped again, opting for blue this time, and sprayed, whipping her trunk swiftly across from left to right.

As she worked, the staff served breakfast. It was a good thing Molly was hungry. A stack of pancakes, plus jam, maple syrup, cream and mixed berries were set in the center of the table. Toast, scrambled eggs, bacon, hash brown, and grilled tomato halves in front of each of them. A jug of orange juice was added to the table, and a cooler stand, with a bottle of champagne, positioned beside them.

Zak lifted the bottle from the ice and held it up for Molly to see. "Would you care for an alcoholic beverage, *m'lady*?" He put on his most formal voice and bowed his head as he awaited her response.

"Why, yes, I believe I would, kind Sir." Playing along with his charade, she grinned.

He handed her a glass and lifted his in a toast. "To *Craze*, for making this possible."

Molly laughed and clinked his glass with hers. "To *Craze*," she repeated.

The finished artwork was more impressive than Molly expected it to be. If the canvas wasn't so big temptation would've got the better of her and she would've left with a Patricia-the-Elephant original.

Hand in hand Molly and Zak strolled the grounds of the zoo, too full from breakfast to pick up the pace. The big cats held their attention for the longest, despite the fact they basked in the sun and hardly moved at all.

The grounds were still secluded; the gate only just opening to the public meant they weren't inundated with onlookers. Front row viewing at each enclosure made for a nice change. As they turned to leave, Zak draped his arm around her waist and pulled her close to his side. Molly glanced up and caught his gaze.

"Thanks for agreeing to today." Zak's voice was low and husky.

"Thanks for inviting me and going to so much trouble. I've had a wonderful time."

"No trouble at all. I hope we can do it again—catch up, that is." Zak didn't break eye contact as he lowered his head, pressing his lips to hers in their first kiss. Sweet and gentle, he lingered before lifting his head slightly, eyes locked on hers.

"I'd like that." Molly didn't wait for him to kiss her again, instead she stretched up and closed the distance between them. Zak folded both arms around her, crushed her to his chest, and deepened the kiss.

## CHAPTER 17

*The Anchor Man*

*What is it about Craze men and extreme sports? Do they not realize that sometimes a build up to hero status is by far sexier than being thrown off the side of a cliff to see if you make or break the fall?*

*A midday date, out and about in nature, was what I was expecting. Never, in my wildest dreams, did I imagine I'd be wearing a seatbelt of sorts, fastened to a line that would direct me over a cliff and down a rock face, apparently for fun.*

*Jack was supposed to be my brake—the anchorman waiting at the bottom to assist my descent. From the top of the cliff I could see him, too caught up in the instructor to worry about where I was at.*

*Now, I'm not normally the jealous type, but when I'm*

*faced with a massive drop, and the guy below, supposedly ensuring my safety, was more wrapped up in the woman in lycra, a surge of something, not unlike jealousy, began to seethe.*

*How I managed to get myself caught up in such a ridiculously dramatic type of date was beyond me. For one thing, heights scare me senseless, and the extent of my past extreme activities are so mild I can't even think of one that exceeded speeding the short distance I had to travel, when my alarm failed to go off, making me late for an appointment.*

*I have come to the conclusion that, in the future, I am going to be far more selective when swiping right. If dead fish, pet kissing, or wild adrenaline pumping sports appear in profile photos, then it's an instant left swipe from me.*

*I turned to the instructor standing next to me at the top of the cliff and frowned. "I don't know which is the most extreme in this case, throwing myself off a cliff, or the lesson in trusting the guy at the other end of the rope." And trust Jack, I did not. "What happens if he's not paying attention?"*

*The instructor peered over the side of the cliff to view the fiasco below. "All I can say is I hope you don't value the skin on your elbows." He offered a smile I think he intended to be reassuring, as if trying to soften his less than appealing response, but he failed miserably.*

*I groaned. I couldn't help it. "A quiet dinner may be boring to some, but I'm starting to appreciate the simplicity of leaving with skin intact." My gut churned, and I knew if they didn't assist me over the edge, and soon, I would remove my harness and make a beeline for my car.*

*I can't believe I turned down an offer to catch up with friends at a barbecue for this. Even before I was about to step off the cliff edge, the offer seemed a much more appealing option.*

*Over the two ways, the guy beside me alerted Jack and his entertainment that we were heading down. The other abseiler, obviously more experienced than me, signaled to Miss Lycra, letting her know he was ready to go.*

*My heart thrummed so hard it would not have surprised me if it created an echo. With eyes closed, I held my breath. The quicker I took that first step, the quicker the experience would be over.*

*I don't remember enough of what happened next to retell the details, but I'm here typing, so I lived. But leaving with skin intact was probably too much to hope for. Battered, bruised and more than a little pissed off, I didn't stick around for long after my descent.*

*It wouldn't have been so bad if the loss of skin was due*

*to my own clumsiness, or even an accident, but as a result of Jack being a jackass and carrying on with Miss. Lycra, I was less than impressed, to say the least.*

*Now, after recent dates, I have come home feeling as if I'm the dud. Running past dates over and over in my head, I've analyzed them from every angle to make sure that I'm not the one in need of an attitude adjustment, to ensure I'm not the one who is high maintenance. But, I keep coming up with the same answer—on date number one, it is more than reasonable to insist on being the focus of your date. If you feel less than special, then get out whilst you can and don't give the connection a second thought. There's someone more suitable out there for both of you.*

There was something to be said for a daytime date that didn't turn out the way she hoped. Plenty of day left to improve her mood meant she'd fall into bed contented rather than agitated about the evening she wasted in the presence of someone she didn't care to spend time with.

Since Zak came on the scene, it was difficult to work up the enthusiasm to go out with anyone. Even Shelley and Karina had been in her neglected pile, something she wasn't proud of.

Glancing at the clock, she saw it was still early enough to rally them together for a movie night. Having kids didn't make last minute girly nights easy, but Matty was great with them and keen for Karina to have time off the demands that came with being a mom.

Wanting to avoid communication via message as much as she possibly could, she dialed Karina's number first. The more notice she had, the more chance there'd be of sorting the kids in time to head over to join them.

"Don't rush, we'll wait for you." Molly reassured her when she insisted it wouldn't take her long to bathe them and settle them ready for bed.

Work had been stressful for Matty of late, and as much as he encouraged her to go out and have fun, Karina never took advantage of his generous nature.

"I'll let you get back to it, Super Mom, and then get your ass over here. I have wine, snacks, and everything sorted, so don't even think about fluffing around for us." Karina had a habit of mothering them as much as she did Matty and her girls, so Molly was quick to nip that one in the bud.

As soon as she finished a simpler conversation with Shelley, she snagged her keys and purse from her desk and ventured out for supplies to pull together a cheese platter, popcorn—a given for any movie night, wine, and the mushiest romantic comedy on offer.

Even though Zak was flourishing her with romantic dates beyond anything she ever expected, she would never have too much romance in her life. No doubt Karina and Shelley would feel the same.

"So, how's the blog going?" Karina took a more roundabout approach to digging the dirt of my private life than what Shelley did.

"Better than I anticipated." There was no doubt, with little effort, her blog had taken off in a way she only dreamed was possible. Molly tucked her feet up onto the couch and leaned into the cushions she'd propped into the corner to make room for when Shelley arrived. She'd been surprised to open the door to Karina first when she had so much else to organize before she was free to venture over.

"Financially or in terms of content and reader response?"

"All of it, actually." Molly sipped her wine before continuing. "The money isn't what I was earning writing articles for the newspaper, but it's climbing. I'm a little blown away by the emails I'm receiving, it won't be long before I can hang up my dating shoes and simply rely on them to sustain the blog entirely."

"Why would you hang up your dating shoes?" Karina raised her eyebrows, and Molly could tell she was hoping to hear a positive outcome on the dating front, but she was still hesitant to share until she had a few more dates under her belt. Zak was such an amazing guy, offering some of the best company she was yet to keep, but it was still aryl days and she didn't want to jinx herself and have it all fall into a heap.

"It's exhausting." She sunk further into her seat and wrinkled her nose as she frowned. "And, if I keep all this restaurant eating, and drinking up, I will resemble the plum pudding by the time Christmas rolls around. I'm actually sick of eating restaurant food—I mean, that's saying something."

"Yeah, I couldn't eat out every night of the week. Too many creamy sauces and side servings of chips, I'd resemble an over stuffed Thanksgiving turkey in no time."

Molly laughed at the thought of Karina's tiny little frame being coated with enough padding to serve her on a silver platter.

The knock at the door saved Molly from any

unanswered questions Shelley would no doubt pry out of her before the night was through.

Setting her glass on the coffee table, she went to open the door. A quick chat prior to the movie was inevitable and would no doubt flow through to the boring bits of the movie, if there were any. Light-hearted banter and teasing was also a given, and, considering the nature of the movie, romantic comedy, they'd direct their comments her way. She didn't need a crystal ball to confirm, because over the years it'd been Shelley on the receiving, Molly guessed it was her turn to cop the flak.

"Sorry I'm late, I got caught up creating a new design." When creativity kicked in, Shelley struggled to kick it out of the way for anything. It was as though she couldn't function until whatever she was working on spilled out of her brain and onto the page, or fabric in front of her. It was interesting to watch, especially when she was working with draping techniques. No pattern to work from, just her artistic flare and knowledge.

"Not late, we were just settling in." Shelley gave a hug as she passed Molly and led the way into the lounge room where Molly poured her a glass of wine without asking if she wanted one.

"Might as well make the most of indulging whilst

I still can." She pulled another bottle of red from her purse and set it on the coffee table, next to the open bottle.

"Damn, I should've got Matty to drop me off." Karina picked up her glass and took a sip.

"I thought ahead, cab for me tonight."

The beauty of playing host meant Molly didn't have to worry, although, after the weeks she'd had, and the amount of alcohol she'd consumed, lemon water might be a more responsible beverage for her.

"So, tell tell, what goss did I miss." Shelley settled on the single recliner, popped the footrest and made herself comfortable.

"Nothing much." Molly looked to Karina for backup. "Karina not long got here, we sat, discussed what we're bringing to the table for Christmas and possibly Thanksgiving, and that's about it." The two of them laughed, which Shelley demanded to be let in on the secret.

"So, any keepers in the midst of all this wining and dining?"

Molly shrugged, not wanting to get into a long-winded conversation about the duds, studs, or keepers in the big sea. Shelley had been there enough to know that the perfect catch wasn't so easy to find—even if she did think Zak was one worth holding on to. "One I'd love to introduce to you, Michael's sweet as."

"And why not the one for you?"

Molly shrugged. There was potential there, and he had contacted her again since their first date, so no doubt he was keen to revisit what they started. With Zak on the scene, Molly didn't feel right to lead him on. He was too nice a guy to be treated poorly.

Dating more than one man at a time wasn't the way in which she would normally conduct herself, but her blog was too new and too profitable to abandon just yet. A few more weeks and she'd offer the positive side of online dating, whilst everyone else provided doom and gloom. She just hoped her carefully structured schedule didn't come unstuck and land her in more trouble than she bargained for.

"Keep him on your list of possibilities, I'm hoping my Italian Stallion is keen for more than a flirty exchange at the sperm bank."

## CHAPTER 18

Getting ready for a date she had no interest in going on was more of a drag than being stood up, but it was too late for her to back out now. Plus, with Zak away for work, there was no chance she would get a better last-minute offer.

The thought alone made her want to pick up her phone and back out, regardless.

As much as she reminded herself that two dates didn't mean she owed Zak exclusivity, she still had her heart set on their connection growing to mean more—like an obsessive teenager, she could already see Zak in her not too distant future, by her side and as keen to explore a relationship with her as she was willing with him.

Molly pulled a pair of black skinny jeans and a black knitted top from her wardrobe and tossed them on the bed, coat hanger still attached. All black wasn't her usual choice of colour for a date, especially when it was so warm out, but there was no denying it matched her mood. *For how long was she going to keep doing this?* Going on dates she had no desire to be on. It wasn't fair on anyone, especially if Zak turned into a permanent fixture in her life.

She sighed as she bent down to retrieve her most comfortable strappy heels from the floor of her wardrobe. Bright red, teamed with red lipstick, would add enough color to drag her from drab to date ready.

*Deal Breaker*

*Ashtray breath is not a delicacy! Nor is it pleasant when out on a first date and you're left sitting alone whilst you wait for him to finish puffing, not once but five times in two hours.*

*Roy was so far from my 'type' that I berated myself for being too quick to swipe right and agree to a date, knowing I had hundreds in my list of matches who were. According to his profile, he was six feet two inches tall—I can vouch for him that two inches shy of six feet was still an exaggeration. How he thought this fact would go unnoticed remains a mystery to me. Just as the well-built body shots were obviously from a time long, long ago, as was his hair. Bald as a bowling ball and thin as a bean, he was difficult to pick in the crowd. Thank goodness my photographs don't lie and he was able to spot me or else he would've been tagged a 'no show'.*

*It wasn't really that he went against the grain of my type, or that he lied about his appearance by uploading misleading photographs—I mean, let's face it, we all want to offer our best when in search for love—and entertaining a conversation about how he was being financially stitched by his ex, unable to see his children, and asking advice on what he should do, wasn't even the worst part of the date.*

*Subject matter aside, he was sweet, genuinely seemed to miss his kids, and was clearly in a predicament that had not only tainted his past, but was encroaching upon his future. Not exactly first date conversation material, but he was clearly nervous and his mouth was running away with him against his will.*

*Relief didn't even cut close to how I felt when my best friend's desperate plea came in the form of a message, begging me to bail her out of a dating disaster of her own. I was delighted for an excuse to escape the evening, although not a complete disaster, I never want to repli-*

*cate. He offered to walk me to my car, hinting that he lived close by and if I was heading in his general direction he needed a lift. Without waiting for him to offer which direction he was referring to, words escaped before I gave them any thought, and I declare the other direction was my route. This guy was still a stranger to me. Despite spending two hours in his presence, the last thing I intended to do was let him in my car to drive him home.*

*As if that wasn't enough of a hint that the date was over and a repeat wasn't likely, he placed one hand on the top of my arm and kissed me on the cheek. "I really like you," he admitted. "You're sweet and smart and as pretty as your pictures."*

*Yes, I was flattered. It's always nice to receive a compliment, but, take it from me, it's also the master weapon to throw your guard off too. Without warning, he gripped the top of both my arms and smacked the sloppiest ashtray tasting kiss on my mouth. When he pulled back, he smiled. It took all my might not to reach up and wipe my lips. Then he said, "as you drive in the opposite direction I want you to think about that, and message me when you're heading my way."*

*The taste of stale cigarettes lingered even after I closed the door and drove away, wiping my mouth with a tissue I plucked from the box in the center console. Non smoker has now advanced to the top of a growing list of deal breakers.*

*What's your deal breaker? Or, like me, do you have a few?*

Molly had reached the point where it wasn't enough to just write a blog post of her experience and hope for the best. She had to start offering her readers more. With her dates growing more disastrous, she was keen to ease up on enduring so many face-to-face encounters. It was tiring having to be switched on and to dine out most nights of the week. She never thought it'd be possible that she'd want to spend a quiet night in, curled up on the couch with a good book, dressed in the daggiest pajamas she owned.

The screen of her cell phone lit up, and she groaned. Craze was the last thing she wanted to deal with. But, when she leaned over to switch her phone to flight mode, an attempt to shut off from the world she was beginning to loath, she saw that it wasn't *Craze*, but a message from Zak.

That silly grin she got whenever he messaged her appeared involuntarily. It was pathetic, really. Twice she'd seen him, yet too much he affected her with crazy feelings she'd not experienced before. It wasn't just that he appealed to her on a physical note, it was the conversations they had and laughter they shared that sealed the deal for her even more.

*<I was thinking about you and wanted to say hi. Hope you had a great day>*

Short, but his message couldn't have been sweeter.

*<It seems great minds think alike...I did have a nice day, thanks. And you?>*

Maybe a slight exaggeration on her behalf. Her day was pretty average, but nice was generic enough not to be considered an outright lie. There was no point throwing herself into the whiner category when she really had nothing to complain about.

*<Busy more than anything else. I'll be glad to be home, that's for sure. You keen to catch up sometime soon? >*

. . .

Molly sucked in a breath and held it for as long as she could, a distraction so as not to come back with an immediate, over eager, yes. There was no doubt she wanted to date him, to skip the uncertainty right to the part where their individual weekend planners were pretty much guaranteed to collide and merge into one.

The temptation to hone in and answer his question and ignore the rest of the message almost got the better of her, but she managed to restrain herself from pressing send on the single word answer—*yes*. Instead, she deleted her declaration of desperate and reworded her response.

*<I hope work eases up and you manage some time for fun. Look forward to catching up when you get back >*

She paused, as she considered adding a couple of kisses to the end of her message, but was quick to deny the urge. Two dates, plus mention of a third, wasn't enough for such a familiar notion.

When she had become so calculated, she didn't

know. Sizing up every word, symbol, or encounter for hidden meanings or miscommunication threatened to claim her easy nature. Too much more of this and she'd become an overthinking hazard in need of wearing a neon warning sign. Nothing more off-putting to a man in the early stages of dating than an analytical woman.

*<Too tight a schedule for fun this trip. Saving that for time spent with you >*

Had the message been sent to anyone else Molly probably would've cringed at how corny it read, but coming from Zak her reaction was anything but cringy. Like millions of tiny bubbles bursting all at once around the center of her core, she clenched, and a wave of desire soared through her. There was no denying her thoughts tipped over the PG rating of his intention. Too long to remember exactly how long it had been since her last intimate encounter with a man was more cringe worthy than any message Zak could ever write.

. . .

*<Sounds like a good plan>*


Encouragement was the only lead she intended to offer Zak. There was no point playing games when she knew exactly what she wanted. Although, she still felt she was playing games by continuing her blog, which not only threatened the relationship she so desperately wanted, but the income she was now counting on.

## CHAPTER 19

"I don't think I can keep doing this," Molly confessed to Shelley before taking a sip of tea. "I'm so over dating—how did you do it for so long?"

Shelley picked a berry off her pancake, popped it in her mouth, chewed and swallowed before answering. "I don't schedule dates like mealtimes." She shrugged as if that was reason enough to justify the two or more years she'd dedicated to the circuit. *Swipe, chat, date, ditch, repeat.*

"It's exhausting."

Shelley rolled her eyes and plucked another berry from her plate. "Ease off a little. Give a guy a chance, risk a second date with one, and see how it goes. Sounds crazy, but guys get nervous too, some of them are quite normal once they get over the stress of being judged for every move they make. Women are the hardest jury to win over, so put yourself in their shoes."

She had a point, but for the most part the first dates she'd been on had been too disastrous to consider a repeat.

"I've been out with Zak twice. He was better than normal from the get-go," she admitted. Part of her was keen to keep Zak to herself for a little longer, but a stronger part of her was up for any advice Shelley could offer on her situation.

"Which one is he?"

"I haven't really mentioned him, but he's the only want I want to mention." She glanced up at Shelley as she scrolled through her list of *Craze* matches.

"Far out. It isn't any wonder you're exhausted. How many of them are you actually communicating with?"

"Not many. I can't keep up with them all." Finding what she was looking for, she touched one finger to Zak's face and he filled her screen. She couldn't help but smile back at him before passing her cell to Shelley.

"Wow. Chris Hemsworth, eat your heart out."

"I know, right?" The smile remained on her face

as Shelley scrolled through the few photos on his profile.

"So, why, if you like this guy so much, are you still entertaining the masses?"

"Because of that stupid blog. I'm actually earning a decent living from my following."

"Can't you make dates up without experiencing them? Who would know the difference?" She cut a mouthful of pancake, scooped up some ice-cream, and stuffed it into her mouth.

Molly followed her lead, needing the time it took to chew to mull over her suggestion. "I'm not sure I could come up with anything that sounded authentic and weird as the dates I've been on. They're so crazy they almost don't seem real."

"I have a confession, I've not read your blog." She looked up sheepishly. "But, from the stories you've told me, you've certainly had your fair share of duds." She paused, as if thinking before she spoke again. "How about you open the blog up for others to contribute to? They can be your disasters and funny stories. You can be the success story with Hottie McHotness by your side, and then you can offer dating tips and bits for the frogs keen to turn into a prince—or, more to the point, princess."

"That was my initial plan, and I have a pile of

great stories I could share, but you don't think it'd be selling out on them?" Molly enjoyed what she was doing. The interaction with readers was fun, so if there was a way to do it and to do it well, she was willing to give it a try. "Are you keen to be my first guest blogger?"

"Honey, I could keep you supplied with stories for an eternity." She popped another berry in her mouth and then wrinkled her nose. "But, what's the audience rating? My PG stories aren't so entertaining."

Molly laughed and shook her head. "Keep it as close to PG as possible—it'll be good practice for the future."

∾

*Drop Dead Gorgeous*

*This post is not for the fainthearted. It comes from a place of sincerity and respect, yet I know that I will struggle to find the right words to capture the heart and soul of this date.*

*A daytime date, something I've found to be more appealing than I anticipated, especially on a Sunday when most guys have to get up for work the following day. There was something limiting about dinner dates when watching the clock, not wanting time to creep up and get away, or else the complete opposite of wishing it'd speed up and you'd be off the hook. Those that leave you at risk of being scarred long enough for your dating days to pass you by, unable to work up the courage to venture out again. If company was good we could extend the date to enjoy a meal together, if not, the night was free to do with as we pleased.*

*Unfortunately, Joel didn't stick around long enough for dinner. But before I get too far ahead of myself, I'll start from the beginning.*

*He was a knockout even from afar, heads turned in his direction as he crossed the park to meet me under the Ferris wheel as planned. Beige shorts, teamed with a white shirt, sleeves rolled to just below his elbow, and brown leather boat shoes. Impeccably dressed to match the rest of his persona. What appealed to me even more was that as soon as he spotted me, glances from admiring passersby seemingly went unnoticed.*

*He greeted me with the usual, polite hand on shoulder, kiss on the cheek. Up close, he was better looking than from afar and smelled every bit as appealing. One of those that wore enough, without drowning himself in cologne to linger even after he took a step back—now and then his scent caught my attention.*

*There was a hint of accent as he spoke, American I discovered upon asking if he grew up near the beach. Skin tanned and sun bleached hair, he was the clean-cut surfer boy that appealed to me now over the more rugged ideal of my younger years. California beaches over Australian, but by the beach all the same.*

*I wish I had more to share with you—we decided to postpone lunch for a little later because it was so nice to be out in the sun. Instead, we talked, we laughed, we strolled a long way before stopping off for an ice cream. Perched on a limestone wall, the conversation continued. Anything and everything we discussed. There was no room for awkward until, mid-sentence, Joel slumped sideward and toppled off the wall. The drop wasn't far, but enough to knock the wind out of someone, that's for sure.*

*At first I thought he was clowning around—a little over the top to initiate a laugh when he'd managed to have me in fits for most of the day. I think I even released a giggle after I gasped, but it was a short burst that didn't last after I peered over the wall to see him in a crumpled heap in the flowerbed below.*

*I road with him in the ambulance, repeated my story to the attending doctor, and answered as many questions as I could in hope he'd be able to provide a few for me.*

*Joel was an angel on earth who could no longer stick around. I feel blessed to have shared his last moments on earth, but I can't help but feel a little cheated out of more.*

*I overheard mention of a suspected brain aneurysm, but the cause of death wasn't something they'd share with a 'Craze' date, no matter how much information I offered them.*

*I caught a cab back to my car, but before I left, there was one thing I had to do—I rode the Ferris wheel and cried for the man who made me laugh for more than two hours straight.*

*You left an impression I will cherish forever, Joel. My thoughts are with you. RIP.*


Molly closed her computer, wandered across the room and flopped down on her bed. Exhaustion claimed her body, yet her mind flooded with the events of the day that wouldn't follow suit.

Knowing there was a family out there, grieving, was enough to break an ironclad heart. As much as hers had been dragged through the wringer of late, empathy engulfed her.

There was no denying the dating game had long since lost its appeal for her. Zak was a huge contributor, as were the duds she encountered, and her most recent encounter with the icing on the cake. Besides, if there was a chance she could have a more steady arrangement with Zak, she might even be willing to grovel at her boss's feet for an assignment or two if income from her blog began to drop off. It wasn't as though she'd be giving up on her dream career; she'd started it on a whim. How was she to know there were so many out there as desperate in the date department as she was?

Not bothering to change into her nightie, Molly squirmed around as she struggled to pull down the covers and crawl beneath them. Sleep was all she craved, but the throb in her temple reinforced her doubt that she'd drift off any time soon.

Although Zak remained at the top of her list of guys, she wanted to pursue a relationship with, which meant that Joel wasn't her keeper. He deserved more than the miserable hand he was dealt.

His death was a wake up call, a harsh reminder that you never know when your time was up, so make the most of what you have. Molly told herself this often, but nothing concreted the belief like the passing of someone so young. The troubles with her blog seemed insignificant, as did her dilemma as to whether or not things would work out with Zak or if she'd be gracing *Craze* with her presence for longer still.

Tugging the duvet high over her shoulder, Molly rolled onto her other side and willed sleep to claim her.

## CHAPTER 20

### Not so Single as He Seems

*It never occurred to me to ask any of my former dates on Craze if they were in fact single. I took their status as a given, and the dog move of cheating never occurred to me as a common occurrence—of course Ainsley should've been a siren at full pitch to set the question in motion. But, with my eye on reaching the fairytale happily ever after result, I didn't consider I'd fall victim to being 'the other woman'.*

*Jason was gorgeous. Perfect fit for a Hollywood RomCom, with a confidence that was neither cocky nor arrogant. Charming to the hilt, but not sleazy or appearing to compensate for other flaws. Conversation flowed freely, as did the drinks we indulged in. Keen to keep the date going beyond the initial suggestion of drinks, we ordered a share platter for lunch and a few more drinks to go with it. There was no doubt about it. For me, Jason was second date material. He ticked all the right boxes and, even more than that, we had fun together.*

*Headed in the same direction after our date was officially over, we continued the laughter and conversation as we walked hand in hand along the edge of the street.*

*Too caught up in the story I was in the middle of sharing, I didn't notice the banshee shrieks meant for us until they were in my ear and Jason dropped my hand and took a couple of steps away from me.*

*It was hard to make out the exact accusations the screaming beauty was making, none of which sounded good, and it took me a few minutes to register that the insults were being flung in my direction.*

*Normally I don't like confrontation, but the things she was accusing me of doing with her 'fiancé' were way off anything I'd be willing to repeat.*

*"I'm really sorry, but you're 'fiancé' is a jerk. Luring unsuspecting women from the 'Craze' dating site seems to be his party trick." With that, I turned back in the direction I was headed and left Jason behind to clean up the mess he'd made.*

*He was so open with our date, holding hands in the*

*street, I didn't see the icing on the date descend. Where had she come from? Had she suspected he was being unfaithful and spied on us from across the room?*

*She seemed too laced with fire to have remained confined for so long. I guess she saw us as we walked passed a cafe or something, her pounce as unexpected to her as it was to us.*

*So much for second dates—seems I am destined to being a one hit wonder.*

*In case you missed the message here...don't forget to confirm relationship status if you're keen to date single people only.*


Whilst there was truth in her post, guilt gripped in the pit of her gut and threatened to never let go. How was she so different to Ainsley, Jason, or any other cheating dog on *Craze*? Although Zak and Molly hadn't spoken of exclusivity, her heart had ideas of its own, and she was no more available than any of the other lying cheats on the app.

She couldn't wait to catch up with Shelley and Karina the following day. A stalker lunch in hope of landing Shelley a date with the hottie Italian Stallion, as he was so fondly known to them.

Wide awake and too restless to sleep, Molly shut

down her computer, grabbed her phone and headed out to watch a girly movie before bed. The only positive about spending most nights alone was that she ruled the remote control. Anything romance and she was set for the evening, even if at times she longed to snuggle on the couch with a man. The temptation to buy a dog passed quickly, especially when Shelley pointed out the hair she'd have to vacuum from her couch on a daily basis. Being a neat freak, she didn't mind cleaning, but adding extra work for the sake of filling a void with a circle instead of a square stamped out the idea before Molly even visited the pet store.

A quick detour via the kitchen for an afternoon snack and cup of tea, and she'd be set until dinnertime. Reasonably stress free, she really couldn't complain—especially when she thought of those without the luxuries of her own life. Too many merely existed in this life, some didn't even know where their next meal was coming from, or when a man to snuggle on the couch with was a minor blip on the radar of life's hardships.

As if on cue, the screen of her phone lit up with a message. The possibility of it being Zak was one in two hundred, but her heart rate jumped and she snatched her phone from the coffee table.

There was no denying she was disappointed when Shelley's profile flashed on the screen. A pang of guilt replaced the disappointment almost immediately. They'd been friends for years, and with all Shelley was going through, deciding to have a baby as a single parent, she was going to need Molly more than ever.

*<I'm so excited about tomorrow. What should I wear? >*

It'd come as a surprise when Karina suggested they meet up for lunch at the little Italian restaurant the following day. A spur of the moment get together they were all able to make. It wasn't any wonder Shelley needed the moral support.

*<Keep it casual...like you're not trying. Feminine, but understated >*

No doubt Shelley's evening would be spent trying on every dress she owned until she came back round to the first. That will be the one she wears, but would insist she had to be certain. She was so predictable—it was the familiarity of their bond Molly cherished most of all.

Her screen lit up again. She glanced down, knowing her response would be a simple thanks sent in hast before she raced off to strip her wardrobe of possibilities.

Instead of Shelley, Zak's name lit the space. Too soon to add a photograph to his contact page, the screenshot she took of his *Craze* profile was the only one she had.

Her heart was off again, increased speed and climbing, as she clicked open the message.

*<Are you free Saturday?>*

Straight to the point—she liked that, so long as the message was intended for her as it seemed out of character not to make small talk first.

*<I'm hoping this wasn't sent to me by accident...or else that would be awkward>*

. . .

She waited, hoping he didn't read into her message and take it for more than playful banter. The worst part of a message-based relationship was text had no tone, and she wasn't keen on using emojis with every message she sent. Although, since *Craze* the smiley face and crying, laughing face was getting a bit of a workout.

*<Ummmm...it's Molly, right? >*

Tone or no tone, he was teasing her, and she knew it.

*<Good guess! >*

Surely punctuation was classed as a tone enhancer, even if most of her friends seemed to leave commas and full stops by the wayside.

*<Far out, that was a close call...So, you free?>*

. . .

Molly grinned back at the screen. He was so adorable, the way he fell into sync with her teasing, taking what she wrote for what it was and not trying to find words that weren't hidden, as so many men seemed to do these days. Always looking for the double meaning, destroying casual interactions and dragging them into the too hard basket even before arrangements to meet could be made.

She wasn't keen on game playing, so she dished up the most obvious, even if a little bit corny, response she could muster.

<Free for you anytime...>

She was glad he didn't leave her waiting, and his reply came through within the minute.

<Great. I'm afraid it'll be another early start, though. Still keen? >

What was it with this guy and early morning meet ups? It'd be easier if he bit the bullet and stayed the night at her house, then they wouldn't have to get up so early to see each other. She groaned, but kept her response light.

*<Ha ha. My former message still applies >*

He was a quick typist which suited her impatient nature perfectly.

*<That was easy. Can I have my driver pick you up at 6am? >*

Really? This better be worth it. Six in the morning was almost enough for her to think he was taking the piss, that he'd be a no show for sure. Who on earth was desperate enough to agree to a date at such a time?

*<Hmmm...that is early. Sure thing. Where are we headed? >*

. . .

Early start time aside, she was intrigued.

*<Former date rules apply…it's a surprise. If you could send me the correct spelling of your full name then we'll be all set >*

She had to break it to him—she didn't enjoy surprises any better coming from him as she did anyone else.

*<Any hint as to what I need bring…or wear…>*

Surely that wasn't too much to ask. Although he was a man, he didn't seem to understand the importance of the outfit.

*<Beachside attire and ID>*

Molly stared at the screen and waited for more. Surely there had to be more of a hint than just that.

But just as she thought it, another message came through.

*<Saturday seems so far away. Are you up for ice-cream and a ride on the Ferris wheel tonight? >*

*Tonight?* Molly released an excited squeal, abandoned her popcorn and tea and stood, responding before she headed to her bedroom to change.

*<Certainly am...seven thirty outside the Esplanade Hotel? >*

He was making all the plans, Molly didn't want to give the impression she didn't have the ability to make decisions too, so she filled in the blanks before he did.

*<Works for me. See you then >*

. . .

She read back over the messages with a grin on her face that widened with each response he'd made. *I think he likes me*, she chanted in her head a she dropped her phone into her purse, slipped a pair of flats on her feet, and headed out for a new swimsuit, sundress, and beach bag. Summer hadn't fully kicked in, so that part of her wardrobe was seriously lacking.

*Was he a bikini or full piece kind of guy?* She shook her head, clearly out of touch with the desires of the opposite sex, and cast her thoughts back over the past ten years. Nowhere in her memory could she grasp a moment where a guy vocalized an appreciation for a full piece over a bikini.

With a few hours before she was due to meet Zak at the Ferris wheel, she had plenty of time to browse.

Molly spread her purchases out on her bed and stood back to admire them. The turquoise bikini caught her eye the moment she walked in the store. As soon as she fastened the top in place, she was convinced it was the perfect choice. The white sundress, flirty short with a fitted bodice and spaghetti straps fitted perfectly. Teamed with a pair of white leather thongs and a navy and white striped beach bag, she was set. Not only was the shopping trip a success, it was the perfect distraction until she had to get ready for her date with Zak. The earlier disaster with Jason now pushed to the back of her thoughts.

Plenty of time for a soak in the tub, Molly added an essential oil blend of lavender, patchouli and ylang-ylang. There was no harm in adding a few aphrodisiac enhancing scents to spice up what she imagined would be a romantic evening out—at least, romance was what she was hoping for, and Zak seemed eager to deliver it in spades.

It didn't take her long to get ready, having opted for blue denims and a simple white and black fitted top teamed with plain black flats, so she left early. To find a car park close to the Ferris wheel on such a beautiful evening may take a while and she didn't want to make Zak wait.

Not wanting to loiter where the families stood, Molly opted for a bench nearby to keep an eye out for Zak. It was warmer than she expected it to be, so close to the water, and wished she'd worn a skirt rather than the jeans that felt as if they were now permanently stuck to her legs.

Zak arrived a few minutes earlier than arrange, but didn't spot her right away, so she sat back a moment and watch. He didn't seem to mind hanging around in the middle of the crowd. Smiling as children ran past, or around him. Molly admired how, even out of place and more gorgeous than a featured display, he looked perfectly at ease.

He spotted her as she stood and grinned. The flutters in her stomach were back in full force. *Would they ever remain settled when he came into view?*

"Hey there, beautiful." His greeting was loud enough for her to hear from two meters away, but soft enough to be intimate in the less than intimate setting. "Hope I haven't kept you waiting long."

"Not at all, I just got here." She took a step toward him as he circled her waist with his arms and drew her close.

"It's really good to see you." He bent his head, forehead rested against hers, and gazed into her eyes before touching his lips to hers.

"It's good to see you too," she admitted as he pulled back slightly. She pressed the palms of her hands to his chest, not to push him away, but to steady herself as she leaned in for another kiss. This one a little more demanding than the last.

Zak followed her lead, pulling her body closer. His hands explored the curves of her waist and her back to her neck where one continued up, fingers tangled in her hair. Molly's skin pricked and her muscles clenched. Despite wanting him never to stop, she slowed the kiss and lessened her hold on him. There was no point denying she wanted him, but in a park filled with families was not the place.

"Ferris wheel before ice cream?" His voice was low and husky.

Molly nodded her response, not trusting her voice to come out as it should. The phrase *he left me breathless* never before held so much meaning as it did right at that moment. She held in a sigh and fell into step beside him.

"Busy day today?" Although they hadn't spent a lot of time together, there was an easiness to being with Zak. He picked up where they left off as if no time had passed, and they'd known each other an age.

"I went shopping." Molly offered after her mind brushed over the date she'd been on earlier. The pang of guilt not so easy to push aside as the details of that part of her day.

"Buy anything exciting."

Whether he was interested or not, he seemed genuine in his curiosity, so she rattled off the list of purchases without going into detail.

"For our date on Saturday?" He snuck a glance her way, a smile teasing the corners of his mouth.

"Maybe—you'll have to wait and see," she teased.

"I look forward to it." He winked, then reached out and brushed a few strands of hair away from her lips and tucked them behind her ear, without breaking stride.

"Still no clues as to where we're going?" She knew she was wasting her breath asking, but a slip up or even the slightest hint was better than the weird guesses churning away in her mind.

"Nope. All you need to know is that our tickets are booked and my driver has strict instructions to keep his lips sealed or else duct tape will become a part of his uniform." Her body responded to his hearty laughter almost as much as she did his kiss. There was something ridiculously sexy about a man who wasn't shy to laugh. Then again, everything about Zak seemed to tick all the right boxes and inspire all the right tummy clenching reactions.

The queue to ride the Ferris wheel was short, which made for a short wait.

Zak stood close, one arm draped across her back, hand resting on her hip. Brushing back and forth with his thumb, he stimulated more than the flesh beneath his touch. Muscles clenched deep, Molly glanced up as he tipped his head to look down at her. Gaze locked, he lowered his head and covered her mouth with his, tracing her bottom lip with his tongue.

"Looks like we're up." He breathed, the husk of his voice giving away the rush of emotion he too was feeling.

Releasing his hold around her waist, he took her hand and led her to the next available cart.

"After you, my lady." He took a step forward, held out his hand and assisted her up the step before him.

Molly settled on one bench, half expecting Zak to sit opposite to balance the load, but he didn't. Sliding up close to her, he draped one arm across her shoulders and nodded for the attending guard to close the door. The wheel jerked to life and moved up a notch to allow for the next cart to be filled.

The process was slow, but Zak was quick to fill the time. The moment they were off the ground, he snaked his other arm around her waist and pulled her close.

Molly sunk into him, tilted her head up and allowed him to claim her kiss. As if starved since their encounter moments before, he nudged her lips apart with his tongue and plunged inside for a taste.

Hands roaming, she slipped one up his top, the

warmth of his flesh on hers made her shudder. Deepening the kiss, he pulled her closer, slipping the hand on her waist down her side to her knee. Changing direction, he pushed the fabric of her dress out the way and dipped to her inner thigh. Inching higher, he continued to massage her tongue with his.

Molly shifted her hand around to his back, fingertips pressed into bare flesh, she clenched in anticipation of his next move.

As if a mind reader, knowing what she wanted, Zak claimed what he sought. Dragging her knickers to one side, he slid two thick fingers between her lips, slick with her moisture, he pressed the deep inside.

Molly gasped, as she bucked under his touch. His rhythm hard and fast, exactly how she liked it. Zak didn't stop until she was panting.

Keen to pleasure him as he was her, she reached down with her free hand and cupped his cock through denim. Hard and wanting, she was eager for flesh to flesh, but he stopped her before she could release the button.

"Just relax. Your pleasure is mine." Zak removed his fingers from inside of her. It took all her will not to protest. Moving to the seat opposite, Zak pushed her knees apart before pushing the skirt of her dress up, exposing her.

"You're beautiful," he breathed, as he leaned forward to grip her hips and drag her ass to the edge of her seat. Drinking in the view a moment he paused before lowering his head between her legs and licking her from back to front. Lapping her opening, he pressed his tongue inside her, tasting. Fingers replacing his tongue, he moved his mouth up to claim her clit, grazing the sensitive bud with his teeth before pressing his lips against hers and sucking hard. Setting a rhythm with his fingers, he licked and sucked in time.

Molly tipped her head back and opened her legs wider. A moan escaped her as he teased the orgasm from deep within. Reaching up, she knotted her fingers in his hair, and began to move in time with his thrust, tilting her pelvis to take him in deeper, and grind her sex into his face. Zak followed her movement. Her muscles clenched around his fingers, and she began to pant as he slipped in another finger, stretching her pussy to accommodate his touch.

"Feels so good." She moaned, pushing forward, her ass off the seat, she supported her weight in a squat, hands pressed either side of her on the bench, allowing her to deepen her movement as Zak continued to feast.

"I'm so close." She panted as her orgasm lingered on the brink of release, teasing her until she burned from wanting.

Zak picked up the pace, taking her clit between his lips, he sucked hard, then shook his head until she shattered around his touch.

## CHAPTER 21

"I'm a horrible person." Molly rest her head in her hands and fought back tears of frustration.

"You're not a horrible person." Shelley soothed, patting her on the shoulder.

"You're just not being a terribly honest person, at the moment." There was nothing comforting about Karina's contribution, but Molly couldn't accuse her of anything but honesty.

"I know, and he's so wonderful. He deserves better than that."

"So tell him." The simplicity of Shelley's words, no doubt, were followed by a shrug as if telling Zak that she's a serial dater was no big deal.

"Tell him?" Molly rolled her head to the side to

see if Shelley appeared to be joking before she retaliated with a sarcastic response. "Are you out of your mind? I want to keep this guy, not scare him off."

"Then stop dating." Karina was clearly the only rational one at the table. "You're not going to keep him if you're flitting off with a different guy every chance you get."

"That was harsh. And, anyway, I don't go on that many dates." There was no point defending herself. One date with a man other than Zak was too many dates for her to fall into the faithful category.

"You're going to have to stop, eventually. If you feel so guilty about it, then pull the pin now."

Shelley was quieter than usual. When Molly glanced in her direction, she saw that she was trying hard not to laugh.

"What's so funny?" No doubt a pout had crept onto her face, but Molly had more important things to worry about than suffering resting bitch face.

Shelley released the burst she'd been holding in. "It's not my fault I have such a visual imagination. You can't blame me for what the two of you inspired."

Karina rolled her eyes. "What a cop out, passing the blame onto us."

"Maybe, but you'd laugh too."

"Don't hold back on us." Karina sat back in her chair and waited for Shelley to share her vision.

"It's not so funny now that I think about it."

"You're not getting out of this one." Molly joined in with the hassling. "Spit it out."

"It's silly—I just pictured you years down the track, Hemsworth lookalike surrounded by three kids, and Molly walking past in her fancy heels and lips painted red, purse in hand, headed for the door." A smile spread across her face and then she giggled.

The vision wasn't too far from one Molly had experienced herself, but it was Karina's snort of laughter that made the biggest impact. "I'm off to work now, honey. Don't wait up." She flipped her wrist in a halfhearted wave and blew a kiss in the air.

Shelley's giggle turned to a hearty belly laugh, and Karina joined in as soon as she was done with her impersonation of Molly.

"You guys are awful." Molly groaned, but she too laughed. It was that or cry, and since meeting Zak tears seemed hard to come by.

"I know, but you love us anyway." Shelley reached out and gripped her forearm. "And we love you, and the entertainment you provide us with." She laughed again, as the Italian Stallion exited the kitchen and walked toward their table with a basket of garlic bread in hand.

"Good afternoon, ladies." He set the basket in the middle of the table. "Compliments of the chef for bringing laughter to my restaurant—and beauty." He winked in Shelley's direction, then turned and left before any of them managed to strike up a conversation.

"Thank you," they chorused, and then giggled like teenagers when he turned and smiled back at them.

"Oh. My. God." Shelley breathed. "He winked at me." She released a muted squeal, then giggled again.

"I told you he was into you." Molly leaned forward and Karina and Shelley copied. "Your mission today is to leave with his number or an arranged date." She snatched a slice of garlic bread from the basket and bit into the crunchy delight. "Oh my god—this is almost as good as sex." She closed her eyes and slumped back in her chair.

"Oh, honey, you are deprived. Keep lining the dates up until one of them is worth sleeping with—a one-night stand would do wonders for you." Karina took a piece and bit. Closing her eyes for a moment before she too sat back. "Okay, I take it back. Think of what he could do in the bedroom if he manages to dish this up in a basket."

"If that's as good as sex, then you're clearly not doing it right." Shelley snatched the last piece and took a bite. "Okay, so it's pretty good, but you two are clearly warped if garlic bread inspires such inappropriate thoughts."

"Oh, for goodness sake, don't start going all *Mary* on us. Italian he may be, a God in the kitchen and the bedroom, but, *honey*, that man is no saint. Don't turn into a libido crusher."

"A what?"

"You heard me—a stuffy old libido crusher." Molly poked her tongue at Shelley and then raised the pitch of her voice as she spoke. *"Such inappropriate thoughts."* She laughed as she picked up her glass and took a sip. "You'd normally set the marker for inappropriate.

Karina snorted. "Doesn't she ever. But, we're getting sidetracked—how do you plan to complete the task at hand."

"Which is?" Shelley picked up her glass and took a sip, looking up at Karina over the rim.

"Oh, for goodness sake." Karina was clearly frustrated. "To land yourself a date so we don't have to dine on Italian food weekly for the next six months." She rolled her eyes and picked up the menu.

Shelley let out a sigh. "I guess we will look like

stalkers if I don't do something soon."

Karina held up her left hand and wiggled her fingers. "Married, remember—so *we* won't look desperate, only you if you don't work up the courage."

"Fine. Fine. I'll do it today." She snatched a menu, frowning as she browsed.

Stomach in knots, thanks to her own dilemmas, Molly didn't bother with a menu. A Caesar salad would suffice. Deep down, she knew what she had to do. Yes, her blog was too new to have a diehard fan base, so there was a good chance no one would really notice if the stories were first or secondhand experiences. Besides, she'd still be the one to sift through and find the best of the bunch to compliment the mood she'd set.

A happily ever after segment might provide hope for those, like Shelley, who'd been caught up in the dating game for too long.

The more time Molly spent with Zak, the more she thought about him, the more she wanted their relationship to work. There were few cases where she'd allow a man to come between her and her career, but this was definitely one of those moments.

"Molly, do you have a pen?" Shelley broke through her thoughts.

"A pen?" Too caught up in her own dilemma, she had no idea where their conversation was at.

"Yeah, like the writing type—honestly, where is your head these days. You're in the clouds more than on the ground."

"You would be too if you had as many thoughts running through your brain as I do."

"What can I say, I like to keep it simple." Shelley laughed, her usual lighthearted self was back.

"What do you need a pen for?" There was no way Molly was going to let her get away with leaving a note as if she were a teenager again.

"I don't need you to give me a lecture. Already heard it whilst you were in la la land. This is me being me—if he doesn't respond to the way I work, then *we* never will."

She made a fair argument, so instead of trying to change her mind, Molly opened her clutch and pulled out the biro and small notebook she carried for story ideas.

"Great. Thanks."

Short, sweet and to the point—*Call Me.* Followed by her number.

"Please tell me you're going to be brave and hand him the note yourself. It'd be a disaster if he thought one of us were making a pass and he didn't call because he was hoping for a date with you." Karina caught the attention of the waitress by the bar, and she wandered over with notebook in hand, pencil poised to take their order.

"I wonder if she's his wife." Shelley said as she watched the perfect hourglass figure walk toward the kitchen, the swing of her hips obvious in the fitted pencil skirt she wore. "She certainly doesn't look like the regular sort of wait staff."

There was no point denying the obvious, but there were other explanations as to who the woman might be—his sister was almost too obvious, but possible.

"She's hot. But, he doesn't look at her like he looks at you, so perhaps she's a relative, or a talented pastry chef." Molly was grasping, at least the part about the pastry chef, but anything to deter Shelley from doubt. If he was married or attached in any way, then they could only hope he was subtle about the note he was about to receive—at least until after they left the restaurant.

The beauty of making a pass was that the few seconds of awkward may be followed by a lifetime of happiness—or else suffering a day of feeling like a dick before moving on with life and never setting foot in the restaurant again.

## CHAPTER 22

*Stalker*

*"All I can do is apologize in advance if my ex-wife turns up here tonight. I'm sure she hacks my account to find out where I'm going to be in the evenings, or else she's psychic."* Mark shook his head and laughed. *"Ten points for me, setting the nerve endings on fire before we even walk through the door. Sorry."*

*He seemed sincere. The laughter brightened his eyes and implied mischief was in his nature. An appealing trait, so long as it didn't go so far as getting caught up in criminal acts of any sorts.*

*I let him lead the way. The last thing I needed was to be the meat in the sandwich if his angry ex-wife was standing on the other side of the door with a butcher's knife, or the neck of a wine bottle she broke out of rage.*

*Not going to lie, I breathed a sigh of relief when he announced the coast was clear. Although, a confrontation would have been an exciting post to share.*

*The waiter greeted him by name, frowned in my direction, and showed us to a table on the far side of the room. There was nothing more embarrassing than being taken on a date to his local hangout, where the staff know him by name and judge me based on the fact that I wasn't his usual handbag. I'm not certain what that says about me, but I think it says a whole lot more about him. My assumption—he's either a cheat or a serial dater.*

*The middle of the room was never a cozy place to sit when out on a first date, but Mark seemed eager to remain exposed. Perhaps his ex really was a nightmare, and this was his way of proving he didn't have anything to hide as it would appear if we were dining in the shadows on the outskirts of the restaurant.*

*No matter where we sat, I felt more on edge than I ever had on a first date. At our age it's pretty much guaranteed that we have ex partners lurking in the past, but I didn't want the hassle of one being dragged into my future. I hadn't been keen to deal with the ghost of a deceased wife that haunted my first 'Craze' date experience, there was no way I'd put up with one in the flesh.*

*Mark seemed a little on edge too, glancing around as if waiting for his ex to materialize at any given moment. The only obvious suggestion seemed that we should order a drink. Something to calm my nerves and to settle his paranoia.*

*The service was prompt, and taking a sip of my gin and tonic, they were generous with their alcohol ratio too. With a vibrant atmosphere, and delicious looking menu, I could see why it appeared a popular spot. If the meal held up, it'd be the perfect place to catch up with my friends. We were always keen to try new places.*

*"Laura, what are the chances?" Mark spoke to the back of the woman passing their table, an older woman and two children in tow. "Care to explain what you're doing here?"*

*The groan she released was audible, despite her back being turned, as was the chorus of 'hi, Daddy', before the children were ushered past their mother by the older woman, to a booth behind me and to my right.*

*If looks could kill, Mark would've been my second experience with death. Something told me his wouldn't have been all together undeserved.*

*"The chances? Are you for real? I told you I'd be here with the kids tonight."* She focused her attention on me, a genuine look of concern upon her face. *"I'm sorry about this. I'm sure you're very nice, but—"* she turned back to Mark. *"Our kids don't need to witness their father with a different woman every time we step foot out of the house."*

*"Then perhaps you should rethink the places you take them. I was a regular here long before you came on the scene, so I should be granted ownership—perhaps we could add it to the court orders."* He glanced over at me and grinned. I don't know if he was looking for my approval or if he was nervous, either way I didn't want to be a part of their marital dispute.

He was like a bulldog after a bone. Not happy with the level he'd stooped to in a public setting, he continued to try to support his position. *"Instead of holding on to the memory of us, you should move on and make new memories."*

*"Honestly, Mark, me move on? What part of 'I told you I'd be here' proves that I'm the one holding on to anything? I wish you'd leave me alone."* The plea in her tone clearly indicated the torture he was bestowing upon her, increasing my desire to miraculously become invisible.

*"Isn't it obvious I'm moving on?"* Mark gestured toward me, and I wished that with his gesture came a

*hook that plucked me off my chair and lifted me away so I didn't have to be a part of the scene that was getting uglier. His sniggering and smartass remarks were enough to make me want to lash out and yell at him, it wasn't any wonder her pleas turned shy of hysteria, causing half the restaurant to turn and stare.*

*"You're unstable, Mark. You need help, not a new woman to use as a prop to try and prove you're over me. I don't care who you're dating, or who you're sleeping with, so long as you leave me alone."*

*Laura turned her attention back to me. "Trust me when I tell you this—run. Don't do what they normally tell you to do, to look over your shoulder—unless it's to check that he's not following you. He's a nightmare. You'll never be free of him."*

*Now, I don't know about you, maybe I'm a scared-cat and melodramatic, I didn't take her warning lightly. I had every intention of following her advice to a tee and leaving them both behind.*

*Opportunity presented itself when Mark stood and began a loud protest, calling for the waiter to remove this woman from his presence. Face bright red, he looked as if fury were about to be unleashed—not my problem. I snatched my purse from the table and took off at the fastest pace I could manage shy of a sprint. I didn't even slow as I reach the front door. A couple coming inside, single file, left room for me to slip out of the open door and into the night. Parked twenty meters or so down the road, I rummaged through my purse for my key, and ensured the door was unlocked before I wrenched it open and slid behind the wheel.*

*Glancing over my shoulder, I checked he wasn't following me. Truth be known, he was probably too caught up with his ex to even notice I left. But I wasn't taking any chances—I don't think I've ever driven so fast in my life. It wasn't until the garage door was shut firm behind me and I was locked inside my house that I managed to settle my heart to a more normal rate.*

*Just in case you were wondering, and for the record, Mark won't be getting a second date...*

Molly stared at the screen, contemplating her options before sending her post out to the world of readers. It wasn't the first time since the second date with Zak that she asked herself why she was still doing this. If he discovered the finer details of what she did for a job, he'd have every right to never speak to her again.

What she was doing, risking the relationship that was growing stronger with Zak for the sake of a blog, didn't make sense. Even Molly recognized it to be out of character for her, but she was in over her head, and felt an obligation to those who'd been supporting her in the past months. Her blog was hitting a heap of the *top read blog* lists, and although it was a huge boost to her confidence, it was the financial rewards that lured her to keep going.

With Zak on the scene, and her feelings for him growing stronger with each encounter, Molly knew the time had come for her to take a step back and look for a fresh approach toward the blog. Ideas she'd discussed with Shelley sprung to mind. Some wouldn't be so easy to pull off without firsthand experience, but there had to be a way she could satisfy her readers without having to date the men herself.

The suggestion of guest posts was proving to be popular. Whether the stories she'd received so far were real or exaggerated, she couldn't be sure. Shelley's idea for her to be creative—to improvise—wasn't a bad one. So, in conversation with the guys she did decide to venture out with, she broached the subject of dating disasters they'd encountered to inspire stories she could recreate, add her own flare, and spice up if necessary. The idea felt deceitful, but with the extra nights she spent at home, she'd be able to dedicate time to adding value to the website so many people seemed compelled to follow.

It wasn't enough that she felt as though she was betraying Zak, but she was leading guys on when they didn't even stand a chance, anyway. Zak had worked his magic on her, no doubt, without even knowing it and, for the time being, Molly couldn't see past him nor did she want to.

Leaning forward, she gave her post a quick once over and hit publish before she was able to overthink her motives and chicken out.

The path she'd chosen, in order to pay her bills, didn't come without questions of her morality, but for one more night she planned to push that aside in hope an alternative approach miraculously manifested whilst she slept.

"I really should be writing fiction, I seem to wish for a life of make-believe," she muttered. "Genie in a bottle, that's what I need." She pushed back from her desk, slipped her feet out of the heels she'd worn out to dinner, then stood and padded barefoot across plush carpet to the bathroom. "Nothing like a long hot bath alone to soothe my cold heart and soul." Talking to herself may've been considered the first sign of crazy, but with the choices she'd been making, she considered herself already on the way.

Feeling sorry for herself didn't help, after all, she only had herself to blame for the mess she'd landed herself in, but it was better than the alternative of beating herself up about mistakes she was yet ready to learn from.

## CHAPTER 23

It's a good thing she was excited to see Zak again, inspiring her to get up before the alarm went off despite her aversion for early mornings. Five minutes before time the driver Zak arranged was parked out the front, patiently waiting for her to surface.

The shiny black car, as sleek as a panther, with windows tinted so dark she struggled to see the driver, was too fancy—rather looked to be waiting for someone of diplomatic status.

Molly smiled as the driver stepped onto the sidewalk and pulled open the backdoor for her to reveal pale grey leather interior, as pristine as the exterior.

"Good morning, Miss Molly." He smiled back, the

white of his teeth startling against the dark tanned skin of his face.

"Good morning. Thank you for picking me up." She had no idea where he was taking her, but was grateful all the same.

She didn't notice Zak sitting on the far side of the back seat until she stooped to slide in. "Oh my goodness, you scared me," she exclaimed, touching a hand to her heart as she laughed. Leaning forward, she brushed his lips with hers. "Good morning, I didn't see you tucked back here," she added, voice lower than before.

Zak laughed, obviously pleased he'd surprised her—he was big on the surprises.

"Did you honestly think I'd let you ride alone?"

"I had no idea—I just assumed you'd be busy trying to be mysterious and keeping your plans concealed."

"Ahh, see, that's where you underestimate me—" He picked up a silky black strip of fabric from the seat beside him and held it up. "I can be much more mysterious at close range than if I was waiting at our destination."

The driver took his position in the front seat, fastened his seatbelt and merged into the traffic.

He'd obviously been issued his orders before picking her up.

"You're going to blindfold me?"

"That is the idea."

"Why?"

"To keep my secret for as long as possible—not sure if I'll be able to pull it off though, for security reasons."

Molly narrowed her eyes and glanced sideways at him to see if there was amusement in his expression, but he remained neutral. "Security reasons?"

Zak met her gaze and winked. "Mysterious, remember."

His comment made her smile. No one could accuse him of being boring, that was for sure.

Still not fully awake, Molly gazed out the window for a few moments without speaking. It was weird how silence was as comfortable as free flowing conversation with Zak. Not feeling the need to talk whilst confined to a small space, especially so early in the morning, scored a huge tick in the keeper category. Awkward silences generally resulted in idle chitchat and superficial topics of conversation—neither of what she wanted for the long term.

"Okay, beautiful, time to cover up." He grinned as

he held the satin strip in each hand and stretched it out tight. "But, first, I need your driver's license."

She frowned at his request, curious if he was trying to mislead her with random additions such as the need for ID, but reached into her purse for it, anyway.

"Great, thanks. Now blindfold time."

"I'm not sure I agreed to this." Molly laughed, and, despite her protest, leaned forward for him to secure it in place.

"You might have to turn around or else I'll knot your hair in it too." He smoothed stray strands back in place and kissed her gently on the lips before she twisted in the seat.

"Okay, I might've made your hair a little bit static—so, there's possibly hair tied up too, sorry."

He was so awkward it was adorable. Big hands fumbling with intricate work. She wondered how he managed the finer details of architecture, although these days it'd be all computer programs rather than ruler and pencil.

"Does that feel secure?"

Molly reached up and touched the satin band covering her eyes. "I think so." The fabric was so thin and smooth that if it wasn't for her vision being impaired, she'd not have noticed the addition.

"Good. Now, no peeping. It'll be so much better if it's a surprise."

"I hope so, because it's really weird having one of your senses stolen whilst the car is in motion."

"You don't suffer motion sickness, do you?"

It would've been the perfect opportunity to grasp hold of the possibility, but he'd gone to so much trouble, and she already felt she was keeping too many secrets to add another to the intricate web of lies. Even is she hadn't directly lied to him, the nag of deceit lingered.

"Not so far."

"That's not very reassuring. I don't want to make you sick."

"I'll be fine." Molly smiled. He was so quick to put her first—accommodating was one of his most notable traits.

"Well, let me know if you start to feel unwell or else the surprise will suck."

She laughed at how honest and simply he put it. No one could accuse Zak of beating around the bush. He was as direct and to the point, in the kindest possible way, that anyone could be.

Round-a-bouts were the most confusing, turning one way and then the other, her balance was off and she flopped around the back seat like a rag doll, fumbling for something to hold on to.

The sound of a seatbelt unbuckling caught her attention. "Are we there?"

"Nope. But, you're going to be battered and bruised if I leave you unsupported for much longer." Zak draped one arm across her shoulders and pulled her tight up against him. "Better?" He kissed the top of her head and then rested his cheek where he left his mark.

"Much. Thank you." She almost sighed out loud, but managed to stop herself before the sound escaped her lips. *Is there such a thing as a perfect man?*

They rode the rest of the trip in silence. Molly focused on keeping her breath even and trying to relax. The disorientation was taking its toll, and she was struggling to fight off the dizziness.

"You still with me?" His voice broke her focus.

"Just." She sucked in a deep breath and exhaled slowly.

"Hang in there, we'll be pulling up in about thirty seconds."

"Oh, thank goodness. Is that my cue to take the blindfold off?"

"Nope. That's your cue to get ready to get out and follow."

Molly groaned inwardly, glad he wasn't able to read minds. Being blindfolded wasn't so mysterious as it was frustrating. She had a whole new appreciation for what the visually impaired must suffer every moment of their life. There was nothing enjoyable about it that was for sure.

"Tell me something though." He'd set himself up for a challenge, and she intended to grasp hold with both hands. "How do I follow if I can't see where I'm going?" she teased.

"Point taken—get ready to be led through crowded streets and tall buildings to the next point toward our final destination."

He was quick on the take up, leaving her with no room to argue the blindfold.

"At least I know crowds and tall buildings won't be hurdles we have to suffer."

"Oh? And, what makes you so sure of that, *Miss Sleuth Solver?*"

"Because if that were the case, then you wouldn't have said it."

"Ahhh, maybe I just want you to think I'm steering you in the wrong direction when, in fact, I'm not—if that makes sense."

Molly went over his tongue twisted sentence in

her head to ensure she'd grasped the gist of what he was saying before she answered.

"Yep. That makes sense, but I still don't believe it."

Zak laughed, deep and throaty. She could only imagine the expression on his face—that alone was enough to make the muscles deep inside clench to her core.

"Looks like you're off the hook. You heard the lady, for security reasons we're about to give away the surprise." He laughed good-naturedly, which was a relief because it was difficult to determine sarcasm without the aid of facial expression.

Zak took his time fumbling with the knot of the blindfold, trying hard not to tug at her hair. The pulling of individual strands as he worked sent shivers down her arms, her skin pricked, and she shuddered.

"Sorry—not the most thought out idea of the day." He sounded nervous, so Molly reached up and took over the untying process.

As soon as the fabric was released, Molly blinked, her eyes adjusting to the brightness before she glanced around the—airport.

A combination of excitement and panic hit as quick as the realization of where she was. Expecting a daytime date, she hadn't packed clothes for more than a trip to the beach required. It was a good thing she'd thought ahead and, at the last minute, grabbed a light jacket for if she came home late. It still got cold out once the sun went down, especially if they lingered by the beach. She was hopeless if there was even the slightest chill to the air, and cold was the last thing she wanted to feel.

"Oh, wow. Now, this I didn't expect," she gasped.

"Surprised?" Zak handed their identification to the attendant.

"That's a bit of an understatement." She let out a breath and a half laugh. "So, where are we going?" Molly glanced up at him through her lashes and smiled.

"For as long as possible, I'll be keeping that detail to myself."

"My guess is that it won't be a secret for long."

Zak laughed and shook his head. "You're probably right. I didn't think that part through very well."

"Are you serious?" She shook her head. Never had she known a guy to be so thoughtful, or extravagant, when it came to organizing dates. "No matter how much longer our destination is kept hidden, this is the biggest surprise anyone has ever organized for me—thank you."

He grinned, then leaned forward and kissed her on the forehead. "It's my pleasure."

"I've booked you in for your return flight at midnight tonight, and printed boarding passes, so no need for you to do anything but show up at the gate." The lady behind the counter returned their driver's licenses and four tickets to Zak, offered directions to their departure gate, and apologized for ruining the surprised.

"No stress. You've got a job to do and her face is too good to keep covered, anyway."

Molly couldn't help but roll her eyes.

"Hey, I saw that." He poked her in the stomach and laughed.

She glanced over her shoulder, then back at him. "Saw what?"

It was his turn to roll his eyes. "Come on, you." With one arm slung across her shoulders, he guided her toward security.

"We're going to Broome?" Molly managed to keep the squeal from her voice, but, inside, it rung loud. The famous sunset camel ride along the beach was high up on her bucket list, not that she'd be announcing that in Zak's presence or else that'd be the next date. She had a feeling *simple* didn't frequent his surprise dates very often, which was more daunting than anything else.

"We are. Have you been before?"

She shook her head. "But I've always wanted to."

"Good, then I chose well."

"Unbelievably well."

"We don't have to board for a while, do you want to grab a cup of—*tea*, right?"

If he wasn't already at the top of the keeper category, then he certainly just made his way there with that one simple word. Tea. No matter how many times she'd expressed her dislike for coffee, Carl had insisted on *coffee* dates.

"Sounds good to me." She slipped her hand into Zak's as he led the way to the *Coffee Club*.

## CHAPTER 24

The dry heat caught in her throat as soon as Molly stepped out of the plane. Although a popular holiday destination, the Broome airport was small and primitive in comparison to what she was used to. Walking across the tarmac to the airport gate, she could feel the heat radiating through the base of her sandals. They were in for a hot day.

Heat waves radiated up from the black surface, emphasizing the temperature that was set to rise. Molly held her face up to the sun, drinking in the summer that had not yet reached its peak back home. Already Broome was a treat beyond her expectations, such weather was like the fruit atop a cocktail.

"Summer. At last." Zak held his arms out for a moment, then dropped one around her waist, the other by his side.

"I know what you mean." Molly pressed her cheek to Zak's shoulder as he tightened his hold around her. "I might actually thaw out today—after the winter we've had, I think my bones are still frozen."

"Remember when we were kids, by September school holidays we were hitting the beach and tanned for the last term back," Zak pointed out.

"Tell me about it." Molly groaned. "We used to smother ourselves in coconut oil and lay for hours baking ourselves."

"I love the smell of that tanning oil, but can't say I ever used it."

"I love it too, and as far as what the weather used to be like, I'm putting that down to climate change and nothing to do with getting old." She laughed. They were far from old, but it was nice to share memories of the past, even if they weren't privy to that time together.

"Have you always lived in the city?" Zak often slipping in questions here and there, seemingly keen to get to know her.

She couldn't deny being curious about him, but was a little more hesitant, not wanting to pry.

"No, I grew up on a large property with horses, four-wheeler motorbikes, and paddock parties. To be honest, I was a bit of a tomboy." Growing up with all boys in the house didn't give her much choice. There was no one to introduce a passion for makeup and fancy clothes, at least not one that exceeded her love of horses, until Shelley.

Roommates at university was like starting life over for her. Shelley was the big sister she never had and taught Molly the girly things in life that would've come from if her mum was in the picture.

"Now that I wouldn't have picked." Zak took a step to the side, his fingertips brushing across the small of her back as he put some distance between them, looking her up and down. "Nah, I don't believe it. You're too much of a girl."

Molly laughed. "Ha. Well, I'm glad you think so." She'd changed a lot since she left home, but the country girl was still in her—if you knew where to look. A bonfire, jacket potatoes cooked in the coals, and toasted marshmallows brought her right back to her roots.

"Do your parents still live on property?" They hadn't spoken much of family on previous dates, details Molly wasn't willing to share unless she was sure there could be more to their relationship.

"Dad's still there. He'll never leave." She looked straight ahead. They were nearly at the car rental and she didn't want to go into a lengthy story as to what her family home meant to her dad. "It was his and Mum's dream to own that place, and after she died, he made it his mission to keep the dream alive."

"Mustn't be easy on his own." His empathy won over sympathy, which meant more to her than if he'd acknowledged the loss of her mum.

"My oldest brother, Nick, lives next door and helps him with the property. It's a lot for one person to manage, that's for sure."

Arriving at the car rental office saw their conversation come to an end. Molly wasn't disappointed, keen to know more about Zak than to elaborate on her own upbringing. Her mom passed when she was five, yet she still felt ripped off—like she missed out on what most classed as a given.

With paperwork and payment sorted online, Molly was seated in the passenger seat of the sporty Holden Commodore in no time. A huge smile spread across Zak's face as he turned the key and the engine purred to life.

"Boys and their toys," Molly teased.

"Not going to argue with you on that one—I treat myself whenever I rent a car, so I don't go out and buy one to have sitting untouched in my garage at home." Zak merged with the flow of traffic. "Can you work out the GPS, I haven't been here before, so we could end up anywhere if I rely on the vague directions given by the lady at the car rental office."

"I'll give it a go. Where are we headed?"

"I hope you don't take this the wrong way, but I booked us a room at Cable Beach Resort, so you have a place to change or if you need to get out of the sun. And, because I thought cocktails by the pool might be nice. Friends of mine told me that besides the beach, bars and restaurants, and the camel ride at sunset, there isn't a great deal to do—unless you fancy feeding the crocodiles or visiting pearl farms."

"Crocodiles are scary, and I'd prefer not to provide them a meal, and although the pearl farms would be interesting, I like the sound of what your friends suggested."

Zak glanced at her and smiled before focusing on the road ahead. They drove in silence for a while.

The expense he'd gone to for one date was somewhat daunting. Either he was too good to be true or else he was distracting her from flaws he appeared not to have. It was early days, of course, but who went to such lengths to impress if they weren't interested in something beyond a few dates. He was either as keen as she was, or else he had more money than sense. She had her hopes fixed on Zak being a big part of her future.

The resort was more than she imagined, exotic in its tropical surrounds. After checking in, with a complimentary glass of champagne in hand, they followed the path woven through lush gardens. Molly inhaled the scent of frangipani blooms added to the ambience.

"Have you been here before?"

"Nope." Zak squeezed her hand in his. "Like you, I've always wanted to, but Bali usually wins me over and so Broome gets put on the back burner."

"Another place I haven't been."

"What? Bali?"

Molly shook her head.

"You're probably one of the few Australians that haven't, you know?"

"Ah huh. After the drug scandals and terrorist bombings, the thought of traveling there freaked me out, so I overlooked the opportunity whenever it came around."

"You should come with me. I know the places to

stay and visit. If you like Broome, then you'll love Bali."

Molly smiled, but refrained from comment. Making plans to go anywhere with Zak seemed bold at such an early stage in their relationship, but the idea was exciting. Even more exciting was that it'd been his suggestion.

Zak squeezed her hand again, then brought it up to his lips and kissed it. "I like spending time with you," he admitted, as he led her to one of the rooms that lined the poolside.

"I like spending time with you, too." There was no hesitation in her response.

"This is us," he said, slipping the room card into the slot and pushing the door open for her to enter first. Spacious, yet homely, with neutral tones and large windows, the room was as beautiful as the rest of the resort.

"You brought your swimsuit, didn't you?" Zak slid the door to the balcony open and stepped outside.

Molly followed. The pool area below was huge with lazy chairs and cabanas two thirds of the way around. The other third was dedicated to the bar and undercover dining area.

"It's an adult only pool—I wasn't sure how

you felt about kids, so thought this would be relaxing and safe in case you aren't so keen on them."

"I haven't had a lot to do with kids, to be honest. One of my best friends has three, and I love them to bits. Kids don't usually bother me, but adults-only sounds nice."

"Good to hear, on both accounts."

"You like them?"

"Yeah, the ones I've spent time with are pretty cool. My niece, Macey, she's the best."

"Pretty name. How old is she?"

"Three." Zak smiled, and took a step forward, wrapping his arms around her, he lowered his mouth to hers. Even through clothing, the warmth of his body was inviting. She moved in closer as he traced her bottom lip with the tip of his tongue, nudging her lips apart to deepen the kiss until her breathing increased and body responded to his touch.

Zak was the first to take a step back. His voice husky when he spoke. "I'll give you some privacy, whilst you get changed." Releasing her from his embrace, he stepped out onto the balcony to wait, which wasn't really necessary. The white glass divider between the room and bathroom was enough to conceal her from full view—silhouette visible at most.

"Thanks. I can meet you out there, if you want? I won't be long."

"Sure thing."

True to her word, no more than ten minutes after he left the room, Molly wandered passed two rows of pool chairs, most of which were vacant, to join Zak who was perched in a partially shaded cabana.

Over the top of a simple black bikini she wore a white lace cover-up, sandals on her feet in case the ground was hot, and her beach bag slung over her shoulder.

Zak watched as she walked over to him, but she pretended not to notice, instead glanced around the poolside.

Pineapple trees set amongst other tropical shrubs along the fence line provided shade and privacy. The perfume of frangipani lingered in the air. Molly inhaled, savoring the fragrance of a vivid childhood memory—five years old, dressed in a puff of a dress, as the flower girl at her parents wedding, she carried a basket of assorted flowers. Fascinated with the waxy feel of the petals, she ran her fingers over them when she was bored during the ceremony, and later at the reception. She didn't remember a lot of that day, except that her mum smiled more than usual, and her dad cried when she walked in front of the bridesmaids and her mom down the aisle. It was the last celebration they shared as a family. Two weeks later was the accident that turned her world upside-down and nearly broke her dad's heart.

Tears pricked at her eyes and she reached into the beach bag for her sunglasses. Now was not the time for a trip down sorrowful lane—a sure way to dampen her vibe.

Zak smiled up at her as she approached. "It gets hot quick sitting in the sun."

"I imagine it would—good score on the cabana." Not a trace of sadness entered her voice as she pushed the thoughts of her past aside. She glanced along the row and noticed that the other cabanas were occupied.

"Yeah. I had to hip and shoulder an old man into the pool or else we would've missed out on this one." Attempting to keep a straight face, a smile teased the corners of his mouth. He tipped his head back and laughed out loud, obviously finding his joke as funny as she imagined the shocked look on her face would've been. Visions of arms and legs failing, and water splashing before swallowing the subject as the center of Zak's joke.

"You're terrible." Molly shook her head as she settled next to him on the cushioned bed.

"I know—pretty mean, but, you have to admit, I'm funny."

Molly laughed. "You're telling the story."

"You better believe it." He continued to blow his own horn. "I'm also thoughtful—drink or dip first?"

"Drink." No thought necessary for what her preference would be. "I'm a wimp when it comes to the water. I need to heat up first."

Zak passed her the drink menu from off the table beside him. "Me too, so don't laugh when I edge in slowly or else you'll go in quicker than the old man."

There was no denying he knew how to keep the mood light.

Molly scanned the cocktail list before opting for a gin and topic. There was no point testing her endurance too early. She had no interest in becoming the biggest joke of the day, especially if a camel ride was on the agenda for later. Toppling off would certainly give them something to laugh about.

It was Molly's turn to watch as Zak walked to the bar to place their order. Tanned skin, despite the summer just beginning, she cringed as she looked down at her glare enhancing body. Lily white legs even more obvious when hit with the glare off the pool and cream pavement, the lack of hours she spent in the sun on display for anyone who dared look her way.

Her eyes flicked back up to Zak, muscular back and torso no longer a guess given his top was beside her, board shorts his only attire. He was beautiful, his body more defined than it felt through clothes, and even better to look at than she imagined.

Almost at the bar, Molly turned her attention to the rooms lining the pool area so as not to get caught perving on him.

The resort definitely measured up to reputation. A touch of paradise in a relatively desolate location.

The hours passed quickly. Sipping cocktails in the sun, taking a dip in the pool when they got too hot, and back on the sun beds when they'd had enough of the water. Relaxed and tipsy, but not too unsteady to ride the camels and enjoy the sunset on the beach. There was no denying Cable beach was the most beautiful she'd ever seen. White sands stretched for kilometers before meeting with red rock cliffs. The contrast, against blue water and sky with a dash of green scattered over the hills, was spectacular.

. . .

Late in the afternoon and it was still hot, although Molly imagined it would have been worse if the all day cocktail binge hadn't taken the edge off.

"How are you holding up?" Zak glanced down at her as they hiked the sand dune to reach the camel ride meeting point on the other side.

"I'm still standing, so that's a positive considering the amount of alcohol I consumed today."

"And you told me you were a Cadbury kid," he teased.

"No joke, a glass and a half, and I'm usually gone." A slight exaggeration, especially of late as she seemed to have developed a tolerance.

"So long as you remain upright on the camel that's all we can hope for."

Molly laughed. She wasn't always the most coordinated person at the best of times, so upright on the camel meant more to her than even Zak realized.

"Have you ridden one before?"

Zak shook his head. "Nah. Horses, yes, but never had the chance to ride a camel."

"Not exactly the most common choice of transport, I guess." She stole a glance as his smile widened and he turned his head to look at her.

"I enjoy spending time with you." His confession out of the blue.

As if a cork released from a bottle of champagne, her stomach felt like hundreds of bubbles fizzed and burst at once. No need to give any thought to how she felt, she didn't hesitate in her response. "I enjoy spending time with you too."

"Glad to hear." Zak reached out and took her hand in his. "I'd really like to spend more time with you and see where things go with this." He squeezed her hand and gave a little tug, pulling her closer to his side, and nudged her shoulder with the top of his arm. "If that's okay with you?" Suddenly seeming shy.

"Hmmm, let me think about that for a bit." Her thoughts flashed to her blog, was this where it all ended, exclusivity granted to Zak and her income diminishing before her eyes. Not fully established in the world of blogging put her in a tricky situation she wasn't completely ready for. But Zak was different to anyone she'd ever dated before, and she didn't want to pass up the opportunity to get to know him—especially when dating duds was the alternative.

"I'm sure that'd be okay." She laughed, despite uncertainty clouding her mind. With any new relationship—or any relationship, for that matter—came uncertainty. But when her career was so closely linked, it threw her whole world into a spin until she could find a way to balance one without the other.

There had to be a way, and she planned to go out on a limb to make it work. Zak already meant too much to her not to try. Besides, bills didn't pay themselves, and she didn't have the luxury of being free of everyday living expenses as some successful bloggers were, she was still new to the game.

"So, why Broome?" Molly was glad they'd etched the top of the incline. Down hill, especially when intoxicate and close to suffering heat stoke was a welcomed change.

"I've heard rave reviews and wanted to see it for myself." Zak shrugged. "Besides, what better place to come for a date. If you wound up to be annoying and we stumbled upon a crocodile, you'd be a great distraction. I'd push you in his path to give myself time to get away." He tipped his head back and a bout of belly laughter burst from within.

"Is that so?" Molly couldn't help but laugh with him. "And here I was thinking you were charming—glad we got that cleared up so early on in the relationship." She tried not to wince as she upped 'spending more time together' to a relationship. Technically it was, but in the dating world it added a whole new layer called commitment. And, in her experience, there wasn't a man around who was keen to get roped in to a serious relationship so soon.

"I am charming." He smiled down at her, draped his arm across her shoulders, and pulled her close to his side. "See, I'm helping you to get safely down the sand dunes."

"I don't think that counts," she laughed. "Especially considering I was managing on my own." Pointing out the obvious was enough to strip the charm from his gesture.

"Ahh, but would you have been able to do this—" he dropped his arm from around her shoulder and scooped her up in his arms. "If I wasn't so charming to assist." With two bounds and a leap from a rock more than a meter high, he landed with feet slightly apart, before pressing his lips to hers.

"Perhaps not, but I'm sure I could've come up with something just as spectacular," she lied.

"Oh, and I suppose you would've kissed yourself once you were done being spectacular," he suggested, the expression on his face serious.

"Something like that." Stretching up to meet his mouth with hers, she kissed him.

## CHAPTER 25

"Well, you certainly look as though you've spent an hour on a camel's back." Molly tried her hardest not to laugh as Zak walked with his legs apart and pulled at the fabric of his shorts.

"I honestly think I have chaffing."

Laughter, from the pit of her belly, burst through her efforts to contain it. "Poor baby." She offered her sympathy, but the laughter dimmed the sincerity.

"Don't laugh, you're the one who'll be suffering too, listening to me whine."

"I think I can handle that." Her tone more serious, but the smile didn't leave her face. "Listening is nowhere near as painful as actually experiencing."

"You can say that again. Who knew a romantic

camel ride on the beach at sunset would turn out to be such a pain in my ass." He laughed through his discomfort, still pulling the fabric of his shorts away from raw skin.

"We can order dinner in the room if you'd prefer not to get dressed to go out."

"Hmmm. I think it would be more uncomfortable to eat dinner nude from the waist down." Eyes wide open as though shocked even by the thought of getting naked in front of her.

She laughed and shook her head. "Not exactly what I had in mind."

Hand over his heart and a look of disappointment on his face, he stopped fidgeting with his shorts and turned to look at her. "Is there something wrong with me—or at least the thought of me naked, that is?"

"Oh. Was I supposed to be thinking of you naked?" She stopped walking and took a step back, as she looked him up and down. "Actually, now that you mention it, I'm pretty sure you'd look alright without your clothes on." She fell into step beside him again.

"Wow. That was convincing."

"How convincing?" She challenged.

"Convincing enough to say we have fifteen

minutes tops to get ready for dinner—at the restaurant where I made a reservation."

"Best we hurry up then."

Zak pulled the room key from his pocket and opened the door, giving her enough space to enter first. "After you, my lady." He dipped his head as she flitted past.

"Why, thank you, kind sir."


With no time to shower, Molly touched up her makeup, changed into the only sundress she brought with her, and sprayed herself with deodorant and perfume. Far from glamorous, she hoped the plain white dress would be appropriate for the restaurant he planned for them. There was nothing she could do about it if it wasn't. In future, if he insisted on more surprise dates, she'd pack a suitcase for the event. That'd be one way to get him to tell her where they were going, for sure.

Zak was dressed in tan denim shorts and a plain white shirt, sleeves rolled to his elbows, and boat shoes on his feet.

"You look nice." There was no denying he was a gorgeous looking man, almost too good-looking and sweet to believe he would stick around for long. As their previous dates, she fully expected by morning he would've turned into a pumpkin, their time together a taste of what could be rather than what would.

"Thanks." He grinned. "And you look as amazing as ever." The appreciation in his tone took her by surprise. All she could hope for now was that he meant what he said about spending more time together.

"Thanks." She felt her cheeks heat and hoped her makeup was doing its job and masked her blush.

"Shall we go?" He either didn't notice or chose to ignore the pink that no doubt tainted her cheeks.

Molly nodded as she slipped her hand into his and followed him out of the room.

As soon as they entered the restaurant, Molly breathed a sigh of relief that she hadn't brought anything fancier than the cute sundress. It seemed casual was the way of life, even at an upmarket restaurant with ocean views. Despite feeling isolated, the casual beach mood was something she could easily get used to.

"Would you like to sit out on the deck or inside?"

"Outside would be nice." Molly didn't hesitate in her preference. The light breezed off the water was cool against her sun-toasted skin.

"Not too cold?"

She shook her head. He was always so considerate, looking out for her above all else.

The waitress led them to a table along the beachside. "Can I get you something to drink?" She was quick and efficient in her service, leaving them alone as soon as she took their drink order.

"I like it here." Molly picked up the menu and held it up in front of her before peering over the top at Zak, who was watching her. "Thank you for bringing me."

"Thanks for coming. Would've been pretty boring on my own—and the view wouldn't have been anywhere near as beautiful as it is currently."

Molly laughed and covered her face with the menu. Her cheeks heated and she knew for sure she was glowing scarlet.

Charming didn't even sum up the mood Zak was in. All day drinking in the sun was probably responsible for his flattery, but Molly enjoyed the flirt and compliments all the same—even if they did make her blush.

Conversation flowed more freely than the drinks, and even without purposely avoiding the topic, details of her work never crept into view. She'd mentioned, on more than one occasion, how she'd worked as a journalist, but that was the extent of it. He either had something against journalists, as many people fell victim to stereotyping as soul sucking leeches, or else he was content with what he knew—keen to know her and not define her by the work she did. As much as she intended on curving the subject matter of her blog, to remove herself from the dating game, she hope the latter to be the case.

Molly struggled to finish her meal, the serving big enough to feed a football team.

"You done?" Zak nodded toward her plate, his already wiped clean.

"About six mouthfuls ago, but it tasted too good to stop." She laughed, clutching her hands to her stomach as if stopping it from protruding—proof she wasn't exaggerating.

"Good to hear. The chicken was my second choice." Zak switched plates and devoured what was left of her food.

It was a good thing he kept so active or else, if he continued to consume so much in one sitting, chaffing would be something he'd need to get used to.

Molly hid her smile so as not to have to explain where her thoughts had gone.

"I was going to suggest we take a stroll along the beach, but it's not very lit up."

"Does that matter." *All the more romantic.*

"Given the wild crocodile population up here, I'd say that could be a bit of an issue."

"Fair point." Molly raised an eyebrow. "But, if we came across one, it'd be a good test as to who runs the fastest."

"As I said before, if we encounter one, it'd be a test on who has the quickest reflexes—me to push, or you to dodge my hand." Out with the charming, he was back to comedian in a flash.

"I'm almost tempted to put you to a challenge." She laughed, no intention to brave the shadow cast beaches, no matter how romantic the notion. "But, crocodiles freak me out, so maybe not."

"Good, because that's one challenge I don't think I'd take you up on."

"So where to now?" Molly didn't want the evening to end, but it was inevitable, with their return flight already booked.

"Seeing as you're a lightweight where food is concerned and you're female, I'm guessing you're regretting being full because the dessert menu has been calling your name from the moment we walked in."

Molly laughed. Playful in his delivery, he hit the nail on the head. Dessert was often her favorite part of the meal, even if she'd ingested enough sugar from her choice of beverages to last her the month. "I think I'll survive, but you're right, dessert is the best part about eating out."

"Well, that's a relief. I have a surprise for a little later, back in the room."

Molly had forgotten they still had the room for the rest of the evening, and it seemed Zak was going to make the most of it. How he managed to pull off such a perfectly planned out date was impressive, to say the least.

"Shall we head back there? We can go for a dip in the pool if you're still hot, or else we can chill out with a bottle of champagne until we have to leave."

"Happy to head back. Doubt I'll swim though—"

"Yes, of course, you're a wimp like me." Zak was more playful than before, and Molly couldn't help but wonder if it had anything to do with the planned activities coming to a close. Whatever the reason, she was enjoying him all the same.

After Zak insisted he pay the bill, they wandered back to their room, hand in hand.

"I feel bad you paying for all of this. Please, can I give you something toward it?"

"Okay—sure."

*That was too easy.* Not that she was complaining, there was nothing worse than the backward and forward argument over who was or wasn't paying.

"Good. Cash or bank transfer?" From past experience, not to the extravagance Zak had gone to with organizing this date, she knew it was best to get in quick before minds were changed and she felt embarrassed, as if she'd ripped someone off intentionally.

"A kiss."

"What?" Distracted by her own thoughts, she wasn't sure she'd heard him correctly.

"Just a kiss. That's what you can give me—oh, wait, did you really think I'd let you pay?" He stopped walking and turned to face her. "Not likely, hottie. This one's on me." Folding her in his arms, he bent his neck until his nose was touching hers. "You really are a hottie." His breath was warm against her face, as were his lips against hers.

The kiss didn't last anywhere near long enough for the sweetness of it. Wanting more, Molly reached one hand up and ran her fingers through his hair. "Not fair, I thought I was supposed to be dishing out the kisses, as payment." Not waiting for him to respond, she stood on tippy toes to claim his mouth.

Time was on their side, yet Molly had no intention of wasting a moment. She wanted to know as much about Zak as she could. The silent file filling fast as the keeper for her, and she was eager to keep adding to it. Fuel to spur her on to quickly make the changes to her blog in order to pull out of the dating game and to declare herself the ultimate winner. Zak was everything she could hope for, and there was nothing she wouldn't do for more time with him.

"We should get back." Zak's tone husky and low. "Don't want to lose track of time and miss out on dessert."

"I don't know about you, but I don't feel like I'm missing out on anything. But, you're right, privacy would be nice." Beating around the bush and pretending she wasn't really into him wasn't her way. There was no point making things difficult for him, and adult guessing games weren't so fun as they were when she was a kid.

As soon as they were behind closed doors, Zak wrapped her in his arms so tight she thought he might crush the air out from her. His mouth finding hers, he deepened the kiss, nudging her tongue with his. Molly all but melted into him. So warm. So strong. It felt good to be in his arms, to be so close to him it was nearly impossible to determine where she ended and he began.

Near breathless, Zak scooped her up and carried her over to the bed.

His kiss was gentle, not so demanding as when they first entered the room. Too long since she'd laid in bed with a man, and the warmth of Zak's skin on hers enticed the minx from within.

She teased him, seeming to meet his kiss, then pulling her head back slightly, denying him a taste. The intensity grew. Her touch more daring, traveling up his shirt, to his back and bare shoulders. Firm, yet not rock solid, his body was as she liked it. *So sexy*. Her muscles clenched, the throb between her legs peaked, and she knew there was no turning back. She wanted him, and as he pressed the pads of his fingers into the flesh of her ass, she knew the feelings were mutual.

Breath quickening, he worked her free of her dress, the complicated wrap around pushed from her body as if an open robe. He didn't wait for her to undress him. In one swift motion, his t-shirt was over his head and flung on to the chair in the corner of the room.

He moved closer, pulling her body until they were chest to chest. The only thing between them was the lace fabric of her bra. She shivered, his body felt good against hers, growing hotter the longer it was pressed to hers. His kiss grew more demanding, and she matched the pace. Reaching one hand up, she raked her fingers through his hair, as Zak pushed her legs apart and settled himself between them. Shorts still in place, but his desire evident through the fabric.

A breath caught in Molly's throat and she released a low moan as Zak rocked his hips, pelvis to pelvis.

There was no denying this man had all the right moves.

"Do you want me to stop?"

Molly shook her head. If there was one thing she was certain of, despite the fact her reality had slipped into a fantasy, it was that she never wanted him to stop. "Not at all," she breathed.

His mouth covered hers, the tip of his tongue nudging her lips apart and plunging in to taste her. Molly wrapped her legs around his waist and pressed the palms of her hands to his back, holding him closer. Zak rolled, pulling her with him until he was settled on his back and she was on top. Trailing a stream of kisses down his neck to his chest, Molly ran her hands down his torso to the button at the waist of his pants. With one hand she worked it open, with the other she unfastened the zip. With both she gripped the fabric and dragged his shorts down to reveal satin boxers.

The thin fabric did nothing to conceal his desire, his thick cock hard and ready, making her crave him all the more. The soft fabric felt cool against her skin as she lowered her body back to meet his. *Warm and cool, the perfect combination.*

Zak pushed the straps off her shoulders, pressing up the moment she was bare to take her nipple between his lips, brushing his tongue over the hardened bud, circling it a few times before biting down, teeth glancing off the end before he moved his attention to the other side.

Molly released a moan, her desire peaking as she ground against him, stimulating her clit as she rubbed up and down his length.

Setting a rhythm, he responded to her movement, entertaining it a moment before switching positions. Flat on her back, him on his side, he snagged her knickers with his thumb and dragged them to one side, slowly sliding two thick fingers between her lips. Slick and wet, he plunged deep inside. Her eyelids flutter shut as he releases a low moan, pivoting his hand to drive deeper.

Reaching down, she grips him through satin, wet with pre-ejaculation, the fabric softens her grip as she works his length. He releases a hiss as the intensity builds, but he doesn't stop. His rhythm set, in out, circle. He teases the hardened bud and she bucks under his touch. Lowering his head, he takes her nipple in his mouth and sucks—hot and wet. He slips in another finger. A sharp burn accompanies the first few thrusts until the third is as slick as the others and her body adapts to the stretch. Opening her legs a little wider, she reaches down and grips his wrist, encouraging him to push a little harder, inviting the burn to radiate through to her core.

Gripping the waistband of his boxers, she dragged them down over his hips. Struggling to get them off with one hand, he removed his fingers to assist. At the same, he moved onto his knees, between her open legs and watched as he circled her clit with one finger. Glancing up, his gaze locked with hers, he lowered his face to replace his finger with tongue. Licking up from her opening to the most sensitive spot he'd been teasing, he groaned as he drank her in, all the while keeping eye contact.

The more he licked, Molly began to pant. Gripping her hips, he restricted her movement as she involuntarily jerked beneath his touch. Dripping wet, her body begged for him to fill her.

"Fuck—that's so good," she moaned, opening her legs a little wider and tilting her pelvis forward. "I want you inside me." Begging wasn't her usual style, but desire took over and controlled her.

Without hesitation, Zak pushes three fingers inside as he continues to lick around them, before taking her clit between his lips and sucking as he begins to pump her orgasm to the brink of release.

"Too soon," she struggles to fight bliss, not wanting it to end so soon.

He shakes his head still pressed against her sex. Seconds before tipping her over, his hands and mouth are replaced with the slam of his cock. She bucks against the force of his possession. Muscles tighten, sucking him in deeper as he attempts to pull back before slamming in again.

Molly cries out, losing the battle of holding off, she gives and shatters around him as he continues to pound until he too finds his release.

## CHAPTER 26

There was nothing like a night of blissful sex to speed up the decision-making process. Such a beautiful date as Zak organized made all others pale in comparison. Nothing about going out with anyone beside him was appealing, and all the inspiration Molly needed to postpone the date she had scheduled for later that day.

Modifying her blog to accommodate for guest posts was going to take some time, but no more time than she was wasting by going out for drinks and dinner dates with guys she had no intention of seeing again. Not now that things were developing with Zak.

She experienced a pang of guilt every time she thought about how deceitful she'd been, putting herself out there as if she were up for grabs when she had no desire to find a man, until Zak.

Molly settled in front of her computer, determined to focus on turning her blog from doom and gloom to a fairy tale overnight. She just hoped that the dates she had already committed to would come and go quickly, or else she'd be pulling the pin on all of them.

*Craze* started as a bit of a joke, but after meeting Zak, her faith in online dating had taken a turn for the better. No more doom and gloom, at least not on a daily basis. A few dating disasters mixed amongst the more appealing headlines from couples who'd found love, including a few posts about her experience with her own keeper to satisfy the readers. Nothing too private, not without Zak's permission. Although, then he would be able to calculate dates and work out that she was seeing other guys whilst he was going to so much effort to impress her.

Molly groaned and, elbows on her desk, she rest her head in her hands. *What a mess.*

*<Hey lovely, are we still on for today? >*

Molly frowned down at her cell on the desk, next to her computer. *Today? What was she supposed to be doing today?*

*<Thought we could grab some lunch after my appointment, if you have time. Been an age since we caught up>*

It was so like Shelley. Twenty-four hours often felt like an age to her if they hadn't spoken or caught up for a chat.

*<Sounds perfect...and I've always got time for you >*

A slight exaggeration on her behalf, as for the past few weeks she knew she hadn't been the best friend Shelley deserved. Too caught up in the dating world to give anyone in her life the time they deserved.

*<Great. I'll pick you up at eleven >*

Molly glanced at the time on the top of the screen. *An hour and a half.* Plenty of time to sort her blog and get ready if she remained focused.

*<Looking forward to it >*

There was something about working to a deadline that inspired Molly to get the job done. Sifting through the emails she'd received from her readers, about their dating disasters, turned out to be more entertaining than she thought it'd be. For the first time in weeks, she was actually excited about her blog again. Variety was by far more appealing than what she'd dished up so far.

She may have had a decent following, but it was nothing in comparison to what she envisaged the future was bound to bring now that she'd given her inbox the attention it deserved.

Dressed and ready, with fifteen minutes to spare, Molly settled on the couch with her laptop and continued the sifting process. There was no denying that a few stories were so exaggerated that she doubted the sincerity of them, but most were funny and surprisingly well written.

No exaggeration, she had enough stories stored in a file to blog daily for the rest of her working life.

Caught up in a boating date gone wrong, the knock at the door startled her and she let out a small yelp.

"You okay in there?" Shelley yelled through the closed door.

Molly laughed as she pressed save on the document she'd been lightly editing, and then shut down her computer, leaving it on the couch next to where she sat. At least she had some interesting and fun reading material for later.

"Won't be a minute," she yelled back, snatching her purse and cell off the coffee table as she hurried out the door.

Shelley was already climbing in her car as Molly pulled the door shut and locked it.

"Far out, I've missed you. Sit your ass down and

fill me in with the gossip." Shelley gushed, leaning over to hug her once she was settled in the passenger seat.

"I've missed you too, and I'm not spilling a word until you tell me about your hottie Italian Stallion."

"Don't even get me started—the man is like a Roman God. Worthy of being worshipped, that's for sure."

Her enthusiasm wasn't so foreign to Molly—not since meeting Zak.

"Good. So it's safe to say you guys have hit it off."

"Hit it off is the understatement of the year, but if downplaying the experience is what you're looking for then sure, you could say that."

Molly laughed. Nothing less than colorful and flamboyant would suit Shelley, not in her designs, not in her choice of clothing, and most certainly not in her relationships. "Downplaying any experience is never what I'm looking for, even less when it's yours and your love life. You deserve so much more than mediocre."

"I do, don't I." Shelley's laughter filled the car before she launched into a full description of her time with Nick, more appropriately titled than *Italian Stallion*.

"This shouldn't take too long." She pulled a face

as if worried Molly might up and leave, as if she had something better to do than support her friend.

"It'll take as long as it takes and then are we headed to a certain someone's restaurant?"

Shelley shook her head. "Nah. I think I'll look a little desperate if we keep going there after my appointments." She shifted the strap of her purse higher on her shoulder as they walked through the doors. "Besides, I don't want him to think I'm totally whipped. It's good for a man to be a little uncertain or else he will stop trying to impress before the courting stage should be over."

"*Courting stage?* How old are you?" Molly teased.

"You know what I mean. There's no point becoming their beck and call girl, at least not until you have a ring on your finger. The way I see it is that if you're not good enough for him to get down on one knee for, then he doesn't deserve to treat you like a wife."

Molly mulled over her point of view. She made a fair point. "I know I keep telling you this, so don't let it go to your head, but you're right. No wife privileges prior to the proposal."

"And, even then there's a limit on expectation—a limit set by us." An outsider listening in wouldn't have had a hard time guessing that Shelley had been messed around in the past, and she just hoped that there was more promise for love in her future.

"We can toast to that over lunch."

Molly hoped that being a good support person didn't include absorbing all the details of what was in store for Shelley if she went through with the whole baby scenario now that Nick was on the scene. Her mind kept wandering off to what Shelley had said about *courting* and how financially strapped Zak would be if he continued with the outrageous dates for any length of time. He'd never be able to afford a ring to accompany a proposal.

"We can do this one of two ways," Dr. Stu sat forward in his seat, arms resting on the desk and hands clasped in front of him. "We can either wait until you've had time to think things through, and to see how things turn out with your new relationship. Or, we can start the ball rolling, run some tests to make sure all is functioning as it should be. Either way, the later will have to be done at some stage, that is, unless nature takes over and bypasses the need for testing."

Shelley turned her head toward Molly as she spoke. "I don't think it'd do any harm to have the tests—I mean, isn't it better if we establish a healthy environment for a baby regardless of how we go about implantation?"

"I'd think so." Molly shrugged, not knowing the correct answer, but guessing what she would do if she were in Shelley's shoes.

Shelley turned back to face Doctor Stu. "What do you think?"

"An entirely personal decision, but from a doctor's viewpoint, I completely agree with you."

"That was easy." Shelley let out a nervous giggle. "Point me in the right direction and I'm there."

"It's fate really, the way we ended up in his restaurant after your first encounter, the two of you making eyes at each other in a fertility clinic—truth be told you'll probably have a dozen kids and live happily ever after," Molly exaggerated.

"Speaking of happily ever after's, how are things with you and Zak?"

"Sheer bliss doesn't even come close to how he makes me feel."

"Elaborate."

"Well, you're never going to guess where he took me—to Broome."

"Broome?" Shelley dropped the fork into her salad. "What the—"

"I know right. Who does that?"

"Is he rich or something?"

"I have no idea. I haven't asked for a printout of his accounts—didn't think it'd be polite."

"You're such a smart ass."

Molly grinned. "He must be keen though, hey?"

"Are you kidding? The guy is hooked. He'll be whisking you down the aisle before you know it."

"Yeah, that won't be happening, but anyway—" Molly all but shuddered. Getting married was the last thing running through her mind. The thought alone was enough to make her cringe.

"Are you kidding? Guys like that don't come along every day, snag him while you still can."

"I don't even feel right about sleeping with him while my life is in such a mess. Some people would see what I'm doing as deceitful—I mean, I do."

"Not all together honest, but it's easy enough for you to take care of."

"I know. I cancelled the date I had scheduled for tonight so I can."

"Oh, was he cute?"

Molly frowned, but didn't respond. What did it matter what he looked like, Zak was the only guy she wanted to spend time with?

"Will you reschedule?"

"Zak's away for a few days with work, so I'll cram the last few dates in to get them over with."

"You don't have to go, you know. You don't owe these guys anything. Just tell them it was nice chatting, but you've met someone. They'll respect that more than you wasting their time."

Molly mulled over what she said. There was no denying she was right, Molly already knew this, but until she committed to the change, there was no way she could take the next step in her connection with Zak.

As much as what Shelley said made sense, there was no way she could cancel on the guy she'd rescheduled, it just didn't seem fair to mess him around more than she had already. A last minute back out of a date would already have his confidence waning. So long as he kept his hands to himself she would treat him a she would a client keen for an interview.

"The only one I'll attend is the reschedule, and I'll cancel the rest of them tonight. As much as I hate to say it, you're right—I have little respect for myself right now, for stringing these guys along with no intention of a second date. That is unless they count their blog appearance."

"Can you imagine if any of these guys got wind

of you writing about their shitty dating deliveries—there'd be a reward on your head." Shelley's eyes widened. "You've kept your identity hidden, haven't you? I mean, someone could jump you in a dark alley if you're not careful."

Molly tipped her head back and laughed. "My measly little blog wouldn't be enough to spark such a wild reaction. But, in answer to your question, hidden identity all the way."

"Well, that's a relief."

Molly rubbed at her eyes, tired from too many hours in front of the computer. She'd been going strong since Shelley dropped her home, racing off to cook dinner for Nick. With a definite direction, and faith in what she was doing, she had the next few weeks covered with scheduled posts. At the rate she was going, there'd be nothing for her to do but to sit back and reap the rewards of her best idea yet.

With a cup of tea in hand, settled on the couch in front of the television, she toyed with the temptation to delete the app from her cell once and for all.

As much as guilt got the better of her where Zak was concerned, it also got the better of her for pulling out of the date she missed earlier. If she had've cancelled from the get go, then she wouldn't have felt so bad, but to reschedule and then cancel, she couldn't bring herself to send the text.

*One last date*, she promised herself, even though she didn't see the meeting as a date at all. Going out with guys, other than Zak, had simply become the downside of her business.

With the following day's blog post scheduled for release the following morning, she was free to watch the end of the romantic comedy movie. Although her mind wasn't on the movie, rather the reaction she'd receive from her readers, stating her intention of the future, followed by the best story she could find as proof her blog was still worth the visit.

## CHAPTER 27

It wasn't difficult to keep the date with Kyle strictly business. He was pleasant enough, but so caught up in his career that he'd need a like-minded person to settle down with or else she'd run the risk of premature death caused from boredom.

Keen to get the date over and done with, Molly continuously bombarded him with questions about the not so fascinating to her world of the pharmaceutical industry. Despite not wanting to be labeled stupid, she knew she'd never get a grasp of what he was talking about. Chemistry wasn't her strongest subject. With thoughts on Zak, it was hard to focus on what Kyle was saying, anyway.

The line of work he was in seemed interesting

enough, at least it would be if she understood more than the fact he was a research scientist in the pharmaceutical industry, but his particular line of research was beyond her understanding.

There was no doubt in her mind he was a workaholic. The conversation didn't stretch beyond his field even when she tried to broaden the scope to the more personal subjects like family and recreational interests.

He was kidding the women he dated just as she was the men. There was no way Kyle was serious about meeting someone he could settle down with. Everything about him screamed lonely, which didn't really support her assumption, but it was the feeling that he liked his life as it was that overruled.

Molly resisted the urge to sigh.

"All I've done is talk about myself, sorry. What is it that you do as a job?"

He obviously thought her as stupid as she felt in his presence, pharmaceuticals being his career and her merely holding down a *job*.

There was no denying she was prickly, more so than usual, but there was something about the guy that enhanced her bad mood. Which really wasn't fair, she'd landed herself in a situation she didn't want to be in, so now she was going to have to suck it up, smile, and be as pleasant as possible.

"I'm a journalist." There was no way she was going to elaborate about the change of direction her *job* had taken, especially not in his company. He, less than any of the guys she'd been out with, wouldn't see the funny side, that was for sure.

"I would never have picked you for a writer, figured you'd be a make-up artist, or something in the beauty industry." He shrugged, obviously uncomfortable about his assumption.

She mulled it over for a moment, not sure whether his comment was meant as a compliment. Deciding she didn't care much for what he thought of her anyway, she took his assessment in the most positive way. "Thanks, but nothing so glamorous for me. Journo for the Times was as good as I got, I'm afraid." There was absolutely nothing to be ashamed of as far as her career had taken her, and she knew it.

"I'm impressed."

*And surprised.* Molly didn't need to voice her opinion, the expression on his face was enough to confirm her thoughts.

Kyle was the best remedy to convince her that this would be her last first date. She was done with the deceit. The sneaking around behind Zak's back.

Even though they hadn't made a formal commitment that they wouldn't see other people, it was the unsaid messages he sent that were stronger than words. She'd come to the conclusion that no one went to so much effort if they didn't have intentions for more than three dates, even if money was no issue.

Relief was only some of what washed over her as her cell phone began to ring. She silently wished it was Shelley to bail her out of her latest disaster. "I'm sorry, this is so rude, but, if you don't mind, I really need to take this call."

He nodded, then gestured toward her phone. "By all means."

Gracious and accommodating, she hoped he had better luck with dating in the future. Guilt gripped as she slipped out of her chair and took a few steps away from the table before answering the call.

"Hello."

"Hey, good-looking." The familiarity of his voice set the butterflies in her stomach into a flurry.

"Hey-y." She grinned, her back to Kyle as she walked to the lobby area for privacy. She wouldn't blame him if he wasn't at their table when she returned. Lousy pretty much summed up her behavior, but she was in too far to back out now. This was it. Her serial dating days were over as soon as she left the restaurant. The decision alone was like a weight had been lifted off her shoulders, and she couldn't wish time away fast enough.

"A vision of you caught my attention and I couldn't help myself. I had to call and say hi."

"Well, I'm glad you did." Molly frowned and glanced around. Was his vision of the memory sort, or was he home early from his trip away? He'd said it'd be a short business trip, but she hadn't expected it'd be less than a few days. "All going well?" She didn't want to be so obvious and ask him if he was back already, instead hoped he would offer his whereabouts in his response.

"Better than I hoped. What about you? Busy day?"

Molly glanced over her shoulder. The restaurant was busy, but nothing else about her day came close. "Out to lunch with a client." Not too far a stretch. Their meeting was merely fodder for her blog.

"Oh, shit. I'll let you get back to it." If you're not too full from lunch, would you like to meet me for dinner later? I'm hoping to finish up early today."

"I'd like that—no matter how full I am."

"Glad to hear. Seven work for you?"

"Perfect."

"I'll text you the address, unless you have a preference."

"I'm happy to go anywhere, so long as you're there." Corny, but true. She didn't often fall victim to the needy side of a relationship, but when her mood was laced with guilt, it was hard not to lather the soppy talk a little thicker.

"I feel the same. But, I'll let you get back to work and I'll talk to you later."

"Look forward to it. Have a good day." She cut connection and stood staring at the wall a few moments before heading back to see if Kyle was as patient as she picked him to be.

"Sorry for making you wait." The apology sounded hollow despite her sincerity. She was glad Zak took the time out to call her in the middle of the day, but she sensed there was more to his call than he let on. At the same time, she felt sorry for Kyle, wasting hours with her when there was no hope of progressing.

"No worries. If you haven't guessed, I'm a patient man."

"I figured you were, but that's no reason to take advantage." If nothing else, she'd learnt a lot about herself since she met Zak. She'd confirmed that more than one man at a time in her life was too much to handle. Yet, at the same time, her work was more important to her than she ever realized. Her newfound passion for storytelling had her hooked—although the subject matter was causing her the grief.

She didn't think it wise to wrap up their lunch so soon after the phone call from Zak. Not only did she get the sense that his vision was in the most literal sense of the word, she didn't want to offend Kyle more than she already thought she had.

"Have you travelled much with your work?" Their conversation was even more stilted than it had been before. Kyle was as much grasping for topics to cover as she was—anything to make the time pass as quickly as possible. She wondered if he suspected the call was of a personal nature and not work as she'd implied.

"Not really. I would've liked to. Health journalism captured my interest of a short time, whilst I was studying, but I found it a little more distressing dealing with grief and sickness, so I changed my focus."

"I was under the impression there was room for travel in all aspects of the job."

That word again, *job*. "I guess there is opportunity, if that's what you're interested in. But, as much as I loved my work, I wanted a life outside of it too." There was no way he'd understand that, but Molly had entertained the date for as long as she could manage, and was now keen to wrap it up.

"Speaking of *job*, sorry to cut our time short, I best get back to it, I have research to do."

"Ah, yes. That makes two of us." She'd never been more grateful for science in her life.

Kyle drained the remaining inch of wine from his glass and was out of his chair before Molly.

"It was lovely to meet you." She extended her hand for him to shake, which he did. Formal to the very last minute, she held back the sigh of relief that the date was finally over.

Poor guy. She really didn't give him a chance—another cross on the list of wrong doings on her part.

Molly didn't wait until she was home to delete the *Craze* app from her cell.

"Good riddance," she muttered. Like a weight lifted from her shoulders, a sense of freedom was almost as obvious as the relief she felt as soon as the icon vanished from her screen.

## CHAPTER 28

Just when she was starting to think she wouldn't hear from him again that day, despite his invitation for them to catch up for dinner, Zak sent through a text.

*<Thought it'd be nice to keep it casual tonight, if that suits. Been a busy few days and I'd love nothing more than to kick back and relax with you tonight >*

She couldn't stop the smile from spreading across her face.

. . .

*<Sounds perfect to me. What did you have in mind? >*

His message said a lot about his desire for keeping it casual, and to share the evening with her, yet nothing about where they were headed. She was curious if his kicking back and casual was out and about, or at his house.

*<The Waterfront Bar for a drink or two and a bite to eat >*

She was a little surprised he was up for going out, especially when he'd been working so hard for the past few days. At least, she thought he'd been working hard. The truth was, she didn't really know what it was he'd been doing—he could be a pimp for all she knew.

Career was probably the safest topic of conversation for newbie relationships, and first time dates, but when that was the one part of your life you had no desire to share, it was an easy topic to avoid. Ultimately, who really wanted to talk about work, anyway?

. . .

*<If you're comfortable to come to mine, then it's a short walk from here >*

Molly had intended to drive, but if his house was anywhere near the bar, as it obviously was, then parking would be a nightmare to find. *A cab it would be.*

*<Completely comfortable. I'll be there just before seven >*

*<Can't wait >*

At least he wasn't one to leave her hanging. Quick responses were so much better than the lag between messages she was used to. Probably because, with Carl, he had to check the coast was clear before he sent her anything. *Cheating bastard.*

It was funny how cut up she was about finding out the truth about him, and yet, lately, he never even made an appearance in her thoughts. She'd known he wasn't right for her, in awe of his achievements and his creativity more than she was over him as a person.

Molly glanced at the time on her cell, a little

under two hours before she needed to leave. Plenty of time to suss out the happenings on her blog after her big announcement earlier that day. It'd been a struggle not to check sooner, but she'd made a promise to give it time and denied herself the urge.

In front of her computer, again—she seemed to be spending half of her time there since working for herself—she opened to the insights page and held her breath. The traffic she expected to be as high as usual, especially considering her readers didn't know what they were in for. It was the likes and comments she was eager to see, and there were plenty of them waiting for her.

Shy of five thousand likes was a record for her, especially in just a few hours. It was the comments she was nervous about reading, but it had to be done sooner rather than later.

Even if her readers weren't happy about the changes, it still didn't mean she would ditch Zak to give them what they wanted. What it did mean was that she'd have to come up with plan B.

After a dozen or more, *great idea, good job, I love your blog,* and *woohoo! I have the best story, pm'img you now*, she began to relax. Where the comments didn't congratulate her on the changes she'd made, readers were curious about the relationship she was entering into, or asked if she'd given up on the dating game as they had.

It was sad really, how so many were holding out for love yet not finding the person they wanted to spend time with. And even sadder that there were people, like Carl, who didn't place a high enough value on love, short changing the person they were with.

As soon as Molly was satisfied that her blog wasn't on the brink of crashing and burning, she shut down her computer and turned her focus to getting ready for her date with Zak. Casual and relaxed may have been his intention, but she was adding sexy to the mix as well. And she knew the perfect little black dress to do the trick.

It always took longer to get ready when you wanted to look as though you weren't trying, and so she was racing around like a madwoman until the very last second when the cab driver blasted the horn to get her attention.

After double-checking her cell was in the nude colored clutch, she chose to match strappy heels, she headed for the door.

She was more nervous about their fourth date than she had been on their first. The urge to check her hair was straight and make up not smudged almost got the better of her. The cab driver didn't help to calm her, arguing in his native tongue with whoever was on the receiving end of his call.

Molly slowly released a deep breath and turned her attention to the buildings they passed. She was glad he only lived fifteen minutes away. Any longer in the presence of the angry ant in the driver's seat, and the option to jump may have been more appealing.

Even from the outside, she could tell that Zak's choice of residence suited him to a tee. Modern and sleek, the building was fitted with a security system she had no idea how to use, so she messaged him for instruction, which was just as well because the driver had dropped her at the side entrance instead of the front.

Always accommodating, Zak volunteered to meet her downstairs to show her the way—or to give her a *tour*, so he put it.

He was already waiting for her as she rounded the corner. Leaning against the wall in denim jeans and a fitted black tee, he looked as casual and relaxed as the night he promised. And more sexy than Molly expected.

"You got down here quick."

"When you come out looking so good as you do, I'd

say it's a good thing I got down here before one of my neighbors tried to lure you in." He couldn't hide the smile for long. By the time she stood in front of him, he was grinning. "You're almost too good to take out."

Molly arched one eyebrow. "*Almost.*"

"Yeah, almost—I'm a cocky bastard sometimes, I like to show you off." He frowned as if not sure he should've shared what he was really thinking.

"Is that so?" She tried to keep a straight face, but was as hopeless as he was at holding back the smile. "Goes both ways, I guess. You look pretty good yourself."

"Why thank you." Zak took her hand and pulled her in for a kiss. "Come on, I'll show you around."

Inside, the apartment complex was even more impressive than the outside.

"Wow." As soon as the door to the lift opened, Molly knew why each and every occupant didn't pass up the chance to live there. Confronted with a resort style pool and surrounding garden, it'd be like being on a permanent vacation. Something she'd quite easily get used to. "Beautiful place."

"Thanks. I'd like to be able to take credit for it, but I was merely the designer. My crew took care of the hard part."

Molly frowned as his words sunk in. "The designer?"

"You noticed how I snuck that in?" He tipped his head back and laughed.

"If I was responsible for designing this place, I'd sky write it in neon for everyone to see." She shook her head in disbelief. "This place is amazing."

"Thanks. I'm glad you like it."

Zak didn't linger long, instead he led the way to the apartment that was his. "We won't stay or else they'll give our booking away, but I'll quickly show you my place."

He was proud, not showy, as he had every right to be. He'd designed a beautiful home not only for himself but for everyone who resided there.

In awe, Molly remained silent as she took it all in. Inside, his apartment was huge. Airy with a lot of natural light. Where she expected a bachelor pad, she was pleasantly surprised by the mostly white and pale grey interior. What she did notice was that he had a lot of cushions and matching lamps throughout. His bed was made, not a crinkle to be seen, and covered with more cushions.

"So, what do you think?" Like a little kid uncertain of whether he'd gained approval, he stood with his hands behind his back. His eyes didn't leave her face.

"I don't know what to say—wow—it's stunning." She glanced around at all the finishing's, taking it in again in hope to come up with a little more satisfying response for him. "Did you design the interior too?"

He nodded, still not looking completely certain by her response.

"I don't think I need to point out what you probably already know, but you have an eye for detail and design. It's completely not what I expected, yet it's by far more spectacular."

A smile replaced the slight frown that haunted him moments before. "I'm intrigued—what did you expect."

Molly shrugged. "A single guy's place. Lots of black or charcoal. Sports memorabilia—a bachelor pad." She shrugged again, not at all apologetic in her response.

"I wonder what your response would've been had you been right," he teased.

"Given your obvious flare for decorating, I still would've been impressed, but this has rendered me a little speechless, and that doesn't happen often."

Seeming content with her comments, he smiled

again and held his hand out for her to take. "Shall we go?"

Molly nodded, although would've been more than happy to stay exactly where they were. If her place looked anything like Zak's she doubted she'd ever leave the house again. The one thing it did highlight was that she had some serious redecorating to do before she invited him over to hers.

True to his word, the bar was only a few minute stroll along the river. They hadn't been out on his balcony, but she had no doubt he could see the table he reserved from his back door.

"Good evening, Mr. Lange, will you have your usual in the bar before your meal?"

"Would you like to start with a drink in the bar?" He looked at Molly for confirmation.

"Sounds good to me." She smiled up at him as he brushed a strand of her hair from her face and tucked it behind her ear.

"Me, too. Thanks, Charlie." He turned his attention back to the seating attendant.

For a Friday night, the place wasn't overly crowded. It seemed Zak was somewhat a VIP client, given first class treatment by all the staff.

"Let me guess, gin and tonic for you?" Zak quizzed when he saw the waitress head their way.

"That'd be great, thank you."

Zak placed their order and then turned his attention back to Molly.

"Will you tell me about the work you do?" As much as she thought it best to avoid career conversation, he had her intrigued, and she wanted to know more.

"Sure. But, I'll warn you first, once I get started you might not shut me up. I love what I do."

"That works for me because, from what I've seen, I love what you do too."

He wasn't wrong. She'd almost finished her drink, and he'd hardly even taken a sip. There was no denying he was passionate and dedicated to design and architecture. His enthusiasm added to his stories, and she was keen to hear more.

"I hope I'm not boring you." Worry crossed his expression.

"Not at all, I'm fascinated by all of this. So, what was the project you were away for?"

"A big hush-hush project, so keep this one to yourself. I've been working on it for a while, a winery, slash resort, in the south-west region." Zak launched into a detailed outline of the project thus far and where they intended it to go in the future.

His willingness to share top-secret information

with her sent the flurry of butterflies wild in the pit of her stomach. Excited and nervous at the same time.

Molly reached into her purse for her lip-gloss and smeared across her lips whilst she listened.

After a few moments, Zak stopped mid-sentence and sniffed the air. "What is that?"

"Just lip tingle gloss." She held it up for him to inspect.

"Does it taste like it smells? Grape, right?"

Molly nodded. "Sure does, and it makes your lips tingle too." She held it out for him and he took it and inhaled deeply.

"It reminds me of the grape bubblegum I used to love as a kid."

"Me too." She grinned. "I used to buy the tape version with my pocket money every week."

"I didn't get it every week, but the tape was the coolest." After another sniff, Zak held the stick of gloss out for her to take.

"You're welcome to try it."

"Nah." He shook his head. "Lip gloss isn't really my thing—especially not in public." He puckered his lips and screwed up his nose.

Molly laughed and smeared her lips with more, even though her lips were already buzzing with the tingle that was intended to plump them. Zak watched as she layered her lips with the clear gel, and as she slipped it back into her purse. Not once did she break eye contact as she shifted to the edge of her seat and leaned forward. Hand cupping his cheek, Molly pressed her lips to Zak's. Mouth closed, her kiss was nonsuggestive to start with, ensuring the gloss transferred before she parted her lips and deepened the kiss. Long. Slow. Deliberate. She increased the intensity, plunging her tongue into his opened mouth as she slid her hand from his cheek to tangle her fingers in his hair.

Zak placed his hand on the small of her back, the pressure intended to pull her closer. Lingering for a few moments longer, Molly resisted the urge to continue. On display for all to see made the decision an easier one.

She licked her lips as she pulled back, as did he.

"Good?"

"Mmmm. Even better than tape bubblegum. Not sure about the tingling though." He frowned and licked his lips again before he leaned forward for another taste.

Molly met him halfway. Shorter, but as intense, she kissed him again.

"Stay with me tonight?" He breathed, lips lightly touching hers.

She covered his mouth with hers as she toyed with his invitation for a few moments. Not because she needed to think about it, but because she didn't want to appear overeager.

"Sounds good to me."

## CHAPTER 29

There was nothing like waking up in Zak's arms to put a smile on her face. Warm and secure, he was still cocooning her from when they drifted off to sleep.

She liked that he was cuddly. Again, not what she expected. There was nothing overly predictable about him, which made their relationship all the more fun. Whether that would change over time, she wasn't sure, but she certainly wanted to be around to witness.

Zak nuzzled into where her shoulder met her neck, his breath hot on her skin. Deeper than usual breaths told her that he was still asleep. She tried to main still so as not to disturb him. How long that would last she didn't know, especially when she was busting for the toilet.

As soon as she moved, Zak was awake.

"Good morning, beautiful." He pressed his lips to her neck. "Did you sleep well?"

"Good morning." She turned her head and dropped her shoulder back so she could kiss him on the tip of his nose. "Well, doesn't even begin to sum it up—I was exhausted, I don't even remember drifting off."

"I'm no help there, I'm sure I was out of it before you." He sucked air in through his nose and pretended to snore. "Sound familiar?"

"Nope. So that proves I was asleep first." Molly wriggled and turned until she was on her back, looking up at him. "So, what are your plans for today?"

Propped up on one elbow, he looked like he was posing for a bedroom setting advertisement.

"Did you bring an overnight bag with you?"

"I wasn't expecting to stay." She wrinkled her nose. Her outfit from the night before wasn't the most casual thing she owned.

"My sister leaves a few clothes in the spare room for when she's in town. You're about the same size, and she won't mind if you borrow a dress or something."

Borrowing his sister's clothes was overly appealing, but she didn't have many options.

"I'm sure I have a new toothbrush in the bathroom. So, shower first, and then we should head out for breakfast—or brunch, depending on what time it is. Unless you have something better to do today—"

"This afternoon I'm helping a friend set up for her birthday party. If you're not busy, I'm sure she wouldn't mind if you came along."

"That would've been great, but I accepted an invitation to a colleague's house a few weeks back. A small gathering, but I'd feel bad if I cancel on him at the last minute."

"Fair enough, I would too." Another tick for Zak —respectful with a solid set of morals.

"I have some work I need to do this afternoon, but we could catch up for lunch tomorrow if you're not busy?"

"Sounds good." Even if she wound up hung over, she should be fine by lunch time.

"Great. Now come on you, shower time. I'm hungry."

. . .

Brunch along the river was the perfect way to start the day off, another eatery where the staff knew Zak by name and treated him like family.

"So, do you use your kitchen or is it for ornamentation purposes only?" There was humor in her tone, and Zak grinned sheepishly.

"What can I say—I'm a guy."

"My best friend is going out with a chef, so that's a cop out." She laughed as he wrinkled his nose.

"True—I'm lazy?"

Molly laughed louder. "It sucks cooking for one."

"Don't I know it? Besides, I get so caught up in my work that if I have to cook for myself, I don't bother eating. I usually think about food when I take a walk or head out to meet a client."

She nodded. "I'm pretty much the same."

"Do you lunch with clients often?"

Molly shrugged, trying to disguise the panic that was building up inside. "Sometimes, or a drink, sometimes even dinner. Breaks the ice and makes for a better story." Molly shrugged again.

"I saw you out with your client yesterday."

Molly opted for surprise rather than admitting she'd guessed that to be the case.

"He looked like a male model that spent all of his spare time in the gym."

"You couldn't be further from the truth." She laughed. "Kyle's a scientist. He works in pharmaceuticals."

"Well, those must be some potent experiments he's conducting. Wonder if he's sampling the goods."

"Maybe. You should've joined us, seems you might be onto something a little more interesting than the science mumbo jumbo he was going on about. My poor little brain went into shutdown mode after three minutes of listening to him."

"Not going to lie, I wasn't thrilled to see him sitting across from you, and that got me thinking about something."

Molly hoped Zak didn't have supersonic hearing or else he would've heard her heart change in rhythm as it skipped into overdrive, pumping so hard it made her a little light-headed. "And what was that?" Elbows on the table, she rest her chin on closed fists she was trying not to clench. *Where was he going with this?*

"Are you still on *Craze*? You don't have to tell me if you don't want to, I'm just curious." The color in his cheeks reddened.

Molly let out a giggle, a little embarrassed to admit she had deleted it, and totally relieved that the app was the something he was thinking about. "No,

I'm not. I wasn't so *crazy* about that app, so I got rid of it."

"Yeah. I know that feeling."

"And you?" Molly took a sip of her tea and peered over the rim of her cup as she awaited his answer.

"Deleted it after our second date." She hoped he didn't ask when she deleted hers, but he seemed content with the answer she'd given.

"Cool." *What else was she supposed to say?* Especially when all she could hope was that they wrapped the conversation up, and soon.

"Why d'you delete it?"

"Seriously?" She set the cup on the saucer and looked up at him with wide eyes. "I was sick of the app running my phone flat. It's so frustrating."

"Seriously?" It was Zak's turn for wide eyes.

"Come on, I bet yours did too." So gorgeous as he was, she could only imagine his phone was running hot all day.

"Not at all. I only had a couple of matches, to be honest."

"You must be really fussy." No other explanation seemed plausible.

"Or, not appealing to the masses."

"Crazy." She'd heard from the men who'd emailed her blog that this was the case, but she hadn't seen their profile, so reserved judgment. "I've heard it's not so easy for men, but never imagined you'd fall into that category." She picked up her cup of tea again. "Their loss."

"Your gain?" He grinned.

"Something like that." She smiled back, more relaxed than she had been when he first sparked up the conversation.

"So, are you seeing anyone else at the moment?" Molly frowned down at her plate and then glanced up at him.

"No, why? Should I be?"

"Not at all. I was just making sure before I make an ass of myself in a public place."

He was confusing her, but she tried to be patient whilst he got to the point. "See, the thing is, I'm not really in to sharing—" he paused as if waiting to gauge her reaction to his confession. She didn't flinch, so he pushed on. "I guess what I'm trying to say is that I really like you and I would like to get to know you better. I hope you feel the same, and if you do, I'd hope I was the only guy on speed dial."

"Not that I use speed dial, but I'm not keen to share you with anyone else either, so exclusivity works for me too."

"Phew. I'm glad I managed to spit that out. Do

you have any idea how nerve-wracking that is for a guy?"

"Probably no different than for a female to face rejection. Trust me, we don't like to feel humiliated any more than you guys do."

"I'm sure you don't." Zak took a sip of freshly squeezed orange juice. "How's the smashed avocado?"

"Delicious. I can see why you wouldn't bother cooking of yourself when you have such fabulous chefs on hand." Zak sat back in his chair, picked his napkin up from off his lap, wiped his mouth and then dropped it on the table beside his plate. "At least it didn't take long for you to start seeing things from my perspective—and, just think, if I don't cook at home then I save on having to hire someone to clean my oven."

"Good point, but I have a solution for the oven cleaning issue. Invest in an oven with a self-cleaning mode inbuilt."

Zak laughed. "Where do you get this stuff from?"

"Ahhh, I'm full of fun facts. You'll have to stick around for a while if you're keen to learn more."

"I might just have to do that." Zak reached out and took her hand in his. "Ready to go?"

Molly gave his hand a light squeeze and nodded.

"So, what project are you working on this afternoon?"

"The secret one." Zak fell into step beside her as they left the cafe to stroll along the river's edge.

"That's exciting. Are you enjoying it?"

He nodded. "I love what I do, and when it's different and I get to leave my mark on something a little more innovative, I love it even more."

"I look forward to visiting once it's built. I can't wait to see what you come up with."

"Ahh, the best part of what I do is the fancy software that's available. We'll have a preview night as soon as I finish putting the virtual video together."

"Oh wow. You can do that?"

"Yeah. It's time consuming, but the end result is always worth the effort."

"That's impressive. I look forward to seeing it." The warmth of the sun on her back was heavenly. Hand in hand with Zak was even better. "Thank you for breakfast, and last night, I really enjoyed myself."

Still walking, he leaned down and pressed his mouth to hers for a quick kiss. "It was my pleasure."

## CHAPTER 30

"Oh wow. Karina, you look stunning," Molly breathed. "Where did you find that dress? It's gorgeous." Forrest green floor length crochet with a mini underskirt was elegant but sexy at the same time.

It was fun getting ready with Karina and Shelley like they were teenagers again.

"Shh, don't tell anyone, but I wore it to a river cruise when I was sixteen and I could never part with it." Karina fussed with the scalloped trim that ran along the edge of the halter and stopped below her bust line, highlighting her cleavage without being distasteful.

"You should talk," Shelley smacked her on the ass

as she wandered over to help Karina with the scalloping at the nape of her neck. "That dress is amazing—oh wait, it's a Shelley Monroe original—" The look of awe on her face was so believable Molly couldn't help but laugh.

"It has nothing to do with the designer, it's all about the figure that wears it." Molly did a full turn and struck a pose that was neither becoming nor complimentary to the exquisitely classy design. The butter yellow wet look dress was cut low in the back and finished with a simple cow neck front. Teamed with strappy heels in the same colour, Molly felt as elegant as her friends looked.

"This was a great idea, Karina." Shelley picked up her dress from on the bed. "At least I have an excuse to get dressed up fancy instead of hanging out washing in my gowns." She laughed despite the fact she wasn't joking. "Nick coming along is like the icing on the cake."

Shelley slipped the red dress over her head. Fabric spilled around her as it fell into place, accentuating her perfect hourglass figure.

"Okay, so you win the award for the showstopper." Molly's eyes widened as she took it all in. "I think that has to be your best design yet."

"Mmmm, I thought the same. Thanks for saying so. I love it." Shelley grinned as she whirled around on the spot.

"You're so talented, maybe I should've taken you up on one of your designs." Karina pressed the palms of her hands to her stomach and sucked in a breath.

"Nonsense, you look amazing—but I'd be happy to make you one anytime. Just say the word."

"Well, hop to it then," she teased, and they all laughed as Karina wandered over to the wine bucket Matty had left by the door whilst they were working on their makeup. "Champagne, ladies?" Karina held up the bottle of *Moet*.

"Ohhh, yes please." Molly and Shelley said in unison and then laughed again.

In turn Karina poured and handed them each a glass and then fixed one for herself before setting the bottle in ice again. "Here's to us, thirty and fabulous." She raised her glass in a toast that applied only to her.

"Not quite thirty, but still fabulous." Molly changed the words to suit herself.

"Old bag of the group, but totally fabulous."

"I would've claimed the toast as it was if I were you," Molly teased.

"Okay, on a serious note—let's get out there and party." Pre drinks were already hitting Karina. From past experience, she'd be in bed before all of her guests left.

The three of them walked out to the family room together. Karina veered off to answer the door. Shelley headed out the back to check that earlier arrivals had a drink in hand, and Molly went to the kitchen to check on the food.

Once she was convinced the caterers had everything under control, she headed out the back to join Shelley.

"Has anyone read that new blog that's taking the Internet by storm? *Craze*, or something?"

Nothing caught her attention quicker than someone out of view talking about her, or in this case, her blog. For the first time, where her career was concerned, she wanted to fall into the pool and sink to the bottom until everyone went home.

"*Join The Craze.*" Matty offered.

"Yeah, that's the one. My wife's addicted to it." The voice boomed. A smile touched the corners of her mouth, but still she didn't turn. It was nice knowing her blog was liked, but even amongst friends, even friends of friends, she didn't want to make a fuss.

"From what I've heard, she's making a bomb from it too." There was admiration, mixed with disdain, in his tone.

"She sure is." Matty was like a proud mother hen. Not a trace of resentment tainted his usual gentle demeanor.

"What makes you so certain?" Another voice piped up, and at that moment she wished she was anywhere other than where she was standing.

"I know her—really well."

"Oh yeah, how well?" The instigator of the conversation was back. "Don't tell me you were the married dog she was talking about." He laughed. Despite not being able to see him, Molly could tell there was nothing more than playful banter in his accusation.

"Did you say *you* or your wife was addicted to it?" A familiar voice she couldn't pick joined the conversation. "What's it about, anyway?"

"This chick organizes dates from that online dating sight, *Craze*, and she spills the dirt on all the shitty dates she goes on. She has categories she slots the date into, dud, stud, or keeper—and let me tell you, there are a lot of duds out there. Some of these guys are a joke."

Molly couldn't say she was disappointed with his description. He certainly saw the humorous side of what she was doing.

"Sounds like crap." The familiar voice interjected.

"I'll call her over in a minute and you can tell her that to her face." Matty laughed, the sound of a slap on someone's back followed.

"She's here. Shit, man, I thought you were joking when you said you knew her," big mouth boomed.

That was Molly's cue to leave. She made a beeline for the house where she would seek refuge until she managed to pull Karina aside and asked her to call Matty and his mates off her tail.

"Molly—" Matty called before she made it to the door.

*Too late.*

She groaned out loud before she fixed a smile on her face and turned in Matty's direction. She froze as soon as she spotted the face that belonged to the familiar voice. Her smile slipped away as she imagined the color had drained from her face. She stood, rooted to the spot, not knowing if she should elaborate on where she was at with her blog, or if she should run and hide.

Zak made the first move, stalking past her as she toyed with her options.

"Zak, it's not what you think." Molly rushed into the house after him, relieved it was still early enough that not everyone had arrived to witness her humiliation.

He reeled around so suddenly she almost bashed into him. He took a step back to put some distance between them. "Really? So, you're saying Luke and Matt lied about what you do? Date blogging? People actually read that stuff?" He shook his head. Molly couldn't tell if he was more disgusted by her or the people who took the time to read her posts.

"Tell me, how many dates have you been on since we've been seeing each other?"

"You never said we were exclusive until this morning—and it wasn't like that." She was grasping, and she knew it as well as he did.

"You're an intelligent woman, I may have confirmed exclusivity this morning, but I really didn't think it needed to be spelled out for you prior to our chat."

"I know I did the wrong thing, but I promise it wasn't done intentionally. I made the blog my career. Since I met you, I have been working on a way to continue earning an income without going on the dates myself."

"You think that justifies what you've done?"

"No, but I'm not the awful person you think I am. Please let me explain, Zak." She reached out to take his hand, but he pulled it out of her way.

"I'm done." Without so much as a glance in her direction, he stalked out of the room.

## CHAPTER 31

"You look like you're in mourning," Shelley announced as soon as Molly sat down. "Could you have found a more depressing outfit if you tried?"

Molly hadn't given a lot of thought to her appearance. Looking down at the heavy fabric, thundercloud colored dress she'd opted to wear, she couldn't blame Shelley for the expression of horror plastered to her face. All about color, no doubt, the drab attire would be painful for her to witness, especially given the storm cloud that seemed to be pissing on Molly's mood since the scene erupted at Karina's birthday party.

"Can we save the I told you so lecture for another

day, I'm not up for that conversation just yet." Molly groaned and let her forehead rest on the tabletop.

"I'm still not over the fact that your Zak is the same Zakary I've been trying to set you up with since he started working with Matty."

She lifted her head and peered up at Karina. "Yeah, well, it would've been good if you had've warned Matty not to elaborate on the content of my blog."

"If I had've known it was a secret, I would never have told him in the first place." Karina's tone turned haughty, but she was kinder in her delivery than Molly knew she deserved. It wasn't Matty, or anyone's fault, and she knew it. She had no one to blame but herself.

"That wasn't fair—sorry." Molly groaned again. "Why did I have to make such a mess of everything?"

It was Shelley's turn to pipe up. "Beats me. All I was trying to get you to do was loosen up and enjoy yourself a little. Who knew your blog would go gangbuster, and you'd screw things up so badly with the only guy who's ever really meant anything to you."

"Way to make me feel worse, thanks for that." She glared at everything and nothing at the same time. "I know I stuffed up, but a little compassion wouldn't go astray."

"Rather than focusing on how badly you stuffed up, why don't you focus on how you're going to fix the mess you've made."

"Fix it? You can't fix something that someone else doesn't want to be a part of." Molly folded her arms across her chest in a self-hug. "It's not like we invested a lot of time in each other. There is very little to focus on. A few extra special dates, and emotions that escalated beyond what I'd consider normal, especially given the short time we spent together."

"All the more reason to fight for it."

"For once, where relationships are concerned, Shelley makes a valid point."

"*Karina.*" Shelley laughed, the backhanded complement came as a surprise.

"Come on, you might have it together now, but—"

"Okay, no need for you to turn this into the *Shelley Show*." She didn't even wait for Karina to explain, she knew as well as all of them that her track record with men was a disaster.

"Regardless, I don't think we have the mileage to

fight for. We weren't even in a proper relationship. We were merely hooking up."

"Hooking up, my ass," Shelley scoffed. "The guy took you to the zoo for breakfast with elephants, and to Broome, for Christ's sake. He had more than hooking up on his mind, and you know it."

"Maybe he did. But now all he has on his mind is that I'm a lying cheat, and a blog to back up the web of deceit. Concrete evidence makes more of an impact than the few memories we created."

"Well, this is going nowhere." Karina picked up the napkin from her lap, crumpled it and dropped it on her empty plate.

"What did Matty say about it—I mean, he knows Zak better than I do. Does he think he'll change his mind about me?"

Karina glanced sideways at Shelley, before attempting to answer. "He doesn't really know him that well."

"Come off it, Karina, I can tell just by the look on your face that he had an opinion about us, so out with it." Molly wasn't in the mood to dance around the facts. As much as she was certain she didn't want to hear what Karina had to share, she wouldn't settle until she spilled.

"He didn't say much. Just that Zak wasn't likely to

give second chances after what his ex fiancé did to him."

"Which was?"

Karina frowned. "I'm not sure it's my place to talk about his private life." She fidgeted in her seat. Matty and Karina shared everything, they'd been together for so long and there had never been secrets between them.

"Oh for goodness sake, I don't even know the guy and the suspense is killing me—just spill, woman."

Molly glanced over at Shelley, grateful she was present to mediate or else she probably would've left without knowing what was said.

"He was with this woman for eight years, or there bouts, and he found out she was cheating on him. He said he'd suspected it wasn't the first time, but catching her red-handed and in the act didn't leave room to deny the truth. Really messed him up apparently." She paused whilst taking a sip of her water. "Matty just mentioned that he didn't even think Zak would be open to an explanation, let alone forgiveness. But that's just him making assumptions. He doesn't know how he feels about you."

"Far out. Trust me to pick one with such deep scars. Why didn't someone hand me a paring knife so I could skin him since he's already been gutted? He'll never forgive me after all that."

"Depends on how much he likes you." Shelley interjected, but even she didn't sound convinced.

"It's alright, Shell. I'm at the point where I told you so would be a more fitting response." Tears welled in her eyes, but there was no way she would let them spill. Feeling sorry for herself wasn't going to help anyone, least of all Zak. She'd hurt him and in turn she was hurting. Given what he'd already suffered, she had nothing to complain about.

"So, Shelley, how are things going between you and the Italian Stallion?" Taking the focus off herself was the only kindness she'd permit, more out of not wanting to spoil everyone else's mood because of her lousy actions.

"Oh, he's wonderful. I don't know what I'd do without him now," she gushed.

Molly winced. She knew exactly what Shelley would do without him—same as she was doing—feel sorry for herself and mope around, making everyone else as miserable as she was.

"I'm so happy for you," Karina, just as gushy, seemed relieved for the change of topic.

"Any talk of future?" As much as Molly wished her own relationship was going strong, she didn't begrudge Shelley's happiness. She'd been waiting a long time and was so deserving of all the good Nick seemed to be bringing her way.

"A bit. He knows I'm keen to have a family, and whilst he's not ready just yet, he wants the same."

"And his donations? What's that all about?"

"Hmmm, long story that may sound a bit weird, but I think it's a lovely gesture on his part."

"Okay, your turn to spill." Karina jumped in as soon as Shelley appeared to be clamming up on the details.

"So long as you don't judge."

"Well, you can guarantee I'm not about to judge anyone."

"Yeah, if we haven't judged Molly then I'm sure the Italian Stallions sperm is safe."

Anything inappropriate coming from Karina's mouth was so much funnier than if it was said by someone else.

"His brother has a low sperm count, so there is a chance he can't father his own children, but there's also a chance he can. So he doesn't have to put his wife through so many failed attempts of IVF, he asked his brothers if they would offer up a sample, as would he. It means that there's a one in four chance he is the natural father—plus, because all the boys look alike, the baby won't look as though it belongs to someone else. Of course, all the brothers agreed, and that's the end of the story."

"Oh my God, what a sweet thing to do." The grin on Karina's face couldn't spread any wider.

"Yeah, makes him all the more special to me."

"I can see why. What a sweetheart—all of them."

Shelley's smile matched Karina's for size. "You guys are the best, you know."

Molly scoffed.

"Okay, so you make bad choices sometimes, but we still love you, bad choices and all."

"Ha, speak for yourself." Sarcasm oozed from Karina's tone and she laughed before Molly could take offence.

"Best not exaggerate. Let's face it, my bad choices have been pretty shit."

Karina and Shelley nodded in unison.

## CHAPTER 32

*Tip Tuesday*

*Honesty and trust should go hand in hand, but too often one exists without the other.*

*In my experience, even a relationship with unbelievable chemistry won't survive the aftermath should one of these traits be burned. And, as much as I have seen couples 'try to make it work' and 'put the hurt behind them' they lose their spark and become another statistic.*

*Be mindful of your actions. Without intention you may be damaging the very core of the foundation you've built, and we all know that an unstable base makes for rocky times to come.*

*Like all areas of your relationship, communication is key. If exclusivity is what you are after from the get go, then say so, instead of thinking your new claimed partner is a mind reader.*

Molly paused to read over her post. "If suicide promotion is my intension, then maybe," she muttered, more pissed off with herself than she was before she started writing. "Just because you're a deceitful relationship wrecker doesn't mean your readership is." Once deleted, Molly closed her laptop and wandered over to flop down on her bed.

Berating herself didn't make her feel any better, but if no one else was going to do it, then she might as well. *What was she trying to achieve from pouring her heart on the page, anyway?* If clearing her conscience through public humiliation was her thing, then even that she was failing at.

She picked up her cell even though she wasn't in the mood to communicate with anyone.

*<If you're not too busy, would you meet me for a cup of tea? >*

. . .

Molly swiped at the tears welling in her eyes, skewing her vision. Even then she didn't quite believe it, so she sat up like that would make all the difference. Nothing changed; the message was definitely from Zak.

"Okay, so you got me here, now what is it I can do for you?" Molly could hear the sigh following, but swallowed in hope Zak didn't catch on to her impatience. What was the point of making her suffer more than she already was? She'd done the wrong thing by him, she knew it, but meeting face to face only emphasized the fact that she was a lying cheat, even if that had not been her intention. How many times did they have to go over the finer details and point out her flaws, when all she saw him as was perfection. It wasn't healthy to place him on the pedestal she had him on, but he was there despite her better judgment.

"Give me a chance—" They both knew it wasn't her needing to give him the chance—in fact, quite the opposite.

"Perhaps that should be my line." He had nothing to explain—nothing to apologize for. No excuses for his reason to give for bailing on her the other night beyond what she had caused, but somehow she sensed that he was feeling guilty.

"How have you been?"

Struggling with tears she wouldn't allow to spill, at least not in his presence. She shrugged. "I've been better, but self-inflicted misery deserves no pity."

"I'm not going to argue with that." Zak didn't break eye contact even after he'd finished speaking. "But something tells me you have a valid explanation for what happened."

"There's no reason good enough for being deceitful, so I don't know what you want me to say."

"I didn't exactly handle your little revolution with grace." He paused, seeming to be searching for the right words. "I apologize for leaving the other night without letting you explain. That was unfair and I want to make it up to you."

"Oh, come off it, Zak, like you're the one who need apologize." Was he playing a game—enjoying the torture he was inflicting, seeing how far he could push before she broke and made a fool of herself in front of a room full of people.

"My behavior was less than gentlemanly, and I have every reason to apologize for that."

"Look, I know this is meant to be a nice gesture and all, but we both know that I'm the one who need apologize. I never expected my blog to replace my income. I never expected to meet someone I would truly care about. All of these things were out of my control, and how to juggle them became my problem." She sucked in a deep breath before continuing. "I tried to fix it, and I never want to be a part of *Craze* ever again. But, to say that I regret any of this would be a lie. Without *Craze,* I may never have met you—and that's the reason I'd do it all over again. Although next time I'd call it quits from the moment I met you." She was rambling, she knew it, but now was all she had, so she was grasping the opportunity with both hands and running with it.

"I don't regret a moment I spent with you either. And, that's the reason I asked you to meet me today —" He leaned forward and grasped both of her hands between his. "I need to know the full story, and I need to hear it directly from you. Karina gave Matty a bit of a rundown, which he shared with me —but I need to hear it from you."

"Ok-ay," she began. "Where do you want me to start?"

"How about you tell me what led you to *Craze*

and then carry on from there." Zak let go of her hands and sat back in his chair.

Molly fidgeted until she was comfortable.

"I want you to tell me about your whole *Craze-y* experience. Help me understand from your perspective to see if it will alter mine." He was trying to lighten the mood, to make her more comfortable, but failed miserably.

He was handing her an olive branch, and all she had was the truth on her side. She had nothing to lose, and everything to gain, so she intended to grasp the branch he offered and give him every detail that led her to where she was at that moment.

"It wasn't my idea to sign up to *Craze* in the first place. I'd been involved with a guy for a few months before I found out he was in a nine-year relationship. I was pretty upset, so my best friend, Shelley, thought it'd be a good idea for me to join—to cheer me up, she said."

"Always the best friend's influence—same for me."

Molly attempted a smile, but she was too nervous for it to be convincing, so she pushed on with her story. "I wasn't happy with the work I was doing—journalism, mostly fashion and event coverage. And, after being stood up and numerous dating disasters,

I was ready to throw the towel in and ignore the dating game for life. Then Shelley joked about a blog. I ignored her and went on another date." She sucked in a deep breath before she continued. "It was such a disaster I decided to turn the dating scene into the game I thought it was, so I started the blog. I never imagined it'd become my source of income."

"You really get paid to write a blog?"

She nodded. "Better than I've ever been paid before."

"Wow." He was clearly impressed, although Molly couldn't take that in as more than a punch in the gut. It's the blog, and her bad decisions regarding it, that landed her where she was at that moment. However, it could've been worse, she may never have seen Zak again.

"In order to keep the blog going, so that I could pay my bills, I scheduled dates as a doctor does patients. After I met you, I searched for a way that I could keep it going without having to go on dates, which I've done—a little too late."

Zak nodded slowly, seemingly taking in what she was saying. "With guest stories?"

Molly nodded. She wasn't surprised he'd read her blog.

"And you haven't lost readers?"

"Nope. If anything, I've gained. It could be that those who've sent me their experience have checked in a little more often so they don't miss their post, or because I've added the success stories and tip page since then too. It's all about value for money." This time she did smile, but it wasn't of the perky kind as she was still too upset that her crazy idea had cost her the connection she had once shared with Zak.

"I get why your blog would be so popular. People are crazy for reality television, why not read about it too?" He seemed more relaxed, as though the thought of what she had done was worse than her actions. She still thought both were as bad.

"I also get why it is you didn't tell me about it, and why you didn't quit the game before we were a sure thing."

"It wasn't that, it was more because I didn't know how I was going to pay my bills if the blog flopped. It's not so easy to pick up where I left off in my industry. I would've been replaced long ago."

"Long ago? How long have you been on *Craze*?" The frown that had left his face was now back, more prominent than before.

"Oh, not that long. A few months, at most. I just meant they would've replaced me the moment I stopped sending articles their way."

The furrow in Zak's brow smoothed, and he seemed to relax more than he had since she arrived. "So, what made you decide to give *Craze* away—that is, I'm presuming you have."

Molly nodded. "I deleted the app the day you phoned me in the middle of the last date I attended—and before you say anything, yes, I did lie, but after I met you, they were all clients to me."

"I saw you that day. Came as a punch to the gut seeing you sit across from that guy. I didn't like it, which is why I had to phone and find out for myself whether you'd snub me or if you'd take my call. Put it this way, a lot goes in your favor for putting me before him and taking my call despite the nature of your meeting."

Relief kicked in, but she knew she was nowhere near in the clear or forgiven for the rest of her deceit.

"I really like you, Molly, and I'm glad we got the chance to talk. I'm just not sure how I feel about all of this—and, as horrible as this is going to sound, if I can trust you."

She had it coming, and she knew it. There was no point arguing with him, and there was no point trying to convince him otherwise. He had proof to back up his reasoning, and she provided it to him in more than one form.

"Perhaps you could take some time to think about how you feel, and if you ever want to catch up again—" she shrugged. "You have my number."

Zak nodded. "So what will you do now? Back to *Craze*?"

She hoped the change in his tone was due to jealousy, but she couldn't be sure. "I've found a way to keep my blog thriving, I have no use for *Craze* or dating anymore. I was done with online dating before I even began. I'll never go back there." She longed to ask if that was where he was headed, but didn't think she had the right to quiz him. "Well, I guess I'll be going." She began to stand, then stopped. "Thank you for the time we spent together, it meant more to me than you'll ever know."

"I noticed you didn't share details about us."

She shook her head. "There are some things that no one else needed to know."

He nodded, but remained quiet.

Zak stood as she stood.

"I'm really sorry, and I do hope to see you again." Stood on her tiptoes, she stretched up to kiss him on the cheek.

His lack of response was enough to confirm her suspicions that he had no intention of seeing her again. Devastation was the understated mix of emotion washing through her, and she knew she had to leave before her tears spilled.

## CHAPTER 33

Two days past and Molly had given up hope that Zak would make contact again. There was no denying she was devastated. A keeper of the best kind, yet obviously not for her. She was relieved the only mutual friend they shared was Matty, so their paths were unlikely to cross in the future. Especially once Zak found the one he was looking for.

Molly wanted to believe that she'd be happy for him, but didn't have to dig too deep to know that'd be a lie. Not that he deserved less than happy, but it was too soon and the only thing she wanted was to be able to prove that she'd never put her career before him again.

The buzz of a message on her cell dragged her

from her thoughts. Even though, deep down, she knew it wouldn't be from Zak, she couldn't help but get her hopes up.

*<I need a huge favor from both of you, urgent lunch at Nick's restaurant? >*

It was unlike Karina to ask for help with anything. Molly hoped there was nothing wrong.

*<Can do, but everything's okay, right? >*

*<Yeah, just can't sort this on my own >*

Karina was quick in her response, which Molly was grateful for. With so much else to worry about, Molly didn't have room for more stress, at least not without having a complete meltdown.

*<Oh, and be prepared to have photos taken >*

. . .

Molly groaned. Photos being taken meant two things. Firstly, she'd have to make herself look presentable when all she felt like doing was watching the saddest movie she owned and continue feeling sorry for herself. Second, there were bound to be children involved—a school project of sorts. Just so long as there was no interview to go with the photos and she'd be fine.

*<Sounds enchanting >*

Karina wouldn't even notice the sarcasm laced comment—why would she. She had such a sweet and gentle nature. Molly scowled, bitterness oozed from her in the most unnecessary and uncalled for moments. Lately, even she didn't much like herself. It wasn't any wonder Zak had taken the opportunity to bail.

*<What time do you need us? >*

. . .

Keen to make amends, regardless of the fact that Karina wasn't even aware of her negative attitude, Molly intended to make an effort, to leave the bitter asshole she'd been behaving like at home.

*<I know it's short notice, but does 1:30 work for a late lunch? >*

*<Suits me fine >*

With Zak out of the picture and her readers taking care of her blog content, time was something she had plenty of. It was amazing how much time dating took up too. Hours she'd never get back, and hours she had no intention of wasting in the future.

She wasn't sure what Shelley's response had been to Karina, but given the meeting point was her boyfriend's restaurant, she didn't doubt she'd be the first one there.

Short notice, when she looked as miserable as she did, was an understatement. Half an hour was all she had to spare if she wanted to arrive on time. Even on a good day, half an hour would push it for her to be photo ready.

Molly wandered over to her wardrobe and pulled out the cutest sundress she owned. She didn't wear it often, but she hoped the bright melon colour, against her lightly tanned skin, would detract from the dark bags that had formed under her eyes.

Even if she applied foundation with a spatula, she'd never be able to cover the dark circles so, after washing off the thick mask she attempted to apply, she ignored the bags and worked with what she had. At least her skin was clear, and her hair streaked with natural highlights from all the time she'd been spending in the sun.

Five minutes late to leave could easily be made up if she got a good run with the traffic lights. If not, they would just have to wait. As shitty as she was feeling about her own life at the moment, it felt good to be out. Especially when it was to help one of her friends.

Having such a short timeframe to make herself presentable was the perfect distraction. Zak hadn't clouded her thoughts once. She knew it'd take time to feel better about how their relationship came to an end, but at least it was still so new that his absence from her life wouldn't seem foreign. She was grateful, so few people in her life even knew he existed, so there wouldn't be questions to repeatedly answer.

Molly pulled into a parking space right out the front of Nick's restaurant and glanced around to see if Shelley or Karina had already arrived. She was right on time, so figured she could be the one waiting after all. Shelley would want to look her best, and Karina—well, Karina was never on time and certainly never early. The thought of her scatterbrain friend made her smile. To think she'd once worked the corporate life. Before kids *organised* was practically her middle name. Amazing how she managed to handle herself against some of the feistiest men in the business, yet three babies could turn her to putty at a moment's notice.

The front desk was unattended when she walked in, but, having been there a number of times, knew it wouldn't be long before she'd be attended to, so she didn't bother to ring the bell on the counter.

"Argh, Molly, *bella*." Nick's thick accent made even the simplest name sound glamorous. "Shelley mentioned you'd be in today." He greeted her as if they'd been friends for years, with a kiss on each cheek. "Come. I'll show you to your table."

Molly followed him to a table in the furthest corner from the kitchen.

"For privacy," he said as he pulled the chair out of her to sit.

She smiled and thanked him, although she was curious to ask what they needed privacy for, but decided against it.

"I'll get you wine? White, yes?" He smiled and ducked off before she could respond.

He was obviously aware Shelley was on her way in. His fussing put Molly on edge, which was ridiculous. He too seemed nervous. She could understand why. Even if he was a chef, a really talented one at that, there was nothing more nerve-wracking than cooking for the person you cared about, and their friends. It'd been a long time since she'd done it, but even the thought was enough to send her into a panic. Good thing she wouldn't have to do it anytime soon. She almost smiled at the positive spin she was starting to have about being single—or at least she was trying to kid herself into believing.

"One glass for you." Nick placed the glass on the table in front of her. "I will be back to take your order soon." He didn't stick around to chat, obviously in the middle of cooking up a storm, not wanting to leave anything to burn in the kitchen.

"Thank you," she said, and he smiled.

As soon as she was alone, Molly took a sip of her wine. She didn't much feel like drinking, but the crisp taste was enough to change her mind. Nick was the best thing that'd ever happened to Shelley. Not only did he light up her life, they got to indulge in her favorite Italian cuisine more often—a win-win situation for all involved.

More than five minutes had passed, and Molly was beginning to fidget. Couples lunching and getting cozy around her was not unlike sitting in a torture chamber. From crisp and refreshing, her wine now resembled vinegar.

A burst of high-pitched laughter behind her caught her attention. Curious as to what was happening, Molly glanced over her shoulder as the couple behind her, too caught up in each other to notice her watching, stole a kiss. Heads together, they continued to giggle.

Despite feeling sorry for herself, she couldn't help but smile. The way that they looked at each other told a story of its own, and it surprisingly warmed her heart. She needed a little warming at that moment, especially when she looked to be the one in the room who's date was a no-show.

"Excuse me, is this seat taken?"

Wide eyed and taken completely by surprise, Molly whipped her head back to face the seat opposite. "Yes—" She shook her head and sucked in a deep breath. "I mean no—not at the moment, at least," she stammered.

"Oh, about that, the girls aren't going to be able to make it today, but said to tell you that they will reschedule soon." Zak grinned and held out the single red rose he'd been carrying before taking a seat. "This is for you."

"Thank you." Too confused to come up with more, she took the rose and attempted to smile back.

"I'm sorry about the short notice—and the deceitful way I got you here, but I wasn't sure if you'd show up if I was the one to message you."

"What gave you that idea?" Nothing he'd ever said to her before had been more stupid than what she was hearing.

"I left you hanging for days. That wasn't exactly kind."

"Failing to be upfront about what influenced me to be on *Craze* wasn't exactly my finest moment either." He had a bad habit of blaming himself when he wasn't the one in the wrong—in the future, if they had a future together, that was something they'd have to work on.

"I'm just going to get to the point. We don't really know each other. We've not even spent a solid week in each other's presence. This may sound crazy to you, but I miss you." Zak leaned forward and reached across the table to take her hands in his. "I miss your smile. I miss the glint in your eyes when you're up to mischief. I miss your lips, your laughter, even the late night text messages." He squeezed her hands then lifted them to his mouth, kissing each of them in turn. "I miss you, and I hope you miss me too."

"If you call this crazy, then I'm guilty of it too, because I don't think I've ever missed anyone so much as I've missed you."

"Does that mean you'd be willing to try this again?"

"I hope you're referring to the you and me dating part, and not the two days of torture."

Zak laughed. "You too, huh?"

"Totally." Molly nodded.

"No more torture therapy."

"Agreed."

"Phew." Zak sat back in his chair and puffed out a breath. "Standing outside for the last ten minutes playing this over in my head, and it went a whole lot different than I expected."

"Good different?"

"Good doesn't even cut it." Pushing his chair back from the table and stood. "Take a walk with me?"

Molly frowned, but began to stand as she spoke. "Aren't we eating lunch?"

Zak tipped his head back and released a loud burst of laughter. "And here I was trying to be subtle." Encircling her waist with both arms, he drew her body close to his. "I just wanted to steal you away for a minute so I didn't put anyone off their meal, but now it's just too bad." He pressed his mouth to hers, deepening the kiss as he dipped her back.

Molly wrapped her arms around his neck and returned the kiss with a passion to match his, knowing she'd found her keeper.

ALSO BY STEFI HART

**Bennett Springs Series**

Country Charm

**Ravens Ridge Series**

Hidden in His Eyes

**Angel Cove Series**

Second Chance Love

**Single Titles**

Dating Game

# MEET STEFI HART

By day, Stefi Hart is a dedicated Literary Curator, but by night, she immerses herself in the world of steamy small-town romance. With a gift for weaving heartfelt stories into country settings, Stefi creates swoon-worthy tales that are her perfect late-night escape.

When she's not writing, Stefi loves unwinding in the Margaret River wine region, savoring a glass of red and a good book. Family is her true anchor, and she cherishes every moment spent with her four children, three grandsons, and her very own real-life hero.

Join Stefi's newsletter for all the *goss* about book releases and author updates.